The Cross-Cut

Courtney Ryley Cooper

Contents

THE CROSS-CUT

BY

Courtney Ryley Cooper

CHAPTER I

It was over. The rambling house, with its rickety, old-fashioned furniture--and its memories--was now deserted, except for Robert Fairchild, and he was deserted within it, wandering from room to room, staring at familiar objects with the unfamiliar gaze of one whose vision suddenly has been warned by the visitation of death and the sense of loneliness that it brings.

Loneliness, rather than grief, for it had been Robert Fairchild's promise that he would not suffer in heart for one who had longed to go into a peace for which he had waited, seemingly in vain. Year after year, Thornton Fairchild had sat in the big armchair by the windows, watching the days grow old and fade into night, studying sunset after sunset, voicing the vain hope that the gloaming might bring the twilight of his own existence,--a silent man except for this, rarely speaking of the past, never giving to the son who worked for him, cared for him, worshiped him, the slightest inkling of what might have happened in the dim days of the long ago to transform him into a beaten thing, longing for the final surcease. And when the end came, it found him in readiness, waiting in the big armchair by the windows. Even now, a book lay on the frayed carpeting of the old room, where it had fallen from relaxing fingers. Robert Fairchild picked it up, and with a sigh restored it to the grim, fumed oak case. His days of petty sacrifices that his father might while away the weary hours with reading were over.

Memories! They were all about him, in the grate with its blackened coals, the old-fashioned pictures on the walls, the almost gloomy rooms, the big chair by the window, and yet they told him nothing except that a white-haired, patient, lovable old man was gone,--a man whom he was wont to call "father." And in that going, the slow procedure of an unnatural existence had snapped for Robert Fairchild. As he roamed about in his loneliness, he wondered what he would do now, where he could go; to whom he could talk. He had worked since sixteen, and since sixteen there had been few times when he had not come home regularly each night, to wait upon the white-haired man in the big chair, to discern his wants instinctively, and to sit with him, often in silence, until the old onyx clock on the mantel had clanged eleven; it had been the same program, day, week, month and year. And now Robert Fairchild was as a person lost. The ordinary pleasures of youth had never been his; he could not turn to them with any sort of grace. The years of servitude to a beloved master had inculcated within him the feeling of self-impelled sacrifice; he had forgotten all thought of personal pleasures for their sake alone. The big chair by the window was vacant, and it created a void which Robert Fairchild could neither combat nor overcome.

What had been the past? Why the silence? Why the patient, yet impatient wait for death? The son did not know. In all his memories was only one faint picture, painted years before in babyhood: the return of his father from some place, he knew not where, a long conference with his mother behind closed doors, while he, in childlike curiosity, waited without, seeking in vain to catch some explanation. Then a sad-faced woman who cried at night when the house was still, who faded and who died. That was all. The picture carried no explanation.

And now Robert Fairchild stood on the threshold of something he almost feared to learn. Once, on a black, stormy night, they had sat together, father and son before the fire, silent for hours. Then the hand of the white-haired man had reached outward and rested for a moment on the young man's knee.

"I wrote something to you, Boy, a day or so ago," he had said. "That little illness I had prompted me to do it. I--I thought it was only fair to you. After I 'm gone, look in the safe. You 'll find the combination on a piece of paper hidden in a hole cut in that old European history in the bookcase. I have your promise, I know--that you 'll not do it until after I 'm gone."

Now Thornton Fairchild was gone. But a message had remained behind; one which the patient lips evidently had feared to utter during life. The heart of the son began to pound, slow and hard, as, with the memory of that conversation, he turned toward the bookcase and unlatched the paneled door. A moment more and the hollowed history had given up its trust, a bit of paper scratched with numbers. Robert Fairchild turned toward the stairs and the small room on the second floor which had served as his father's bedroom.

There he hesitated before the little iron safe in the corner, summoning the courage to unlock the doors of a dead man's past. At last he forced himself to his knees and to the numerals of the combination.

The safe had not been opened in years; that was evident from the creaking of the plungers as they fell, the gummy resistance of the knob as Fairchild turned it in accordance with the directions on the paper. Finally, a great wrench, and the bolt was drawn grudgingly back; a strong pull, and the safe opened.

A few old books; ledgers in sheepskin binding. Fairchild disregarded these for the more important things that might lie behind the little inner door of the cabinet. His hand went forward, and he noticed, in a hazy sort of way, that it was trembling. The door was unlocked; he drew it open and crouched a moment, staring, before he reached for the thinner of two envelopes which lay before him. A moment later he straightened and turned toward the light. A crinkling of paper, a quick-drawn sigh between clenched teeth; it was a letter; his strange, quiet, hunted-appearing father was talking to him through the medium of ink and paper, after death.

Closely written, hurriedly, as though to finish an irksome task in as short a space as possible, the missive was one of several pages,--pages which Robert Fairchild hesitated to read. The secret--and he knew full well that there was a secret--had been in the atmosphere about him ever since he could remember. Whether or not this was the solution of it, Robert Fairchild did not know, and the natural reticence with which he had always approached anything regarding his father's life gave him an instinctive fear, a sense of cringing retreat from anything that might now open the doors of mystery. But it was before him, waiting in his father's writing, and at last his gaze centered; he read:

My son:

Before I begin this letter to you I must ask that you take no action whatever until you have seen my attorney--he will be yours from now on. I have never mentioned him to you before; it was not necessary and would only have brought you curiosity which I could not have satisfied. But now, I am afraid, the doors must be unlocked. I am gone. You are young, you have been a faithful son and you are deserving of every good fortune that may possibly come to you. I am praying that the years have made a difference, and that Fortune may smile upon you as she frowned on me. Certainly, she can injure me no longer. My race is run; I am beyond earthly fortunes.

Therefore, when you have finished with this, take the deeds inclosed in the larger envelope and go to St. Louis. There, look up Henry F. Beamish, attorney-at-law, in the Princess Building. He will explain them to you.

Beyond this, I fear, there is little that can aid you. I cannot find the strength, now that I face it, to tell you what you may find if you follow the lure that the other envelope holds forth to you.

There is always the hope that Fortune may be kind to me at last, and smile upon my memory by never letting you know why I have been the sort of man you have known, and not the jovial, genial companion that a father should be. But there are certain things, my son, which defeat a man. It killed your mother--every day since her death I have been haunted by that fact; my prayer is that it may not kill you, spiritually, if not physically. Therefore is it not better that it remain behind a cloud until such time as Fortune may reveal it--and hope that such a time will never come? I think so--not for myself, for when you read this, I shall be gone; but for you, that you may not be handicapped by the knowledge of the thing which whitened my hair and aged me, long before my time.

If he lives, and I am sure he does, there is one who will hurry to your aid as soon as he knows you need him. Accept his counsels, laugh at his little eccentricities if you will, but follow his judgment implicitly. Above all, ask him no questions that he does not care to answer--there are things that he may not deem wise to tell. It is only fair that he be given the right to choose his disclosures.

There is little more to say. Beamish will attend to everything for you--if you care to go. Sell everything that is here; the house, the furniture, the belongings. It is my wish, and you will need the capital--if you go. The ledgers in the safe are only old accounts which would be so much Chinese to you now. Burn them. There is nothing else to be afraid of--I hope you will never find anything to fear. And if circumstances should arise to bring before you the story of that which has caused me so much darkness, I have nothing to say in self-extenuation. I made one mistake--that of fear--and in committing one error, I shouldered every blame. It makes little difference now. I am dead--and free.

My love to you, my son. I hope that wealth and happiness await you. Blood of my blood flows in your veins--and strange though it may sound to you--it is the blood of an adventurer. I can almost see you smile at that! An old man who sat by the window, staring out; afraid of every knock at the door--and yet an adventurer! But they say, once in the blood, it never dies. My wish is that you succeed where I failed--and God be with you!

Your father.

For a long moment Robert Fairchild stood staring at the letter, his heart pounding with excitement, his hands grasping the foolscap paper as though with a desire to tear through the shield which the written words had formed about a mysterious past and disclose that which was so effectively hidden. So much had the letter told--and yet so little! Dark had been the hints of some mysterious, intangible thing, great enough in its horror and its far-reaching consequences to cause death for one who had known of it and a living panic for him who had perpetrated it. As for the man who stood now with the letter clenched before him, there was promise of wealth, and the threat of sorrow, the hope of happiness, yet the foreboding omen of discoveries which might ruin the life of the reader as the existence of the writer had been blasted,--until death had brought relief. Of all this had the letter told, but when Robert Fairchild read it again in the hope of something tangible, something that might give even a clue to the reason for it all, there was nothing. In that super-calmness which accompanies great agitation, Fairchild folded the paper, placed it in its envelope, then slipped it into an inside pocket. A few steps and he was before the safe once more and reaching for the second envelope.

Heavy and bulky was this, filled with tax receipts, with plats and blueprints and the reports of surveyors. Here was an assay slip, bearing figures and notations which Robert Fairchild could not understand. Here a receipt for money received, here a vari-colored map with lines and figures and conglomerate designs which Fairchild believed must relate in some manner to the location of a mining camp; all were aged and worn at the edges, giving evidence of having been carried, at some far time of the past, in a wallet. More receipts, more blueprints, then a legal document, sealed and stamped, and bearing the words:

County of Clear Creek,) ss.
State of Colorado.   )

DEED PATENT.

KNOW ALL MEN BY THESE PRESENTS: That on this day of our Lord, February 22, 1892, Thornton W. Fairchild, having presented the necessary affidavits and statements of assessments accomplished in accordance with--

On it trailed in endless legal phraseology, telling in muddled, attorney-like language, the fact that the law had been fulfilled in its requirements, and that the claim for which Thornton Fairchild had worked was rightfully his, forever. A longer statement full of figures, of diagrams and surveyor's calculations which Fairchild could neither decipher nor understand, gave the location, the town site and the property included within the granted rights. It was something for an attorney, such as Beamish, to interpret, and Fairchild reached for the age-yellowed envelope to return the papers to their resting place. But he checked his motion involuntarily and for a moment held the envelope before him, staring at it with wide eyes. Then, as though to free by the stronger light of the window the haunting thing which faced him, he rose and hurried across the room, to better light, only to find it had not been imagination; the words still were before him, a sentence written in faint, faded ink proclaiming the contents to be "Papers relating to the Blue Poppy Mine", and written across this a word in the bolder, harsher strokes of a man under stress of emotion, a word which held the eyes of Robert Fairchild fixed and staring, a word which spelled books of the past and evil threats of the future, the single, ominous word:

"Accursed!"

CHAPTER II

One works quickly when prodded by the pique of curiosity. And in spite of all that omens could foretell, in spite of the dull, gloomy life which had done its best to fashion a matter-of-fact brain for Robert Fairchild, one sentence in that letter had found an echo, had started a pulsating something within him that he never before had known:

"--It is the blood of an adventurer."

And it seemed that Robert Fairchild needed no more than the knowledge to feel the tingle of it; the old house suddenly became stuffy and prison-like as he wandered through it. Within his pocket were two envelopes filled with threats of the future, defying him to advance and fight it out,--whatever *it* might be. Again and again pounded through his head the fact that only a night of travel intervened between Indianapolis and St. Louis; within twelve hours he could be in the office of Henry Beamish. And then--

A hurried resolution. A hasty packing of a traveling bag and the cashing of a check at the cigar store down on the corner. A wakeful night while the train clattered along upon its journey. Then morning and walking of streets until office hours. At last:

"I 'm Robert Fairchild," he said, as he faced a white-haired, Cupid-faced man in the rather dingy offices of the Princess Building. A slow smile spread over the pudgy features of the genial appearing attorney, and he waved a fat hand toward the office's extra chair.

"Sit down, Son," came casually. "Need n't have announced yourself. I 'd have known you--just like your father, Boy. How is he?" Then his face suddenly sobered. "I 'm afraid your presence is the answer. Am I right?"

Fairchild nodded gravely. The old attorney slowly placed his fat hands together, peaking the fingers, and stared out of the window to the grimy roof and signboards of the next building.

"Perhaps it's better so," he said at last. "We had n't seen each other in ten years--not since I went up to Indianapolis to have my last talk with him. Did he get any cheerier before--he went?"

"No."

"Just the same, huh? Always waiting?"

"Afraid of every step on the veranda, of every knock at the door."

Again the attorney stared out of the window.

"And you?"

"I?" Fairchild leaned forward in his chair. "I don't understand."

"Are you afraid?"

"Of what?"

The lawyer smiled.

"I don't know. Only--" and he leaned forward--"it's just as though I were living my younger days over this morning. It doesn't seem any time at all since your father was sitting just about where you are now, and gad, Boy, how much you look like he looked that morning! The same gray-blue, earnest eyes, the same dark hair, the same strong shoulders, and good, manly chin, the same build--and look of determination about him. The call of adventure was in his blood, and he sat there all enthusiastic, telling me what he intended doing and asking my advice--although he would n't have followed it if I had given it. Back home was a baby and the woman he loved, and out West was sudden wealth, waiting for the right man to come along and find it. Gad!" White-haired old Beamish chuckled with the memory of it. "He almost made me throw over the law business that morning and go out adventuring with him! Then four years later," the tone changed suddenly, "he came back."

"What then?" Fairchild was on the edge of his chair. But Beamish only spread his hands.

"Truthfully, Boy, I don't know. I have guessed--but I won't tell you what. All I know is that your father found what he was looking for and was on the point of achieving his every dream, when something happened. Then three men simply disappeared from the mining camp, announcing that they had failed and were going to hunt new diggings. That was all. One of them was your father--"

"But you said that he 'd found--"

"Silver, running twenty ounces to the ton on an eight-inch vein which gave evidences of being only the beginning of a bonanza! I know, because he had written me that, a month before."

"And he abandoned it?"

"He 'd forgotten what he had written when I saw him again. I did n't question him. I did n't want to--his face told me enough to guess that I would n't learn. He went home then, after giving me enough money to pay the taxes on the mine for the next twenty years, simply as his attorney and without divulging his whereabouts. I did it. Eight years or so later, I saw him in Indianapolis. He gave me more money--enough for eleven or twelve years--"

"And that was ten years ago?" Robert Fairchild's eyes were reminiscent. "I remember--I was only a kid. He sold off everything he had, except the house."

Henry Beamish walked to his safe and fumbled there a moment, to return at last with a few slips of paper.

"Here 's the answer," he said quietly, "the taxes are paid until 1922."

Robert Fairchild studied the receipts carefully--futilely. They told him nothing. The lawyer stood looking down upon him; at last he laid a hand on his shoulder.

"Boy," came quietly, "I know just about what you 're thinking. I 've spent a few hours at the same kind of a job myself, and I 've called old Henry Beamish more kinds of a fool than you can think of for not coming right out flat-footed and making Thornton tell me the whole story. But some way, when I 'd look into those eyes with the fire all dead and ashen within them, and see the lines of an old man in his young face, I--well, I guess I 'm too soft-hearted to make folks suffer. I just couldn't do it!"

"So you can tell me nothing?"

"I 'm afraid that's true--in one way. In another I 'm a fund of information. To-night you and I will go to Indianapolis and probate the will--it's simple enough; I 've had it in my safe for ten years. After that, you become the owner of the Blue Poppy mine, to do with as you choose."

"But--"

The old lawyer chuckled.

"Don't ask my advice, Boy. I have n't any. Your father told me what to do if you decided to try your luck--and silver 's at $1.29. It means a lot of money for anybody who can produce pay ore--unless what he said about the mine pinching out was true."

Again the thrill of a new thing went through Robert Fairchild's veins, something he never had felt until twelve hours before; again the urge for strange places, new scenes, the fire of the hunt after the hidden wealth of silver-seamed hills. Somewhere it lay awaiting him; nor did he even know in what form. Robert Fairchild's life had been a plodding thing of books and accounts, of high desks which as yet had failed to stoop his shoulders, of stuffy offices which had been thwarted so far in their grip at his lung power; the long walk in the morning and the tired trudge homeward at night to save petty carfare for a silent man's pettier luxuries had looked after that. But the recoil had not exerted itself against an office-cramped brain, a dusty ledger-filled life that suddenly felt itself crying out for the free, open country, without hardly knowing what the term meant. Old Beamish caught the light in the eyes, the quick contraction of the hands, and smiled.

"You don't need to tell me, Son," he said slowly. "I can see the symptoms. You 've got the fever--You 're going to work that mine. Perhaps," and he shrugged his shoulders, "it's just as well. But there are certain things to remember."

"Name them."

"Ohadi is thirty-eight miles from Denver. That's your goal. Out there, they 'll tell you how the mine caved in, and how Thornton Fairchild, who had worked it, together with his two men, Harry Harkins, a Cornishman, and 'Sissie' Larsen, a Swede, left town late one night for Cripple Creek--and that they never came back. That's the story they 'll tell you. Agree with it. Tell them that Harkins, as far as you know, went back to Cornwall, and that you have heard vaguely that Larsen later followed the mining game farther out West."

"Is it the truth?"

"How do I know? It 's good enough--people should n't ask questions. Tell nothing more than that--and be careful of your friends. There is one man to watch--if he is still alive. They call him 'Squint' Rodaine, and he may or may not still be there. I don't know--I 'm only sure of the fact that your father hated him, fought him and feared him. The mine tunnel is two miles up Kentucky Gulch and one hundred yards to the right. A surveyor can lead you to the very spot. It's been abandoned now for thirty years. What you 'll find there is more than I can guess. But, Boy," and his hand clenched tight on Robert Fairchild's shoulder, "whatever you do, whatever you run into, whatever friends or enemies you find awaiting you, don't let that light die out of your eyes and don't pull in that chin! If you find a fight on your hands, whether it's man, beast or nature, sail into it! If you run into things that cut your very heart out to learn--beat 'em down and keep going! And win! There--that's all the advice I know. Meet me at the 11:10 train for Indianapolis. Good-by."

"Good-by--I 'll be there." Fairchild grasped the pudgy hand and left the office. For a moment afterward, old Henry Beamish stood thinking and looking out over the dingy roof adjacent. Then, somewhat absently, he pressed the ancient electric button for his more ancient stenographer.

"Call a messenger, please," he ordered when she entered, "I want to send a cablegram."

CHAPTER III

Two weeks later, Robert Fairchild sat in the smoking compartment of the Overland Limited, looking at the Rocky Mountains in the distance. In his pocket were a few hundred dollars; in the bank in Indianapolis a few thousand, representing the final proceeds of the sale of everything that had connected him with a rather dreary past. Out before him--

The train had left Limon Junction on its last, clattering, rushing leg of the journey across the plains, tearing on through a barren country of tumbleweed, of sagebrush, of prairie-dog villages and jagged arroyos toward the great, crumpled hills in the distance,--hills which meant everything to Robert Fairchild. Two weeks had created a metamorphosis in what had been a plodding, matter-of-fact man with dreams which did not extend beyond his ledgers and his gloomy home--but now a man leaning his head against the window of a rushing train, staring ahead toward the Rockies and the rainbow they held for him. Back to the place where his father had gone with dreams aglow was the son traveling now,--back into the rumpled mountains where the blue haze hung low and protecting as though over mysteries and treasures which awaited one man and one alone. Robert Fairchild momentarily had forgotten the foreboding omens which, like murky shadows, had been cast in his path by a beaten, will-broken father. He only knew that he was young, that he was strong, that he was free from the drudgery which had sought to claim him forever; he felt only the surge of excitement that can come with new surroundings, new country, new life. Out there before him, as the train rattled over culverts spanning the dry arroyos, or puffed gingerly up the grades toward the higher levels of the plains, were the hills, gray and brown in the foreground, blue as the blue sea farther on, then fringing into the sun-pinked radiance of the snowy range, forming the last barrier against a turquoise sky. It thrilled Fairchild, it caused his heart to tug and pull,--nor could he tell exactly why.

Still eighty miles away, the range was sharply outlined to Fairchild, from the ragged hump of Pikes Peak far to the south, on up to where the gradual lowering of the mighty upheaval slid away into Wyoming. Eighty miles, yet they were clear with the clearness that only altitudinous country can bring; alluring, fascinating, beckoning to him until his being rebelled against the comparative slowness of the train, and the minutes passed in a dragging, long-drawn-out sequence that was al-most an agony to Robert Fairchild.

Hours! The hills came closer. Still closer; then, when it seemed that the train must plunge straight into them, they drew away again, as though through some optical illusion, and brooded in the background, as the long, transcontinental train began to bang over the frogs and switches as it made its entrance into Denver. Fairchild went through the long chute and to a ticket window of the Union Station.

"When can I get a train for Ohadi?"

The ticket seller smiled. "You can't get one."

"But the map shows that a railroad runs there--"

"Ran there, you mean," chaffed the clerk.

"The best you can do is get to Forks Creek and walk the rest of the way. That's a narrow-gauge line, and Clear Creek 's been on a rampage. It took out about two hundred feet of trestle, and there won't be a train into Ohadi for a week."

The disappointment on Fairchild's face was more than apparent, almost boyish in its depression. The ticket seller leaned closer to the wicket.

"Stranger out here?"

"Very much of one."

"In a hurry to get to Ohadi?"

"Yes."

"Then you can go uptown and hire a taxi--they 've got big cars for mountain work and there are good roads all the way. It 'll cost fifteen or twenty dollars. Or--"

Fairchild smiled. "Give me the other system if you 've got one. I 'm not ter-ribly long on cash--for taxis."

"Certainly. I was just going to tell you about it. No use spending that money if you 've got a little pep, and it is n't a matter of life or death. Go up to the Central Loop--anybody can direct you--and catch a street car for Golden. That eats up fifteen miles and leaves just twenty-three miles more. Then ask somebody to point out the road over Mount Lookout. Machines go along there every few minutes--no trouble at all to catch a ride. You 'll be in Ohadi in no time."

Fairchild obeyed the instructions, and in the baggage room rechecked his trunk to follow him, lightening his traveling bag at the same time until it carried only necessities. A luncheon, then the street car. Three quarters of an hour later, he began the five-mile trudge up the broad, smooth, carefully groomed automobile highway which masters Mount Lookout. A rumbling sound behind him, then as he stepped to one side, a grimy truck driver leaned out to shout as he passed:

"Want a lift? Hop on! Can't stop--too much grade."

A running leap, and Fairchild seated himself on the tailboard of the truck, swinging his legs and looking out over the fading plains as the truck roared and clattered upward along the twisting mountain road.

Higher, higher, while the truck labored along the grade, and while the buildings in Golden below shrank smaller and smaller. The reservoir lake in the center of the town, a broad expanse of water only a short time before, began to take on the appearance of some great, blue-white diamond glistening in the sun. Gradually a stream outlined itself in living topography upon a map which seemed as large as the world itself. Denver, fifteen miles away, came into view, its streets showing like seams in a well-sewn garment, the sun, even at this distance, striking a sheen from the golden dome of the capitol building. Higher! The chortling truck gasped at the curves and tugged on the straightaway, but Robert Fairchild had ceased to hear. His every attention was centered on the tremendous stage unfolded before him, the vast stretches of the plains rolling away beneath, even into Kansas and Wyoming and Nebraska, hundreds of miles away, plains where once the buffalo had roamed in great, shaggy herds, where once the emigrant trains had made their slow, rocking progress into a Land of Heart's Desire; and he began to understand something of the vastness of life, the great scope of ambition; new things to a man whose world, until two weeks before, had been the four chalky walls of an office.

Cool breezes from pine-fringed gulches brushed his cheek and smoothed away the burning touch of a glaring sun; the truck turned into the hairpin curves of the steep ascent, giving him a glimpse of deep valleys, green from the touch of flowing streams, of great clefts with their vari-hued splotches of granite, and on beyond, mound after mound of pine-clothed hills, fringing the peaks of eternal snow, far away. The blood suddenly grew hot in Fairchild's veins; he whistled, he repressed a wild, spasmodic desire to shout. The spirit that had been the spirit of the determined men of the emigrant trains was his now; he remembered that he was traveling slowly toward a fight--against whom, or what, he knew not--but he welcomed it just the same. The exaltation of rarefied atmosphere was in his brain; dingy offices were gone forever. He was free; and for the first time in his life, he appreciated the meaning of the word.

Upward, still upward! The town below became merely a checkerboard thing, the lake a dot of gleaming silver, the stream a scintillating ribbon stretching off into the foothills. A turn, and they skirted a tremendous valley, its slopes falling away in sheer descents from the roadway. A darkened, moist stretch of road, fringed by pines, then a jogging journey over rolling table-land. At last came a voice from the driver's seat, and Fairchild turned like a man suddenly awakened.

"Turn off up here at Genesee Mountain. Which way do you go?"

"Trying to get to Ohadi." Fairchild shouted it above the roar of the engine. The driver waved a hand forward.

"Keep to the main road. Drop off when I make the turn. You 'll pick up another ride soon. Plenty of chances."

"Thanks for the lift."

"Aw, forget it."

The truck wheeled from the main road and chugged away, leaving Fairchild afoot, making as much progress as possible toward his goal until good fortune should bring a swifter means of locomotion. A half-mile he walked, studying the constant changes of the scenery before him, the slopes and rises, the smooth valleys and jagged crags above, the clouds as they drifted low upon the higher peaks, shielding them from view for a moment, then disappearing. Then suddenly he wheeled. Behind him sounded the swift droning of a motor, cut-out open, as it rushed forward along the road,--and the noise told a story of speed.

Far at the brow of a steep hill it appeared, seeming to hang in space for an instant before leaping downward. Rushing, plunging, once skidding dangerously at a small curve, it made the descent, bumped over a bridge, was lost for a second in the pines, then sped toward him, a big touring car, with a small, resolute figure clinging to the wheel. The quarter of a mile changed to a furlong, the furlong to a hundred yards,--then, with a report like a revolver shot, the machine suddenly slewed in drunken fashion far to one side of the road, hung dangerously over the steep cliff an instant, righted itself, swayed forward and stopped, barely twenty-five yards away. Staring, Robert Fairchild saw that a small, trim figure had leaped forth and was waving excitedly to him, and he ran forward.

His first glance had proclaimed it a boy; the second had told a different story. A girl--dressed in far different fashion from Robert Fairchild's limited specifications of feminine garb--she caused him to gasp in surprise, then to stop and stare. Again she waved a hand and stamped a foot excitedly; a vehement little thing in a snug, whipcord riding habit and a checkered cap pulled tight over closely braided hair, she awaited him with all the impatience of impetuous womanhood.

"For goodness' sake, come here!" she called, as he still stood gaping. "I 'll give you five dollars. Hurry!"

Fairchild managed to voice the fact that he would be willing to help without remuneration, as he hurried forward, still staring at her, a vibrant little thing with dark-brown wisps of hair which had been blown from beneath her cap straying about equally dark-brown, snapping eyes and caressing the corners of tightly pressed, momentarily impatient lips. Only a second she hesitated, then dived for the tonneau, jerking with all her strength at the heavy seat cushion, as he stepped to the running board beside her.

"Can't get this dinged thing up!" she panted. "Always sticks when you 're in a hurry. That's it! Jerk it. Thanks! Here!" She reached forward and a small, sun-tanned hand grasped a greasy jack, "Slide under the back axle and put this jack in place, will you? And rush it! I 've got to change a tire in nothing flat! Hurry!"

Fairchild, almost before he knew it, found himself under the rear of the car, fussing with a refractory lifting jack and trying to keep his eyes from the view of trimly clad, brown-shod little feet, as they pattered about at the side of the car, hurried to the running board, then stopped as wrenches and a hammer clattered to the ground. Then one shoe was raised, to press tight against a wheel; metal touched metal, a feminine gasp sounded as strength was exerted in vain, then eddying dust as the foot stamped, accompanied by an exasperated ejaculation.

"Ding these old lugs! They 're rusted! Got that jack in place yet?"

"Yes! I'm raising the car now."

"Oh, please hurry." There was pleading in the tone now. "Please!"

The car creaked upward. Out came Fairchild, brushing the dust from his clothes. But already the girl was pressing the lug wrench into his hands.

"Don't mind that dirt," came her exclamation. "I 'll--I 'll give you some extra money to get your suit cleaned. Loosen those lugs, while I get the spare tire off the back. And for goodness' sake, please hurry!"

Astonishment had taken away speech for Fairchild. He could only wonder--and obey. Swiftly he twirled the wrench while lug after lug fell to the ground, and while the girl, struggling with a tire seemingly almost as big as herself, trundled the spare into position to await the transfer. As for Fairchild, he was in the midst of a task which he had seen performed far more times than he had done it himself. He strove to remove the blown-out shoe with the cap still screwed on the valve stem; he fussed and swore under his breath, and panted, while behind him a girl in whip-cord riding habit and close-pulled cap fidgeted first on one tan-clad foot, then on the other, anxiously watching the road behind her and calling constantly for speed.

At last the job was finished, the girl fastening the useless shoe behind the machine while Fairchild tightened the last of the lugs. Then as he straightened, a small figure shot to his side, took the wrench from his hand and sent it, with the other tools, clattering into the tonneau. A tiny hand went into a pocket, something that crinkled was shoved into the man's grasp, and while he stood there gasping, she leaped to the driver's seat, slammed the door, spun the starter until it whined, and with open cutout roaring again, was off and away, rocking down the mountain side, around a curve and out of sight--while Fairchild merely stood there, staring wonderingly at a ten-dollar bill!

A noise from the rear, growing louder, and the amazed man turned to see a second machine, filled with men, careening toward him. Fifty feet away the brakes creaked, and the big automobile came to a skidding, dust-throwing stop. A sun-browned man in a Stetson hat, metal badge gleaming from beneath his coat, leaned forth.

"Which way did he go?"

"He?" Robert Fairchild stared.

"Yeh. Did n't a man just pass here in an automobile? Where'd he go--straight on the main road or off on the circuit trail?"

"It--it was n't a man."

"Not a man?" The four occupants of the machine stared at him. "Don't try to bull us that it was a woman."

"Oh, no--no--of course not." Fairchild had found his senses. "But it was n't a man. It--it was a boy, just about fifteen years old."

"Sure?"

"Oh, yes--" Fairchild was swimming in deep water now. "I got a good look at him. He--he took that road off to the left."

It was the opposite one to which the hurrying fugitive in whipcord had taken. There was doubt in the interrogator's eyes.

"Sure of that?" he queried. "I 'm the sheriff of Arapahoe County. That's an auto bandit ahead of us. We--"

"Well, I would n't swear to it. There was another machine ahead, and I lost 'em both for a second down there by the turn. I did n't see the other again, but I did get a glimpse of one off on that side road. It looked like the car that passed me. That's all I know."

"Probably him, all right." The voice came from the tonneau. "Maybe he figured to give us the slip and get back to Denver. You did n't notice the license number?" This to Fairchild. That bewildered person shook his head.

"No. Did n't you?"

"Could n't--covered with dust when we first took the trail and never got close enough afterward. But it was the same car--that's almost a cinch."

"Let's go!" The sheriff was pressing a foot on the accelerator. Down the hill went the car, to skid, then to make a short turn on to the road which led away from the scent, leaving behind a man standing in the middle of the road, staring at a ten-dollar bill,--and wondering why he had lied!

CHAPTER IV

Wonderment which got nowhere. The sheriff's car returned before Fairchild reached the bottom of the grade, and again stopped to survey the scene of defeat, while Fairchild once more told his story, deleting items which, to him, appeared unnecessary for consumption by officers of the law. Carefully the sheriff surveyed the winding road before him and scratched his head.

"Don't guess it would have made much difference which way he went," came ruefully at last, "I never saw a fellow turn loose with so much speed on a mountain road. We never could have caught him!"

"Dangerous character?" Fairchild hardly knew why he asked the question. The sheriff smiled grimly.

"If it was the fellow we were after, he was plenty dangerous. We were trailing him on word from Denver--described the car and said he 'd pulled a daylight hold-up on a pay-wagon for the Smelter Company--so when the car went through Golden, we took up the trail a couple of blocks behind. He kept the same speed for a little while until one of my deputies got a little anxious and took a shot at a tire. Man, how he turned on the juice! I thought that thing was a jack rabbit the way it went up the hill! We never had a chance after that!"

"And you 're sure it was the same person?"

The sheriff toyed with the gear shift.

"You never can be sure about nothing in this business," came finally. "But there 's this to think about: if that fellow was n't guilty of something, why did he run?"

"It might have been a kid in a stolen machine," came from the back seat.

"If it was, we 've got to wait until we get a report on it. I guess it's us back to the office."

The automobile went its way then, and Fairchild his, still wondering; the sheriff's question, with a different gender, recurring again and again:

"If she was n't guilty of something, why did she run?"

And why had she? More, why had she been willing to give ten dollars in payment for the mere changing of a tire? And why had she not offered some explanation of it all? It was a problem which almost wiped out for Robert Fairchild the zest of the new life into which he was going, the great gamble he was about to take. And so thoroughly did it engross him that it was not until a truck had come to a full stop behind him, and a driver mingled a shout with the tooting of his horn, that he turned to allow its passage.

"Did n't hear you, old man," he apologized. "Could you give a fellow a lift?"

"Guess so." It was friendly, even though a bit disgruntled; "hop on."

And Fairchild hopped, once more to sit on the tailboard, swinging his legs, but this time his eyes saw the ever-changing scenery without noticing it. In spite of himself, Fairchild found himself constantly staring at a vision of a pretty girl in a riding habit, with dark-brown hair straying about equally dark-brown eyes, almost frenzied in her efforts to change a tire in time to elude a pursuing sheriff. Some way, it all did n't blend. Pretty girls, no doubt, could commit infractions of the law just as easily as ones less gifted with good looks. Yet if this particular pretty girl had held up a pay wagon, why did n't the telephoned notice from Denver state the fact, instead of referring to her as a man? And if she had n't committed some sort of depredation against the law, why on earth was she willing to part with ten dollars, merely to save a few moments in changing a tire and thus elude a sheriff? If there had been nothing wrong, could not a moment of explanation have satisfied any one of the fact? Anyway, were n't the officers looking for a man instead of for a woman? And yet:

"If she was n't guilty of something, why did she run?"

It was too much for any one, and Fairchild knew it. Yet he clung grimly to the mystery as the truck clattered on, mile after mile, while the broad road led along the sides of the hills, finally to dip downward and run beside the bubbling Clear Creek,--clear no longer in the memory of the oldest inhabitant; but soiled by the silica from ore deposits that, churned and rechurned, gave to the stream a whitish, almost milk-like character, as it twisted in and out of the tortuous canon on its turbulent journey to the sea. But Fairchild failed to notice either that or the fact that ancient, age-whitened water wheels had begun to appear here and there, where gulch miners, seekers after gold in the silt of the creek's bed, had abandoned them years before; that now and then upon the hills showed the gaunt scars of mine openings,--reminders of dreams of a day long past; or even the more important fact that in the distance, softened by the mellowing rays of a dying sun, a small town gradually was coming into view. A mile more, then the truck stopped with a jerk.

"Where you bound for, pardner?"

Fairchild turned absently, then grinned in embarrassment.

"Ohadi."

"That's it, straight ahead. I turn off here. Stranger?"

"Yep."

"Miner?"

Fairchild shrugged his shoulders and nodded noncommittally. The truck driver toyed with his wheel.

"Just thought I 'd ask. Plenty of work around here for single and double jackers. Things are beginning to look up a bit--at least in silver. Gold mines ain't doing much yet--but there 's a good deal happening with the white stuff."

"Thanks. Do you know a good place to stop?"

"Yeh. Mother Howard's Boarding House. Everybody goes there, sooner or later. You 'll see it on the left-hand side of the street before you get to the main block. Good old girl; knows how to treat anybody in the mining game from operators on down. She was here when mining was mining!"

Which was enough recommendation for Mother Howard. Fairchild lifted his bag from the rear of the vehicle, waved a farewell to the driver and started into the village. And then--for once--the vision of the girl departed, momentarily, to give place to other thoughts, other pictures, of a day long gone.

The sun was slanting low, throwing deep shadows from the hills into the little valley with its chattering, milk-white stream, softening the scars of the mountains with their great refuse dumps; reminders of hopes of twenty years before and as bare of vegetation as in the days when the pick and gad and drill of the prospector tore the rock loose from its hiding place under the surface of the ground. Nature, in the mountainous country, resents any outrage against her dignity; the scars never heal; the mine dumps of a score of years ago remain the same, without a single shrub or weed or blade of grass growing in the big heaps of rocky refuse to shield them.

But now it was all softened and aglow with sunset. The deep red buildings of the Argonaut tunnel--a great, criss-crossing hole through the hills that once connected with more than thirty mines and their feverish activities--were denuded of their rust and lack of repair. The steam from the air-compressing engine, furnishing the necessary motive power for the drills that still worked in the hills, curled upward in billowy, rainbow-like coloring. The scrub pines of the almost barren mountains took on a fluffier, softer tone; the jutting rocks melted away into their own shadows, it was a picture of peace and of memories.

And it had been here that Thornton Fairchild, back in the nineties, had dreamed his dreams and fought his fight. It had been here--somewhere in one of the innumerable canons that led away from the little town on every side--that Thornton Fairchild had followed the direction of "float ore" to its resting place, to pursue the vagrant vein through the hills, to find it at last, to gloat over it in his letters to Beamish and then to--what?

A sudden cramping caught the son's heart, and it pounded with something akin to fear. The old foreboding of his father's letter had come upon him, the mysterious thread of that elusive, intangible Thing, great enough to break the will and resistance of a strong man and turn him into a weakling--silent, white-haired--sitting by a window, waiting for death. What had it been? Why had it come upon his father? How could it be fought? All so suddenly, Robert Fairchild had realized that he was in the country of the invisible enemy, there to struggle against it without the slightest knowledge of what it was or how it could be combated. His forehead felt suddenly damp and cold. He brushed away the beady perspiration with a gesture almost of anger, then with a look of relief, turned in at a small white gate toward a big, rambling building which proclaimed itself, by the sign on the door, to be Mother Howard's Boarding House.

A moment of waiting, then he faced a gray-haired, kindly faced woman, who stared at him with wide-open eyes as she stood, hands on hips, before him.

"Don't you tell me I don't know you!" she burst forth at last.

"I 'm afraid you don't."

"Don't I?" Mother Howard cocked her head. "If you ain't a Fairchild, I 'll never feed another miner corned beef and cabbage as long as I live. Ain't you now?" she persisted, "ain't you a Fairchild?"

The man laughed in spite of himself. "You guessed it."

"You 're Thornton Fairchild's boy!" She had reached out for his handbag, and then, bustling about him, drew him into the big "parlor" with its old-fashioned, plush-covered chairs, its picture album, its glass-covered statuary on the old, onyx mantel. "Did n't I know you the minute I saw you? Land, you're the picture of your dad! Sakes alive, how is he?"

There was a moment of silence. Fairchild found himself suddenly halting and boyish as he stood before her.

"He 's--he 's gone, Mrs. Howard."

"Dead?" She put up both hands. "It don't seem possible. And me remembering him looking just like you, full of life and strong and--"

"Our pictures of him are a good deal different. I--I guess you knew him when everything was all right for him. Things were different after he got home again."

Mother Howard looked quickly about her, then with a swift motion closed the door.

"Son," she asked in a low voice, "did n't he ever get over it?"

"It?" Fairchild felt that he stood on the threshold of discoveries. "What do you mean?"

"Didn't he ever tell you anything, Son?"

"No. I--"

"Well, there was n't any need to." But Mother Howard's sudden embarrassment, her change of color, told Fairchild it was n't the truth. "He just had a little bad luck out here, that was all. His--his mine pinched out just when he thought he 'd struck it rich--or something like that."

"Are you sure that is the truth?"

For a second they faced each other, Robert Fairchild serious and intent, Mother Howard looking at him with eyes defiant, yet compassionate. Suddenly they twinkled, the lips broke from their straight line into a smile, and a kindly old hand reached out to take him by the arm.

"Don't you stand there and try to tell Mother Howard she don't know what she 's talking about!" came in tones of mock severity. "Hear me? Now, you get up them steps and wash up for dinner. Take the first room on the right. It's a nice, cheery place. And get that dust and grime off of you. The dinner bell will ring in about fifteen minutes, and they 's always a rush for the food. So hurry!"

In his room, Fairchild tried not to think. His brain was becoming too crammed with queries, with strange happenings and with the aggravating mysticisms of the life into which his father's death had thrown him to permit clearness of vision. Even in Mother Howard, he had not been able to escape it; she told all too plainly, both by her actions and her words, that she knew something of the mystery of the past,--and had falsified to keep the knowledge from him.

It was too galling for thought. Robert Fairchild hastily made his toilet, then answered the ringing of the dinner bell, to be introduced to strong-shouldered men who gathered about the long tables; Cornishmen, who talked an "h-less" language, ruddy-faced Americans, and a sprinkling of English, all of whom conversed about things which were to Fairchild as so much Greek,--of "levels" and "stopes" and "winzes", of "skips" and "manways" and "raises", which meant nothing to the man who yet must master them all, if he were to follow his ambition. Some ate with their knives, meeting the food halfway from their plates; some acted and spoke in a manner revealing a college education and the poise that it gives. But all were as one, all talking together; the operator no more enthusiastic than the man whose sole recompense was the five dollars a day he received for drilling powder holes; all happy, all optimistic, all engrossed in the hopes and dreams that only mining can give. And among them Mother Howard moved, getting the latest gossip from each, giving her views on every problem and incidentally seeing that the plates were filled to the satisfaction of even the hungriest.

As for Robert Fairchild, he spoke but seldom, except to acknowledge the introductions as Mother Howard made him known to each of his table mates. But it was not aloofness; it was the fact that these men were talking of things which Fairchild longed to know, but failed, for the moment, to master. From the first, the newcomer had liked the men about him, liked the ruggedness, the mingling of culture with the lack of it, liked the enthusiasm, the muscle and brawn, liked them all,--all but two.

Instinctively, from the first mention of his name, he felt they were watching him, two men who sat far in the rear of the big dining room, older than the other occupants, far less inviting in appearance. One was small, though chunky in build, with sandy hair and eyebrows; with weak, filmy blue eyes over which the lids blinked constantly. The other, black-haired with streaks of gray, powerful in his build, and with a walrus-like mustache drooping over hard lips, was the sort of antithesis naturally to be found in the company of the smaller, sandy complexioned man. Who they were, what they were, Fairchild did not know, except from the general attributes which told that they too followed the great gamble of mining. But one thing was certain; they watched him throughout the meal; they talked about him in low tones and ceased when Mother Howard came near; they seemed to recognize in him some one who brought both curiosity and innate enmity to the surface. And more; long before the rest had finished their meal, they rose and left the room, intent, apparently, upon some important mission.

After that, Fairchild ate with less of a relish. In his mind was the certainty that these two men knew him--or at least knew about him--and that they did not relish his presence. Nor were his suspicions long in being fulfilled. Hardly had he reached the hall, when the beckoning eyes of Mother Howard signaled to him. Instinctively he waited for the other diners to pass him, then looked eagerly toward Mother Howard as she once more approached.

"I don't know what you 're doing here," came shortly, "but I want to."

Fairchild straightened. "There is n't much to tell you," he answered quietly. "My father left me the Blue Poppy mine in his will. I 'm here to work it."

"Know anything about mining?"

"Not a thing."

"Or the people you 're liable to have to buck up against?"

"Very little."

"Then, Son," and Mother Howard laid a kindly hand on his arm, "whatever you do, keep your plans to yourself and don't talk too much. And what's more, if you happen to get into communication with Blindeye Bozeman and Taylor Bill, lie your head off. Maybe you saw 'em, a sandy-haired fellow and a big man with a black mustache, sitting at the back of the room?" Fairchild nodded. "Well, stay away from them. They belong to 'Squint' Rodaine. Know him?"

She shot the question sharply. Again Fairchild nodded.

"I 've heard the name. Who is he?"

A voice called to Mother Howard from the dining room. She turned away, then leaned close to Robert Fairchild. "He 's a miner, and he 's always been a miner. Right now, he 's mixed up with some of the biggest people in town. He 's always been a man to be afraid of--and he was your father's worst enemy!"

Then, leaving Fairchild staring after her, she moved on to her duties in the kitchen.

CHAPTER V

Impatiently Fairchild awaited Mother Howard's return, and when at last she came forth from the kitchen, he drew her into the old parlor, shadowy now in the gathering dusk, and closed the doors.

"Mrs. Howard," he began, "I--"

"Mother Howard," she corrected. "I ain't used to being called much else."

"Mother, then--although I 'm not very accustomed to using the title. My own mother died--shortly after my father came back from out here."

She walked to his side then and put a hand on his shoulders. For a moment it seemed that her lips were struggling to repress something which strove to pass them, something locked behind them for years. Then the old face, dim in the half light, calmed.

"What do you want to know, Son?"

"Everything!"

"But there is n't much I can tell."

He caught her hand.

"There is! I know there is. I--"

"Son--all I can do is to make matters worse. If I knew anything that would help you--if I could give you any light on anything, Old Mother Howard would do it! Lord, did n't I help out your father when he needed it the worst way? Did n't I--"

"But tell me what you know!" There was pleading in Fairchild's voice. "Can't you understand what it all means to me? Anything--I 'm at sea, Mother Howard! I 'm lost--you 've hinted to me about enemies, my father hinted to me about them-- but that's all. Is n't it fair that I should know as much as possible if they still exist, and I 'm to make any kind of a fight against them?"

"You 're right, Son. But I 'm as much in the dark as you. In those days, if you were a friend to a person, you didn't ask questions. All that I ever knew was that your father came to this boarding house when he was a young man, the very first day that he ever struck Ohadi. He did n't have much money, but he was enthusiastic--and it was n't long before he 'd told me about his wife and baby back in Indianapolis and how he 'd like to win out for their sake. As for me--well, they always called me Mother Howard, even when I was a young thing, sort of setting my cap for every good-looking young man that came along. I guess that's why I never caught one of 'em--I always insisted on darning their socks and looking after all their troubles for 'em instead of going out buggy-riding with some other fellow and making 'em jealous." She sighed ever so slightly, then chuckled. "But that ain't getting to the point, though, is it?"

"If you could tell me about my father--"

"I 'm going to--all I know. Things were a lot different out here then from what they were later. Silver was wealth to anybody that could find it; every month, the Secretary of the Treasury was required by law to buy three or four million ounces for coining purposes, and it meant a lot of money for us all. Everywhere around the hills and gulches you could see prospectors, with their gads and little picks, fooling around like life did n't mean anything in the world to 'em, except to grub around in those rocks. That was the idea, you see, to fool around until they 'd found a bit of ore or float, as they called it, and then follow it up the gorge until they came to rock or indications that 'd give 'em reason to think that the vein was around there somewhere. Then they 'd start to make their tunnel--to drift in on the vein. I 'm telling you all this, so you 'll understand."

Fairchild was listening eagerly. A moment's pause and the old lodging-house keeper went on.

"Your father was one of these men. 'Squint' Rodaine was another--they called him that because at some time in his life he 'd tried to shoot faster than the other fellow--and did n't do it. The bullet hit right between his eyes, but it must have had poor powder behind it--all it did was to cut through the skin and go straight up his forehead. When the wound healed, the scar drew his eyes close together, like a Chinaman's. You never see Squint's eyes more than half open.

"And he's crooked, just like his eyes--" Mother Howard's voice bore a touch of resentment. "I never liked him from the minute I first saw him, and I liked him less afterward. Then I got next to his game.

"Your father had been prospecting just like everybody else. He 'd come on float up Kentucky Gulch and was trying to follow it to the vein. Squint saw him--and what's more, he saw that float. It looked good to Squint--and late that night, I heard him and his two drinking partners, Blindeye Bozeman and Taylor Bill--they just reverse his name for the sound of it--talking in Blindeye's room. I 'm a woman--" Mother Howard chuckled--"so I just leaned my head against the door and listened. Then I flew downstairs to wait for your father when he came in from sitting up half the night to get an assay on that float. And you bet I told him--folks can't do sneaking things around me and get away with it, and it was n't more 'n five minutes after he 'd got home that your father knew what was going on--how Squint and them two others was figuring on jumping his claim before he could file on it and all that.

"Well, there was a big Cornishman here that I was kind of sweet on--and I guess I always will be. He 's been gone now though, ever since your father left. I got him and asked him to help. And Harry was just the kind of a fellow that would do it. Out in the dead of night they went and staked out your father's claim--Harry was to get twenty-five per cent--and early the next morning your dad was waiting to file on it, while Harry was waiting for them three. And what a fight it must have been--that Harry was a wildcat in those younger days." She laughed, then her voice grew serious. "But all had its effect. Rodaine did n't jump that claim, and a few of us around here filed dummy claims enough in the vicinity to keep him off of getting too close--but there was one way we couldn't stop him. He had power, and he 's always had it--and he 's got it now. A lot of awful strange things happened to your father after that--charges were filed against him for things he never did. Men jumped on him in the dark, then went to the district attorney's office and accused him of making the attack. And the funny part was that the district attorney's office always believed them--and not him. Once they had him just at the edge of the penitentiary, but I--I happened to know a few things that--well, he did n't go." Again Mother Howard chuckled, only to grow serious once more. "Those days were a bit wild in Ohadi--everybody was crazy with the gold or silver fever; out of their head most of the time. Men who went to work for your father and Harry disappeared, or got hurt accidentally in the mine or just quit through the bad name it was getting. Once Harry, coming down from the tunnel at night, stepped on a little bridge that always before had been as secure and safe as the hills themselves. It fell with him--they went down together thirty feet, and there was nothing but Nature to blame for it, in spite of what we three thought. Then, at last, they got a fellow who was willing to work for them in spite of what Rodaine's crowd--and it consisted of everybody in power--hinted about your father's bad reputation back East and--"

"My father never harmed a soul in his life!" Fairchild's voice was hot, resentful. Mother Howard went on:

"I know he did n't, Son. I 'm only telling the story. Miners are superstitious as a general rule, and they 're childish at believing things. It all worked in your father's case--with the exception of Harry and 'Sissie' Larsen, a Swede with a high voice, just about like mine. That's why they gave him the name. Your father offered him wages and a ten per cent. bonus. He went to work. A few months later they got into good ore. That paid fairly well, even if it was irregular. It looked like the bad luck was over at last. Then--"

Mother Howard hesitated at the brink of the very nubbin of it all, to Robert Fairchild. A long moment followed, in which he repressed a desire to seize her and wrest it from her, and at last--

"It was about dusk one night," she went on. "Harry came in and took me with him into this very room. He kissed me and told me that he must go away. He asked me if I would go with him--without knowing why. And, Son, I trusted him, I would have done anything for him--but I was n't as old then as I am now. I refused--and to this day, I don't know why. It--it was just woman, I guess. Then he asked me if I would help him. I said I would.

"He did n't tell me much; except that he had been uptown spreading the word that the ore had pinched out and that the hanging rock had caved in and that he and 'Sissie' and your father were through, that they were beaten and were going away that night. But--and Harry waited a long time before he told me this--'Sissie' was not going with them.

"'I'm putting a lot in your hands,' he told me, 'but you 've got to help us. "Sissie" won't be there--and I can't tell you why. The town must think that he is. Your voice is just like "Sissie's." You 've got to help us out of town.'

"And I promised. Late that night, the three of us drove up the main street, your father on one side of the seat. Harry on the other, and me, dressed in some of

Sissie's clothes, half hidden between them. I was singing; that was Sissie's habit,--to get roaring drunk and blow off steam by yodelling song after song as he rolled along. Our voices were about the same; nobody dreamed that I was any one else but the Swede--my head was tipped forward, so they couldn't see my features. And we went our way with the miners standing on the curb waving to us, and not one of them knowing that the person who sat between your father and Harry was any one except Larsen. We drove outside town and stopped. Then we said good-by, and I put on an old dress that I had brought with me and sneaked back home. Nobody knew the difference."

"But Larsen--?"

"You know as much as I do, Son."

"But did n't they tell you?"

"They told me nothing and I asked 'em nothing. They were my friends and they needed help. I gave it to them--that's all I know and that's all I 've wanted to know."

"You never saw Larsen again?"

"I never saw any of them. That was the end."

"But Rodaine--?"

"He 's still here. You 'll hear from him--plenty soon. I could see that, the minute Blindeye Bozeman and Taylor Bill began taking your measure. You noticed they left the table before the meal was over? It was to tell Rodaine."

"Then he'll fight me too?"

Mother Howard laughed,--and her voice was harsh.

"Rodaine's a rattlesnake. His son 's a rattlesnake. His wife 's crazy--Old Crazy Laura. He drove her that way. She lives by herself, in an old house on the Georgeville road. And she 'd kill for him, even if he does beat her when she goes to his house and begs him to take her back. That's the kind of a crowd it is. You can figure it out for yourself. She goes around at night, gathering herbs in graveyards; she thinks she 's a witch. The old man mutters to himself and hates any one who doesn't do everything he asks,--and just about everybody does it, simply through fear. And just to put a good finish on it all, the young 'un moves in the best society in town and spends most of his time trying to argue the former district judge's daughter into marrying him. So there you are. That's all Mother Howard knows,

Son."

She reached for the door and then, turning, patted Fairchild on the shoulder.

"Boy," came quietly, "you 've got a broad back and a good head. Rodaine beat your father--don't let him beat you. And always remember one thing: Old Mother Howard 's played the game before, and she 'll play it with you--against anybody. Good night. Go to bed--dark streets are n't exactly the place for you."

Robert Fairchild obeyed the instructions, a victim of many a conjecture, many an attempt at reasoning as he sought sleep that was far away. Again and again there rose before him the vision of two men in an open buggy, with a singing, apparently maudlin person between them whom Ohadi believed to be an effeminate-voiced Swede; in reality, only a woman. And why had they adopted the expedient? Why had not Larsen been with them in reality? Fairchild avoided the obvious conclusion and turned to other thoughts, to Rodaine with his squint eyes, to Crazy Laura, gathering herbs at midnight in the shadowy, stone-sentineled stretches of graveyards, while the son, perhaps, danced at some function of Ohadi's society and made love in the rest periods. It was all grotesque; it was fantastic, almost laughable,--had it not concerned him! For Rodaine had been his father's enemy, and Mother Howard had told him enough to assure him that Rodaine did not forget. The crazed woman of the graveyards was Squint's lunatic wife, ready to kill, if necessary, for a husband who beat her. And the young Rodaine was his son, blood of his blood; that was enough. It was hours before Fairchild found sleep, and even then it was a thing of troubled visions.

Streaming sun awakened him, and he hurried to the dining room to find himself the last lodger at the tables. He ate a rather hasty meal, made more so by an impatient waitress, then with the necessary papers in his pocket, Fairchild started toward the courthouse and the legal procedure which must be undergone before he made his first trip to the mine.

A block or two, and then Fairchild suddenly halted. Crossing the street at an angle just before him was a young woman whose features, whose mannerisms he recognized. The whipcord riding habit had given place now to a tailored suit which deprived her of the boyishness that had been so apparent on their first meeting. The cap had disappeared before a close-fitting, vari-colored turban. But the straying brown hair still was there, the brown eyes, the piquant little nose and the prettily formed lips. Fairchild's heart thumped,--nor did he stop to consider why. A quickening of his pace, and he met her just as she stepped to the curbing.

"I 'm so glad of this opportunity," he exclaimed happily. "I want to return that money to you. I--I was so fussed yesterday I did n't realize--"

"Aren't you mistaken?" She had looked at him with a slight smile. Fairchild did not catch the inflection.

"Oh, no. I 'm the man, you know, who helped you change that tire on the Denver road yesterday."

"Pardon me." This time one brown eye had wavered ever so slightly, indicating some one behind Fairchild. "But I was n't on the Denver road yesterday, and if you 'll excuse me for saying it, I don't remember ever having seen you before."

There was a little light in her eyes which took away the sting of the denial, a light which seemed to urge caution, and at the same time to tell Fairchild that she trusted him to do his part as a gentleman in a thing she wished forgotten. More fussed than ever, he drew back and bent low in apology, while she passed on. Half a block away, a young man rounded a corner and, seeing her, hastened to join her. She extended her hand; they chatted a moment, then strolled up the street together. Fairchild watched blankly, then turned at a chuckle just behind him emanating from the bearded lips of an old miner, loafing on the stone coping in front of a small store.

"Pick the wrong filly, pardner?" came the query. Fairchild managed to smile.

"Guess so." Then he lied quickly. "I thought she was a girl from Denver."

"Her?" The old miner stretched. "Nope. That's Anita Richmond, old Judge Richmond's daughter. Guess she must have been expecting that young fellow--or she would n't have cut you off so short. She ain't usually that way."

"Her fiance?" Fairchild asked the question with misgiving. The miner finished his stretch and added a yawn to it. Then he looked appraisingly up the street toward the retreating figures. "Well, some say he is and some say he ain't. Guess it mostly depends on the girl, and she ain't telling yet."

"And the man--who is he?"

"Him? Oh, he 's Maurice Rodaine. Son of a pretty famous character around here, old Squint Rodaine. Owns the Silver Queen property up the hill. Ever hear of him?"

The eyes of Robert Fairchild narrowed, and a desire to fight--a longing to grapple with Squint Rodaine and all that belonged to him--surged into his heart. But his voice, when he spoke, was slow and suppressed.

"Squint Rodaine? Yes, I think I have. The name sounds rather familiar."

Then, deliberately, he started up the street, following at a distance the man and the girl who walked before him.

CHAPTER VI

There was no specific reason why Robert Fairchild should follow Maurice Rodaine and the young woman who had been described to him as the daughter of Judge Richmond, whoever he might be. And Fairchild sought for none--within two weeks he had been transformed from a plodding, methodical person into a creature of impulses, and more and more, as time went on, he was allowing himself to be governed by the snap judgment of his brain rather than by the carefully exacting mind of a systematic machine, such as he had been for the greater part of his adult life. All that he cared to know was that resentment was in his heart,--resentment that the family of Rodaine should be connected in some way with the piquant, mysterious little person he had helped out of a predicament on the Denver road the day before. And, to his chagrin, the very fact that there *was* a connection added a more sinister note to the escapade of the exploded tire and the pursuing sheriff; as he walked along, his gaze far ahead, Fairchild found himself wondering whether there could be more than mere coincidence in it all, whether she was a part of the Rodaine schemes and the Rodaine trickery, whether--

But he ceased his wondering to turn sharply into a near-by drug store, there absently to give an order at the soda fountain and stand watching the pair who had stopped just in front of him on the corner. She was the same girl; there could be no doubt of that, and he raged inwardly as she chatted and chaffed with the man who looked down upon her with a smiling air of proprietorship which instilled instant rebellion in Fairchild's heart. Nor did he know the reason for that, either.

After a moment they parted, and Fairchild gulped at his fountain drink. She had hesitated, then with a quick decision turned straight into the drug store.

"Buy a ticket, Mr. McCauley?" she asked of the man behind the counter. "I 've sold twenty already, this morning. Only five more, and my work 's over."

"Going to be pretty much of a crowd, is n't there?" The druggist was fishing in his pocket for money. Fairchild, dallying with his drink now, glanced sharply toward the door and went back to his refreshment. She was standing directly in the entrance, fingering the five remaining tickets.

"Oh, everybody in town. Please take the five, won't you? Then I 'll be through."

"I 'll be darned if I will, 'Nita!" McCauley backed against a shelf case in mock self-defense. "Every time you 've got anything you want to get rid of, you come in here and shove it off on me. I 'll be gosh gim-swiggled if I will. There 's only four in my family and four 's all I 'm going to take. Fork 'em over--I 've got a prescription to fill." He tossed four silver dollars on the showcase and took the tickets. The girl demurred.

"But how about the fifth one? I 've got to sell that too--"

"Well, sell it to him!" And Fairchild, looking into the soda-fountain mirror, saw himself indicated as the druggist started toward the prescription case. "I ain't going to let myself get stuck for another solitary, single one!"

There was a moment of awkward silence as Fairchild gazed intently into his soda glass, then with a feeling of queer excitement, set it on the marble counter and turned. Anita Richmond had accepted the druggist's challenge. She was approaching--in a stranger-like manner--a ticket of some sort held before her.

"Pardon me," she began, "but would you care to buy a ticket?"

"To--to what?" It was all Fairchild could think of to say.

"To the Old Timers' Dance. It's a sort of municipal thing, gotten up by the bureau of mines--to celebrate the return of silver mining."

"But--but I 'm afraid I 'm not much on dancing."

"You don't have to be. Nobody 'll dance much--except the old-fashioned affairs. You see, everybody 's supposed to represent people of the days when things were booming around here. There 'll be a fiddle orchestra, and a dance caller and everything like that, and a bar--but of course there 'll only be imitation liquor. But," she added with quick emphasis, "there 'll be a lot of things really real--real keno and roulette and everything like that, and everybody in the costume of thirty or forty years ago. Don't you want to buy a ticket? It's the last one I 've got!" she added prettily. But Robert Fairchild had been listening with his eyes, rather than his ears. Jerkily he came to the realization that the girl had ceased speaking.

"When's it to be?"

"A week from to-morrow night. Are you going to be here that long?"

She realized the slip of her tongue and colored slightly. Fairchild, recovered now, reached into a pocket and carefully fingered the bills there. Then, with a quick motion, as he drew them forth, he covered a ten-dollar bill with a one-dollar note and thrust them forward.

"Yes, I 'll take the ticket."

She handed it to him, thanked him, and reached for the money. As it passed into her hand, a corner of the ten-dollar bill revealed itself, and she hastily thrust it toward him as though to return money paid by mistake. Just as quickly, she realized his purpose and withdrew her hand.

"Oh!" she exclaimed, almost in a whisper, "I understand." She flushed and stood a second hesitant, flustered, her big eyes almost childish as they looked up into his. "You--you must think I 'm a cad!" Then she whirled and left the store, and a slight smile came to the lips of Robert Fairchild as he watched her hurrying across the street. He had won a tiny victory, at least.

Not until she had rounded a corner and disappeared did Fairchild leave his point of vantage. Then, with a new enthusiasm, a greater desire than ever to win out in the fight which had brought him to Ohadi, he hurried to the courthouse and the various technicalities which must be coped with before he could really call the Blue Poppy mine his own.

It was easier than he thought. A few signatures, and he was free to wander through town to where idlers had pointed out Kentucky gulch and to begin the steep ascent up the narrow road on a tour of prospecting that would precede the more legal and more safe system of a surveyor.

The ascent was almost sheer in places, for in Kentucky gulch the hills huddled close to the little town and rose in precipitous inclines almost before the city limits had been reached. Beside the road a small stream chattered, milk-white from the silica deposits of the mines, like the waters of Clear Creek, which it was hastening to join. Along the gullies were the scars of prospect holes, staring like dark, blind eyes out upon the gorge;--reminders of the lost hopes of a day gone by. Here and there lay some discarded piece of mining machinery, rust-eaten and battered now, washed down inch by inch from the higher hill where it had been abandoned when the demonetization of silver struck, like a rapier, into the hearts of grubbing men, years before. It was a canon of decay, yet of life, for as he trudged along, the roar of great motors came to Fairchild's ears; and a moment later he stepped aside to allow the passage of ore-laden automobile trucks, loaded until the springs had flattened and until the engines howled with their compression as they sought to hold back their burdens on the steep grade. And it was as he stood there, watching the big vehicles travel down the mountain side, that Fairchild caught a glimpse of a human figure which suddenly darted behind a clump of scrub pine and skirted far to one side, taking advantage of every covering. A new beat came into Fairchild's heart. He took to the road again, plodding upward apparently without a thought of his pursuer, stopping to stare at the bleak prospect holes, or to admire the pink-white beauties of the snowy range in the far distance, seemingly a man entirely bereft of suspicion. A quarter of a mile he went, a half. Once, as the road turned beside a great rock, he sought its shelter and looked back. The figure still was following, running carefully now along the bank of the stream in an effort to gain as much ground as possible before the return of the road to open territory should bring the necessity of caution again.

A mile more, then, again in the shelter of rocks, he swerved and sought a hiding place, watching anxiously from his concealment for evidences of discovery. There were none. The shadower came on, displaying more and more caution as he approached the rocks, glancing hurriedly about him as he moved swiftly from cover to cover. Closer--closer--then Fairchild repressed a gasp. The man was old, almost white-haired, with hard, knotted hands which seemed to stand out from his wrists; thin and wiry with the resiliency that outdoor, hardened muscles often give to age, and with a face that held Fairchild almost hypnotized. It was like a hawk's; hook-beaked, colorless, toneless in all expressions save that of a malicious tenacity; the eyes were slanted until they resembled those of some fantastic Chinese image, while just above the curving nose a blue-white scar ran straight up the forehead,-- Squint Rodaine!

So he was on the trail already! Fairchild watched him pass, sneak around the corner of the rocks, and stand a moment in apparent bewilderment as he surveyed the ground before him. A mumbling curse and he went on, his cautious gait discarded, walking briskly along the rutty, boulder-strewn road toward a gaping hole in the hill, hardly a furlong away. There he surveyed the ground carefully, bent and stared hard at the earth, apparently for a trace of footprints, and finding none, turned slowly and looked intently all about him. Carefully he approached the mouth of the tunnel and stared within. Then he straightened, and with another glance about him, hurried off up a gulch leading away from the road, into the hills. Fairchild lay and watched him until he was out of sight, and he knew instinctively that a surveyor would only cover beaten territory now. Squint Rodaine, he felt sure, had pointed out to him the Blue Poppy mine.

But he did not follow the direction given by his pursuer. Squint Rodaine was in the hills. Squint Rodaine might return, and the consciousness of caution bade that Fairchild not be there when he came back. Hurriedly he descended the rocks once more to turn toward town and toward Mother Howard's boarding house. He wanted to tell her what he had seen and to obtain her help and counsel.

Quickly he made the return trip, crossing the little bridge over the turbulent Clear Creek and heading toward the boarding house. Half a block away he halted, as a woman on the veranda of the big, squarely built "hotel" pointed him out, and the great figure of a man shot through the gate, shouting, and hurried toward him.

A tremendous creature he was, with red face and black hair which seemed to scramble in all directions at once, and with a mustache which appeared to scamper in even more directions than his hair. Fairchild was a large man; suddenly he felt himself puny and inconsequential as the mastodonic thing before him swooped forward, spread wide the big arms and then caught him tight in them, causing the breath to puff over his lips like the exhaust of a bellows.

A release, then Fairchild felt himself lifted and set down again. He pulled hard at his breath.

"What's the matter with you?" he exclaimed testily. "You 've made a mistake!"

"I 'm blimed if I 'ave!" bellowed a tornado-like voice. "Blime! You look just like 'im!"

"But you 're mistaken, old man!"

Fairchild was vaguely aware that the spray-like mustache was working like a dust-broom, that snappy blue eyes were beaming upon him, that the big red nose was growing redder, while a tremendous paw had seized his own hand and was doing its best to crush it.

"Blimed if I 'ave!" came again. "You're your Dad's own boy! You look just like 'im! Don't you know me?"

He stepped back then and stood grinning, his long, heavily muscled arms hanging low at his sides, his mustache trying vainly to stick out in more directions than ever. Fairchild rubbed a hand across his eyes.

"You 've got me!" came at last. "I--"

"You don't know me? 'Onest now, don't you? I 'm Arry! Don't you know now? 'Arry from Cornwall!"

CHAPTER VII

It came to Fairchild then,--the sentence in his father's letter regarding some one who would hurry to his aid when he needed him, the references of Beamish, and the allusion of Mother Howard to a faithful friend. He forgot the pain as the tremendous Cornishman banged him on the back, he forgot the surprise of it all; he only knew that he was laughing and welcoming a big man old enough in age to be his father, yet young enough in spirit to want to come back and finish a fight he had seen begun, and strong enough in physique to stand it. Again the heavy voice boomed:

"You know me now, eh?"

"You bet! You 're Harry Harkins!"

"'Arkins it is! I came just as soon as I got the cablegram!"

"The cablegram?"

"Yeh." Harry pawed at his wonderful mustache. "From Mr. Beamish, you know. 'E sent it. Said you 'd started out 'ere all alone. And I could n't stand by and let you do that. So 'ere I am!"

"But the expense, the long trip across the ocean, the--"

"'Ere I am!" said Harry again. "Ain't that enough?"

They had reached the veranda now, to stand talking for a moment, then to go within, where Mother Howard awaited, eyes glowing, in the parlor. Harry flung out both arms.

"And I still love you!" he boomed, as he caught the gray-haired, laughing woman in his arms. "Even if you did run me off and would n't go back to Cornwall!"

Red-faced, she pushed him away and slapped his cheek playfully; it was like the tap of a light breeze against granite. Then Harry turned.

"'Ave you looked at the mine?"

The question brought back to Fairchild the happenings of the morning and the memory of the man who had trailed him. He told his story, while Mother Howard listened, her arms crossed, her head bobbing, and while Harry, his big grin still on his lips, took in the details with avidity. Then for a moment a monstrous hand scrambled vaguely about in the region of the Cornishman's face, grasping a hair of that radiating mustache now and then and pulling hard at it, at last to drop,--and the grin faded.

"Le 's go up there," he said quietly.

This time the trip to Kentucky gulch was made by skirting town; soon they were on the rough, narrow roadway leading into the mountains. Both were silent for the most part, and the expression on Harry's face told that he was living again the days of the past, days when men were making those pock-marks in the hills, when the prospector and his pack jack could be seen on every trail, and when float ore in a gulley meant riches waiting somewhere above. A long time they walked, at last to stop in the shelter of the rocks where Fairchild had shadowed his pursuer, and to glance carefully ahead. No one was in sight. Harry jabbed out a big finger.

"That's it," he announced, "straight a'ead!"

They went on, Fairchild with a gripping at his throat that would not down. This had been the hope of his father--and here his father had met--what? He swerved quickly and stopped, facing the bigger man.

"Harry," came sharply, "I know that I may be violating an unspoken promise to my father. But I simply can't stand it any longer. What happened here?"

"We were mining--for silver."

"I don't mean that--there was some sort of tragedy."

Harry chuckled,--in concealment, Fairchild thought, of something he did not want to tell him.

"I should think so! The timbers gave way and the mine caved in!"

"Not that! My father ran away from this town. You and Mother Howard helped him. You didn't come back. Neither did my father. Eventually it killed him."

"So?" Harry looked seriously and studiously at the young man. "'E did n't write me of'en."

"He did n't need to write you. You were here with him--when it happened."

"No--" Harry shook his head. "I was in town."

"But you knew--"

"What's Mother Howard told you?"

"A lot--and nothing."

"I don't know any more than she does."

"But--"

"Friends did n't ask questions in those days," came quietly. "I might 'ave guessed if I 'd wanted to--but I did n't want to."

"But if you had?"

Harry looked at him with quiet, blue eyes.

"What would you guess?"

Slowly Robert Fairchild's gaze went to the ground. There was only one possible conjecture: Sissie Larsen had been impersonated by a woman. Sissie Larsen had never been seen again in Ohadi.

"I--I would hate to put it into words," came finally. Harry slapped him on the shoulder.

"Then don't. It was nearly thirty years ago. Let sleeping dogs lie. Take a look around before we go into the tunnel."

They reconnoitered, first on one side, then on the other. No one was in sight. Harry bent to the ground, and finding a pitchy pine knot, lighted it. They started cautiously within, blinking against the darkness.

A detour and they avoided an ore car, rusty and half filled, standing on the little track, now sagging on moldy ties. A moment more of walking and Harry took the lead.

"It's only a step to the shaft now," he cautioned. "Easy--easy--look out for that 'anging wall--" he held the pitch torch against the roof of the tunnel and displayed a loose, jagged section of rock, dripping with seepage from the hills above. "Just a step now--'ere it is."

The outlines of a rusty "hoist", with its cable leading down into a slanting hole in the rock, showed dimly before them,--a massive, chunky, deserted thing in the shadows. About it were clustered drills that were eaten by age and the dampness of the seepage; farther on a "skip", or shaft-car, lay on its side, half buried in mud and muck from the walls of the tunnel. Here, too, the timbers were rotting; one after another, they had cracked and caved beneath the weight of the earth above, giving the tunnel an eerie aspect, uninviting, dangerous. Harry peered ahead.

"It ain't as bad as it looks," came after a moment's survey. "It's only right 'ere at the beginning that it's caved. But that does n't do us much good."

"Why not?" Fairchild was staring with him, on toward the darkness of the farther recesses. "If it is n't caved in farther back, we ought to be able to repair this spot."

But Harry shook his head.

"We did n't go into the vein 'ere," he explained. "We figured we 'ad to 'ave a shaft anyway, sooner or later. You can't do under'and stoping in a mine--go down on a vein, you know. You 've always got to go up--you can't get the metal out if you don't. That's why we dug this shaft--and now look at it!"

He drew the flickering torch to the edge of the shaft and held it there, staring downward. Fairchild beside him. Twenty feet below there came the glistening reflection of the flaring flame. Water! Fairchild glanced toward his partner.

"I don't know anything about it," he said at last. "But I should think that would mean trouble."

"Plenty!" agreed Harry lugubriously. "That shaft's two 'unnerd feet deep and there 's a drift running off it for a couple o' 'unnerd feet more before it 'its the vein. Four 'unnerd feet of water. 'Ow much money 'ave you got?"

"About twenty-five hundred dollars."

Harry reached for his waving mustache, his haven in time of storm. Thoughtfully he pulled at it, staring meanwhile downward. Then he grunted.

"And I ain't got more 'n five 'unnerd. It ain't enough. We 'll need to repair this 'oist and put the skip in order. We 'll need to build new track and do a lot of things. Three thousand dollars ain't enough."

"But we 'll have to get that water out of there before we can do anything." Fairchild interposed. "If we can't get at the vein up here, we 'll have to get at it from below. And how 're we going to do that without unwatering that shaft?"

Again Harry pulled at his mustache.

"That's just what 'Arry 's thinking about," came his answer finally. "Le 's go back to town. I don't like to stand around this place and just look at water in a 'ole."

They turned for the mouth of the tunnel, sliding along in the greasy muck, the torch extinguished now. A moment of watchfulness from the cover of the darkness, then Harry pointed. On the opposite hill, the figure of a man had been outlined for just a second. Then he had faded. And with the disappearance of the watcher, Harry nudged his partner in the ribs and went forth into the brighter light. An hour more and they were back in town. Harry reached for his mustache again.

"Go on down to Mother 'Oward's," he commanded. "I 've got to wander around and say 'owdy to what's left of the fellows that was 'ere when I was. It's been twenty years since I 've been away, you know," he added, "and the shaft can wait."

Fairchild obeyed the instructions, looking back over his shoulder as he walked along toward the boarding house, to see the big figure of his companion loitering up the street, on the beginning of his home-coming tour. It was evident that Harry was popular. Forms rose from the loitering places on the curbings in front of the stores, voices called to him; even as the distance grew greater, Fairchild could hear the shouts of greeting which were sounding to Harry as he announced his return.

The blocks passed. Fairchild turned through the gate of Mother Howard's boarding house and went to his room to await the call for dinner. The world did not look exceptionally good to him; his brilliant dreams had not counted upon the decay of more than a quarter of a century, the slow, but sure dripping of water which had seeped through the hills and made the mine one vast well, instead of the free open gateway to riches which he had planned upon. True, there had been before him the certainty of a cave-in, but Fairchild was not a miner, and the word to him had been a vague affair. Now, however, it was taking on a new aspect; he was beginning to realize the full extent of the fight which was before him if the Blue Poppy mine ever were to turn forth the silver ore he hoped to gain from it, if the letter of his father, full of threats though it might be, were to be realized in that part of it which contained the promise of riches in abundance.

Pitifully small his capital looked to Fairchild now. Inadequate--that was certain--for the needs which now stood before it. And there was no person to whom he could turn, no one to whom he could go, for more. To borrow, one must have security; and with the exception of the faith of the red-faced Harry, and the promise of a silent man, now dead, there was nothing. It was useless; an hour of thought and Fairchild ceased trying to look into the future, obeying, instead, the insistent clanging of the dinner bell from downstairs. Slowly he opened the door of his room, trudged down the staircase,--then stopped in bewilderment. Harry stood before him, in all the splendor that a miner can know.

He had bought a new suit, brilliant blue, almost electric in its flashiness, nor had he been careful as to style. The cut of the trousers was somewhat along the lines of fifteen years before, with their peg tops and heavy cuffs. Beneath the vest, a glowing, watermelon-pink shirt glared forth from the protection of a purple tie. A wonderful creation was on his head, dented in four places, each separated with almost mathematical precision. Below the cuffs of the trousers were bright, tan, bump-toed shoes. Harry was a complete picture of sartorial elegance, according to his own dreams. What was more, to complete it all, upon the third finger of his right hand was a diamond, bulbous and yellow and throwing off a dull radiance like the glow of a burnt-out arclight; full of flaws, it is true, off color to a great degree, but a diamond nevertheless. And Harry evidently realized it.

"Ain't I the cuckoo?" he boomed, as Fairchild stared at him. "Ain't I? I 'ad to 'ave a outfit, and--

"It might as well be now!" he paraphrased, to the tune of the age-whitened sextette from "Floradora." "And look at the sparkler! Look at it!"

Fairchild could do very little else but look. He knew the value, even in spite of flaws and bad coloring. And he knew something else, that Harry had confessed to having little more than five hundred dollars.

"But--but how did you do it?" came gaspingly. "I thought--"

"Installments!" the Cornishman burst out. "Ten per cent. down and the rest when they catch me. Installments!" He jabbed forth a heavy finger and punched Fairchild in the ribs. "Where's Mother 'Oward? Won't I knock 'er eyes out?"

Fairchild laughed--he couldn't help it--in spite of the fact that five hundred dollars might have gone a long way toward unwatering that shaft. Harry was Harry--he had done enough in crossing the seas to help him. And already, in the eyes of Fairchild, Harry was swiftly approaching that place where he could do no wrong.

"You're wonderful, Harry," came at last. The Cornishman puffed with pride.

"I'm a cuckoo!" he admitted. "Where's Mother 'Oward? Where's Mother 'Oward? Won't I knock 'er eyes out, now?"

And he boomed forward toward the dining room, to find there men he had known in other days, to shake hands with them and to bang them on the back, to sight Blindeye Bozeman and Taylor Bill sitting hunched over their meal in the corner and to go effusively toward them. "'Arry" was playing no favorites in his "'ome-coming." "'Arry" was "'appy", and a little thing like the fact that friends of his enemies were present seemed to make little difference.

Jovially he leaned over the table of Bozeman and Bill, after he had displayed himself before Mother Howard and received her sanction of his selections in dress. Happily he boomed forth the information that Fairchild and he were back to work the Blue Poppy mine and that they already had made a trip of inspection.

"I 'm going back this afternoon," he told them. "There 's water in the shaft. I 've got to figure a wye to get it out."

Then he returned to his table and Fairchild leaned close to him.

"Is n't that dangerous?"

"What?" Harry allowed his eyes to become bulbous as he whispered the question. "Telling them two about what we 're going to do? Won't they find it out anyway?"

"I guess that's true. What time are you going to the mine?"

"I don't know that I 'm going. And then I may. I 've got to kind of sye 'ello around town first."

"Then I 'm not to go with you?"

Harry beamed at him.

"It's your day off, Robert," he announced, and they went on with their meal.

That is, Fairchild proceeded. Harry did little eating. Harry was too busy. Around him were men he had known in other days, men who had stayed on at the little silver camp, fighting against the inevitable downward course of the price of the white metal, hoping for the time when resuscitation would come, and now realizing that feeling of joy for which they had waited a quarter of a century. There were a thousand questions to be answered, all asked by Harry. There was gossip to relate and the lives of various men who had come and gone to be dilated upon. Fairchild finished his meal and waited. But Harry talked on. Bozeman and Bill left the dining room again to make a report to the narrow-faced Squint Rodaine. Harry did not even notice them. And as long as a man stayed to answer his queries, just so long did Harry remain, at last to rise, brush a few crumbs from his lightning-like suit, press his new hat gently upon his head with both hands and start forth once more on his rounds of saying hello. And there was nothing for Fairchild to do but to wait as patiently as possible for his return.

The afternoon grew old. Harry did not come back. The sun set and dinner was served. But Harry was not there to eat it. Dusk came, and then, nervous over the continued absence of his eccentric partner, Fairchild started uptown.

The usual groups were in front of the stores, and before the largest of them Fairchild stopped.

"Do any of you happen to know a fellow named Harry Harkins?" he asked somewhat anxiously. The answer was in the affirmative. A miner stretched out a foot and surveyed it studiously.

"Ain't seen him since about five o'clock," he said at last. "He was just starting up to the mine then."

"To the mine? That late? Are you sure?"

"Well--I dunno. May have been going to Center City. Can't say. All I know is he said somethin' about goin' to th' mine earlier in th' afternoon, an' long about five I seen him starting up Kentucky Gulch."

"Who 's that?" The interruption had come in a sharp, yet gruff voice. Fairchild turned to see before him a man he recognized, a tall, thin, wiry figure, with narrowed, slanting eyes, and a scar that went straight up his forehead. He evidently had just rounded the corner in time to hear the conversation. Fairchild straightened, and in spite of himself his voice was strained and hard.

"I was merely asking about my partner in the Blue Poppy mine."

"The Blue Poppy?" the squint eyes narrowed more than ever. "You 're Fairchild, ain't you? Well, I guess you 're going to have to get along without a partner from now on."

"Get along without--?"

A crooked smile came to the other man's lips.

"That is, unless you want to work with a dead man. Harry Harkins got drowned, about an hour ago, in the Blue Poppy shaft!"

CHAPTER VIII

The news caused Fairchild to recoil and stand gasping. And before he could speak, a new voice had cut in, one full of excitement, tremulous, anxious. "Drowned? Where 's his body?"

"How do I know?" Squint Rodaine turned upon his questioner. "Guess it's at the foot of the shaft. All I saw was his hat. What 're you so interested for?"

The questioner, small, goggle-eyed and given to rubbing his hands, stared a moment speechlessly. Then he reached forward and grasped at the lapels of Rodaine's coat.

"He--he bought a diamond from me this morning--on the installment plan!"

Rodaine smiled again in his crooked fashion. Then he pushed the clawlike hands of the excited jeweler away from his lapels.

"That's your own fault, Sam," he announced curtly. "If he 's at the bottom of the shaft, your diamond 's there too. All I know about it is that I was coming down from the Silver Queen when I saw this fellow go into the tunnel of the Blue Poppy. He was all dressed up, else I don't guess I would have paid much attention to him. But as it was, I kind of stopped to look, and seen it was Harry Harkins, who used to work the mine with this"--he pointed to Fairchild--"this fellow's father. About a minute later, I heard a yell, like somebody was in trouble, then a big splash. Naturally I ran in the tunnel and struck a match. About twenty feet down, I could see the water was all riled up, and a new hat was floating around on top of it. I yelled a couple of times and struck a lot of matches--but he did n't come to the surface. That's all I know. You can do as you please about your diamond. I 'm just giving you the information."

He turned sharply and went on then, while Sam the jeweler, the rest of the loiterers clustered around him, looked appealingly toward Fairchild.

"What 'll we do?" he wailed.

Fairchild turned. "I don't know about you--but I 'm going to the mine."

"It won't do any good--bodies don't float. It may never float--if it gets caught down in the timbers somewheres."

"Have to organize a bucket brigade." It was a suggestion from one of the crowd.

"Why not borry the Argonaut pump? They ain't using it."

"Go get it! Go get it!" This time it was the wail of the little jeweler. "Tell 'em Sam Herbenfelder sent you. They 'll let you have it."

"Can't carry the thing on my shoulder."

"I 'll get the Sampler's truck"--a new volunteer had spoken--"there won't be any kick about it."

Another suggestion, still another. Soon men began to radiate, each on a mission. The word passed down the street. More loiterers--a silver miner spends a great part of his leisure time in simply watching the crowd go by--hurried to join the excited throng. Groups, en route to the picture show, decided otherwise and stopped to learn of the excitement. The crowd thickened. Suddenly Fairchild looked up sharply at the sound of a feminine voice.

"What is the matter?"

"Harry Harkins got drowned." All too willingly the news was dispersed. Fairchild's eyes were searching now in the half-light from the faint street bulbs. Then they centered. It was Anita Richmond, standing at the edge of the crowd, questioning a miner, while beside her was a thin, youthful counterpart of a hard-faced father, Maurice Rodaine. Just a moment of queries, then the miner's hand pointed to Fairchild as he turned toward her.

"It's his partner."

She moved forward then and Fairchild went to meet her.

"I 'm sorry," she said, and extended her hand. Fairchild gripped it eagerly.

"Thank you. But it may not be as bad as the rumors."

"I hope not." Then quickly she withdrew her hand, and somewhat flustered, turned as her companion edged closer. "Maurice, this is Mr. Fairchild," she announced, and Fairchild could do nothing but stare. She knew his name! A second more and it was explained; "My father knew his father very well."

"I think my own father was acquainted too," was the rejoinder, and the eyes of the two men met for an instant in conflict. The girl did not seem to notice.

"I sold him a ticket this morning to the dance, not knowing who he was. Then father happened to see him pass the house and pointed him out to me as the son of a former friend of his. Funny how those things happen, is n't it?"

"Decidedly funny!" was the caustic rejoinder of the younger Rodaine. Fairchild laughed, to cover the air of intensity. He knew instinctively that Anita Richmond was not talking to him simply because she had sold him a ticket to a dance and because her father might have pointed him out. He felt sure that there was something else behind it,--the feeling of a debt which she owed him, a feeling of companionship engendered upon a sunlit road, during the moments of stress, and the continuance of that meeting in those few moments in the drug store, when he had handed her back her ten-dollar bill. She had called herself a cad then, and the feeling that she perhaps had been abrupt toward a man who had helped her out of a disagreeable predicament was prompting her action now; Fairchild felt sure of that. And he was glad of the fact, very glad. Again he laughed, while Rodaine eyed him narrowly. Fairchild shrugged his shoulders.

"I 'm not going to believe this story until it's proven to me," came calmly. "Rumors can be started too easily. I don't see how it was possible for a man to fall into a mine shaft and not struggle there long enough for a man who had heard his shout to see him."

"Who brought the news?" Rodaine asked the question.

Fairchild deliberately chose his words:

"A tall, thin, ugly old man, with mean squint eyes and a scar straight up his forehead."

A flush appeared on the other man's face. Fairchild saw his hands contract, then loosen.

"You 're trying to insult my father!"

"Your father?" Fairchild looked at him blankly. "Would n't that be a rather difficult job--especially when I don't know him?"

"You described him."

"And you recognized the description."

"Maurice! Stop it!" The girl was tugging at Rodaine's sleeve. "Don't say anything more. I 'm sorry--" and she looked at Fairchild with a glance he could not interpret--"that anything like this could have come up."

"I am equally so--if it has caused you embarrassment."

"You 'll get a little embarrassment out of it yourself--before you get through!" Rodaine was scowling at him. Again Anita Richmond caught his arm.

"Maurice! Stop it! How could the thing have been premeditated when he did n't even know your father? Come--let's go on. The crowd's getting thicker."

The narrow-faced man obeyed her command, and together they turned out into the street to avoid the constantly growing throng, and to veer toward the picture show, Fairchild watching after them, wondering whether to curse or luck himself. His temper, his natural enmity toward the two men whom he knew to be his enemies, had leaped into control, for a moment, of his tongue and his senses, and in that moment what had it done to his place in the estimation of the woman whom he had helped on the Denver road? Yet, who was she? What connection had she with the Rodaines? And had she not herself done something which had caused a fear of discovery should the pursuing sheriff overtake her? Bewildered, Robert Fairchild turned back to the more apparent thing which faced him: the probable death of Harry--the man upon whom he had counted for the knowledge and the perspicacity to aid him in the struggle against Nature and against mystery--who now, according to the story of Squint Rodaine, lay dead in the black waters of the Blue Poppy shaft.

Carbide lights had begun to appear along the street, as miners, summoned by hurrying gossip mongers, came forward to assist in the search for the missing man. High above the general conglomeration of voices could be heard the cries of the instigator of activities, Sam Herbenfelder, bemoaning the loss of his diamond, ninety per cent. of the cost of which remained to be paid. To Sam, the loss of Harry was a small matter, but that loss entailed also the disappearance of a yellow, carbon-filled diamond, as yet unpaid for. His lamentations became more vociferous than ever. Fairchild went forward, and with an outstretched hand grasped him by the collar.

"Why don't you wait until we 've found out something before you get the whole town excited?" he asked. "All we 've got is one man's word for this."

"Yes," Sam spread his hands, "but look who it was! Squint Rodaine! Ach--will I ever get back that diamond?"

"I 'm starting to the mine," Fairchild released him. "If you want to go along and look for yourself, all right. But wait until you 're sure about the thing before you go crazy over it."

However, Sam had other thoughts. Hastily he shot through the crowd, organizing the bucket brigade and searching for news of the Argonaut pump, which had not yet arrived. Half-disgusted, Fairchild turned and started up the hill, a few miners, their carbide lamps swinging beside them, following him. Far in the rear sounded the wails of Sam Herbenfelder, organizing his units of search.

Fairchild turned at the entrance of the mine and waited for the first of the miners and the accompanying gleam of his carbide. Then, they went within and to the shaft, the light shining downward upon the oily, black water below. Two objects floated there, a broken piece of timber, torn from the side of the shaft, where some one evidently had grasped hastily at it in an effort to stop a fall, and a new, four-dented hat, gradually becoming water-soaked and sinking slowly beneath the surface. And then, for the first time, fear clutched at Fairchild's heart,--fear which hope could not ignore.

"There 's his hat." It was a miner staring downward.

Fairchild had seen it, but he strove to put aside the thought.

"True," he answered, "but any one could lose a hat, simply by looking over the edge of the shaft." Then, as if in proof of the forlorn hope which he himself did not believe; "Harry 's a strong man. Certainly he would know how to swim. And in any event he should have been able to have kept afloat for at least a few minutes. Rodaine says that he heard a shout and ran right in here; but all that he could see was ruffled water and a floating hat. I--" Then he paused suddenly. It had come to him that Rodaine might have helped in the demise of Harry!

Shouts sounded from outside, and the roaring of a motor truck as it made its slow, tortuous way up the boulder-strewn road with its gullies and innumerable ruts. Voices came, rumbling and varied. Lights. Gaining the mouth of the tunnel. Fairchild could see a mass of shadows outlined by the carbides, all following the leadership of a small, excited man, Sam Herbenfelder, still seeking his diamond.

The big pump from the Argonaut tunnel was aboard the truck, which was followed by two other auto vehicles, each loaded with gasoline engines and smaller pumps. A hundred men were in the crowd, all equipped with ropes and buckets. Sam Herbenfelder's pleas had been heard. The search was about to begin for the body of Harry and the diamond that circled one finger. And Fairchild hastened to do his part.

Until far into the night they worked and strained to put the big pump into position; while crews of men, four and five in a group, bailed water as fast as possible, that the aggregate might be lessened to the greatest possible extent before the pumps, with their hoses, were attached. Then the gasoline engines began to snort, great lengths of tubing were let down into the shaft, and spurting water started down the mountain side as the task of unwatering the shaft began.

But it was a slow job. Morning found the distance to the water lengthened by twenty or thirty feet, and the bucket brigades nearly at the end of their ropes. Men trudged down the hills to breakfast, sending others in their places. Fairchild stayed on to meet Mother Howard and assuage her nervousness as best he could, dividing his time between her and the task before him. Noon found more water than ever tumbling down the hills--the smaller pumps were working now in unison with the larger one--for Sam Herbenfelder had not missed a single possible outlet of aid in his campaign; every man in Ohadi with an obligation to pay, with back interest due, or with a bill yet unaccounted for was on his staff, to say nothing of those who had volunteered simply to still the tearful remonstrances of the hand-wringing, diamond-less, little jeweler. Afternoon--and most of Ohadi was there. Fairchild could distinguish the form of Anita Richmond in the hundreds of women and men clustered about the opening of the tunnel, and for once she was not in the company of Maurice Rodaine. He hurried to her and she smiled at his approach.

"Have they found anything yet?"

"Nothing--so far. Except that there is plenty of water in the shaft. I 'm trying not to believe it."

"I hope it is n't true." Her voice was low and serious. "Father was talking to me--about you. And we hoped you two would succeed--this time."

Evidently her father had told her more than she cared to relate. Fairchild caught the inflection in her voice but disregarded it.

"I owe you an apology," he said bluntly.

"For what?"

"Last night. I could n't resist it--I forgot for a moment that you were there. But I--I hope that you 'll believe me to be a gentleman, in spite of it."

She smiled up at him quickly.

"I already have had proof of that. I--I am only hoping that you will believe me--well, that you 'll forget something."

"You mean--"

"Yes," she countered quickly, as though to cut off his explanation. "It seemed like a great deal. Yet it was nothing at all. I would feel much happier if I were sure you had disregarded it."

Fairchild looked at her for a long time, studying her with his serious, blue eyes, wondering about many things, wishing that he knew more of women and their ways. At last he said the thing that he felt, the straightforward outburst of a straightforward man:

"You 're not going to be offended if I tell you something?"

"Certainly not."

"The sheriff came along just after you had made the turn. He was looking for an auto bandit."

"A what?" She stared at him with wide-open, almost laughing eyes. "But you don't believe--"

"He was looking for a man," said Fairchild quietly. "I--I told him that I had n't seen anything but--a boy. I was willing to do that then--because I could n't believe that a girl like you would--" Then he stumbled and halted. A moment he sought speech while she smiled up at him. Then out it came: "I--I don't care what it was. I--I like you. Honest, I do. I liked you so much when I was changing that tire that I did n't even notice it when you put the money in my hand. I--well, you 're not the kind of a girl who would do anything really wrong. It might be a prank--or something like that--but it would n't be wrong. So--so there 's an end to it."

Again she laughed softly, in a way tantalizing to Robert Fairchild, as though she were making game of him.

"What do you know about women?" she asked finally, and Fairchild told the truth:

"Nothing."

"Then--" the laugh grew heartier, finally, however, to die away. The girl put forth her hand. "But I won't say what I was going to. It would n't sound right. I hope that I--I live up to your estimation of me. At least--I 'm thankful to you for being the man you are. And I won't forget!"

And once more her hand had rested in his,--a small, warm, caressing thing in spite of the purely casual grasp of an impersonal action. Again Robert Fairchild felt a thrill that was new to him, and he stood watching her until she had reached the motor car which had brought her to the big curve, and had faded down the hill. Then he went back to assist the sweating workmen and the anxious-faced Sam Herbenfelder. The water was down seventy feet.

That night Robert Fairchild sought a few hours' sleep. Two days after, the town still divided its attention between preparations for the Old Times Dance and the progress in the dewatering of the Blue Poppy shaft. Now and then the long hose was withdrawn, and dynamite lowered on floats to the surface of the water, far below, a copper wire trailing it. A push of the plunger, a detonation, and a wait of long moments; it accomplished nothing, and the pumping went on. If the earthly remains of Harry Harkins were below, they steadfastly refused to come to the surface.

The volunteers had thinned now to only a few men at the pumps and the gasoline engine, and Sam Herbenfelder was taking turns with Fairchild in overseeing the job. Spectators were not as frequent either; they came and went,--all except Mother Howard, who was silently constant. The water had fallen to the level of the drift, two hundred feet down; the pumps now were working on the main flood which still lay below, while outside the townspeople came and went, and twice daily the owner and proprietor and general assignment reporter of the *Daily Bugle* called at the mouth of the tunnel for news of progress. But there was no news, save that the water was lower. The excitement of it began to dim. Besides, the night of the dance was approaching, and there were other calls for volunteers, for men to set up the old-time bar in the lodge rooms of the Elks Club; for others to dig out ancient roulette wheels and oil them in preparation for a busy play at a ten-cent limit instead of the sky-high boundaries of a day gone by; for some one to go to Denver and raid the costume shops, to say nothing of buying the innumerable paddles which must accompany any old-time game of keno. But Sam stayed on--and Fairchild with him--and the loiterers, who would refuse to work at anything else for less than six dollars a day, freely giving their services at the pumps and the engines in return for a share of Sam's good will and their names in the papers.

A day more and a day after that. Through town a new interest spread. The water was now only a few feet high in the shaft; it meant that the whole great opening, together with the drift tunnel, soon would be dewatered to an extent sufficient to permit of exploration. Again the motor cars ground up the narrow roadway. Outside the tunnel the crowds gathered. Fairchild saw Anita Richmond and gritted his teeth at the fact that young Rodaine accompanied her. Farther in the background, narrow eyes watching him closely, was Squint Rodaine. And still farther--

Fairchild gasped as he noticed the figure plodding down the mountain side. He put out a hand, then, seizing the nervous Herbenfelder by the shoulder, whirled him around.

"Look!" he exclaimed. "Look there! Did n't I tell you! Did n't I have a hunch?"

For, coming toward them jauntily, slowly, was a figure in beaming blue, a Fedora on his head now, but with the rest of his wardrobe intact, yellow, bump-toed shoes and all. Some one shouted. Everybody turned. And as they did so, the figure hastened its pace. A moment later, a booming voice sounded, the unmistakable voice of Harry Harkins:

"I sye! What's the matter over there? Did somebody fall in?"

The puffing of gasoline engines ceased. A moment more and the gurgling cough of the pumps was stilled, while the shouting and laughter of a great crowd sounded through the hills. A leaping form went forward, Sam Herbenfelder, to seize Harry, to pat him and paw him, as though in assurance that he really was alive, then to grasp wildly at the ring on his finger. But Harry waved him aside.

"Ain't I paid the installment on it?" he remonstrated. "What's the rumpus?"

Fairchild, with Mother Howard, both laughing happily, was just behind Herbenfelder. And behind them was thronging half of Ohadi.

"We thought you were drowned!"

"Me?" Harry's laughter boomed again, in a way that was infectious. "Me drowned, just because I let out a 'oller and dropped my 'at?"

"You did it on purpose?" Sam Herbenfelder shook a scrawny fist under Harry's nose. The big Cornishman waved it aside as one would brush away an obnoxious fly. Then he grinned at the townspeople about him.

"Well," he confessed, "there was an un'oly lot of water in there, and I didn't 'ave any money. What else was I to do?"

"You--!" A pumpman had picked up a piece of heavy timbering and thrown it at him in mock ferocity. "Work us to death and then come back and give us the laugh! Where you been at?"

"Center City," confessed Harry cheerily.

"And you knew all the time?" Mother Howard wagged a finger under his nose.

"Well," and the Cornishman chuckled, "I did n't 'ave any money. I 'ad to get that shaft unwatered, did n't I?"

"Get a rail!" Another irate--but laughing--pumpman had come forward. "Think you can pull that on us? Get a rail!"

Some one seized a small, dead pine which lay on the ground near by. Others helped to strip it of the scraggly limbs which still clung to it. Harry watched them and chuckled--for he knew that in none was there malice. He had played his joke and won. It was their turn now. Shouting in mock anger, calling for all dire things, from lynchings on down to burnings at the stake, they dragged Harry to the pine tree, threw him astraddle of it, then, with willing hands volunteering on every side, hoisted the tree high above them and started down the mountain side, Sam Herbenfelder trotting in the rear and forgetting his anger in the joyful knowledge that his ring at last was safe.

Behind the throng of men with their mock threats trailed the women and children, some throwing pine cones at the booming Harry, juggling himself on the narrow pole; and in the crowd, Fairchild found some one he could watch with more than ordinary interest,--Anita Richmond, trudging along with the rest, apparently remonstrating with the sullen, mean-visaged young man at her side. Instinctively Fairchild knew that young Rodaine was not pleased with the return of Harkins. As for the father--

Fairchild whirled at a voice by his side and looked straight into the crooked eyes of Thornton Fairchild's enemy. The blue-white scar had turned almost black now, the eyes were red from swollen, blood-stained veins, the evil, thin, crooked lips were working in sullen fury. They were practically alone at the mouth of the mine, Fairchild with a laugh dying on his lips, Rodaine with all the hate and anger and futile malice that a human being can know typified in his scarred, hawklike features. A thin, taloned hand came upward, to double, leaving one bony, curved finger extending in emphasis of the words which streamed from the slit of a mouth:

"Funny, weren't you? Played your cheap jokes and got away with 'em. But everybody ain't like them fools!" he pointed to the crowd just rounding the rocks, Harry bobbing in the foreground. "There 's some that remember--and I 'm one of 'em. You 've put over your fake; you 've had your laugh; you 've framed it so I 'll be the butt of every numbskull in Ohadi. But just listen to this--just listen to this!" he repeated, the harsh voice taking on a tone that was almost a screech. "There's another time coming--and that time 's going to be mine!"

And before Fairchild could retort, he had turned and was scrambling down the mountain side.

CHAPTER IX

It was just as well. Fairchild could have said nothing that would have helped matters. He could have done nothing that would have damaged them. The cards were still the same; the deck still bore its markings, and the deal was going on without ever a change, except that now the matter of concealment of enmities had turned to an open, aboveboard proposition. Whether Harry had so intended it or not, he had forced Squint Rodaine to show his hand, and whether Squint realized it, that amounted to something. Fairchild was almost grateful for the fact as he went back into the tunnel, spun the flywheels of the gasoline engines and started them revolving again, that the last of the water might be drained from the shaft before the pumps must be returned to their owners.

Several hours passed, then Harry returned, minus his gorgeous clothing and his diamond ring, dressed in mining costume now, with high leather boots into which his trousers were tucked, and carrying a carbide lantern. Dolefully he looked at the vacant finger where once a diamond had sparkled. Then he chuckled.

"Sam took it back," he announced. "And I took part of the money and paid it out for rent on these pumps. We can keep 'em as long as we want 'em. It's only costing about a fourth of what it might of. Drowning 's worth something," he laughed again. Fairchild joined him, then sobered.

"It brought Rodaine out of the bushes," he said. "Squint threatened us after they 'd hauled you down town on the rail."

Harry winked jovially.

"Ain't it just what I expected? It's better that wye than to 'ave 'im snoopin' around. When I came up to the mine, 'e was right behind me. I knew it. And I 'd figured on it. So I just gave 'im something to get excited about. It was n't a minute after I 'd thrown a rock and my 'at in there and let out a yell that he came thumping in, looking around. I was 'iding back of the timbers there. Out 'e went, muttering to 'imself, and I--well, I went to Center City and read the papers."

They chuckled together then; it was something to know that they had not only forced Squint Rodaine to show his enmity openly, but it was something more to make him the instrument of helping them with their work. The pumps were going steadily now, and a dirty stream of water was flowing down the ditch that had been made at one side of the small tram track. Harry looked down the hole, stared intently at nothing, then turned to the rusty hoist.

"'Ere 's the thing we 've got to fix up now. This 'ere chiv wheel's all out of gear."

"What makes your face so red?" Fairchild asked the question as the be-mus-tached visage of Harry came nearer to the carbide. Harry looked up.

"Mother 'Oward almost slapped it off!" came his rueful answer. "For not telling 'er what I was going to do, and letting 'er think I got drownded. But 'ow was I to know?"

He went to tinkering with the big chiv wheel then, supported on its heavy timbers, and over which the cable must pass to allow the skip to travel on its rails down the shaft. Fairchild absently examined the engines and pumps, supplying water to the radiators and filling an oil cup or two. Then he turned swiftly, voicing that which was uppermost in his mind.

"When you were here before, Harry, did you know a Judge Richmond?"

"Yeh." Harry pawed his mustache and made a greasy, black mark on his face. "But I don't think I want to know 'im now."

"Why not?"

"'E's mixed up with the Rodaines."

"How much?"

"They own 'im--that's all."

There was silence for a moment. It had been something which Fairchild had not expected. If the Rodaines owned Judge Richmond, how far did that ownership extend? After a long time, he forced himself to a statement.

"I know his daughter."

"You?" Harry straightened. "'Ow so?"

"She sold me a ticket to a dance," Fairchild carefully forgot the earlier meeting.

"Then we 've happened to meet several times after that. She said that her father had told her about me--it seems he used to be a friend of my own father."

Harry nodded.

"So 'e was. And a good friend. But that was before things 'appened--like they 've 'appened in the last ten years. Not that I know about it of my own knowledge. But Mother 'Oward--she knows a lot."

"But what's caused the change? What--?"

Harry's intent gaze stopped him.

"'Ow many times 'ave you seen the girl when she was n't with young Rodaine?"

"Very few, that's true."

"And 'ow many times 'ave you seen Judge Richmond?"

"I have n't ever seen him."

"You won't--if Mother 'Oward knows anything. 'E ain't able to get out. 'E's sick--apoplexy--a stroke. Rodaine's taken advantage of it."

"How?"

"'Ow does anybody take advantage of somebody that's sick? 'Ow does anybody get a 'old on a person? Through money! Judge Richmond 'ad a lot of it. Then 'e got sick. Rodaine, 'e got 'old of that money. Now Judge Richmond 'as to ask 'im for every penny he gets--and 'e does what Rodaine says."

"But a judge--"

"Judges is just like anybody else when they're bedridden and only 'arf their faculties working. The girl, so Mother 'Oward tells me, is about twenty now. That made 'er just a little kid, and motherless, when Rodaine got in 'is work. She ain't got a thing to sye. And she loves 'er father. Suppose," Harry waved a hand, "that you loved somebody awful strong, and suppose that person was under a influence? Suppose it meant 'is 'appiness and 'is 'ealth for you to do like 'e wanted you? Wouldn't you go with a man? What's more, if 'e don't die pretty soon, you 'll see a wedding!"

"You mean--?"

"She 'll be Mrs. Maurice Rodaine. She loves 'er father enough to do it--after 'er will's broken. And I don't care 'oo it is; there ain't a woman in the world that's got the strength to keep on saying no to a sick father!"

Again Robert Fairchild filled an oil cup, again he tinkered about the pumps. Then he straightened.

"How are we going to work this mine?" he asked shortly. Harry stared at him.

"'Ow should I know? You own it!"

"I don't mean that way. We were fifty-fifty from the minute you showed up. There never has been any other thought in my mind--"

"Fifty-fifty? You're making me a bloated capitalist!"

"I hope I will. Or rather, I hope that you 'll make such a thing possible for both of us. But I was talking about something else; are we going to work hard and fight it out day and night for awhile until we can get things going, or are we just going at it by easy stages?"

"Suppose," answered Harry after a communication with his magic mustache, "that we go dye and night 'til we get the water out? It won't be long. Then we 'll 'ave to work together. You 'll need my vast store of learning and enlightenment!" he grinned.

"Good. But the pumping will last through tomorrow night. Can you take the night trick?"

"Sure. But why?"

"I want to go to that dance!"

Harry whistled. Harry's big lips spread into a grin.

"And she 's got brown eyes!" he chortled to himself. "And she 's got brown 'air, and she 's a wye about 'er. Oh! She's got a wye about 'er! And I 'll bet she 's going with Maurice Rodaine! Oh! She's got a wye about'er!"

"Oh, shut up!" growled Fairchild, but he grinned in schoolboy fashion as he said it. Harry poured half a can of oil upon the bearings of the chiv wheel with almost loving tenderness.

"She 's got a wye about 'er!" he echoed. Fairchild suddenly frowned.

"Just what do you mean? That she 's in love with Rodaine and just--"

"'Ow should I know? But she 's got a wye about 'er!"

"Well," the firm chin of the other man grew firmer, "it won't be hard to find out!"

And the next night he started upon his investigations. Nor did he stop to consider that social events had been few and far between for him, that his dancing had progressed little farther than the simple ability to move his feet in unison to music. Years of office and home, home and office, had not allowed Robert Fairchild the natural advantages of the usual young man. But he put that aside now; he was going to that dance, and he was going to stay there as long as the music sounded, or rather as long as the brown eyes, brown hair and laughing lips of Anita Richmond were apparent to him. What's more, he carried out his resolution.

The clock turned back with the entrance to that dance hall. Men were there in the rough mining costumes of other days, with unlighted candles stuck through patent holders into their hats, and women were there also, dressed as women could dress only in other days of sudden riches, in costumes brought from Denver, be-spangled affairs with the gorgeousness piled on until the things became fantastic instead of the intensely beautiful creations that the original wearers had believed them to be. There was only one idea in the olden mining days, to buy as much as possible and to put it all on at once. High, Spanish combs surmounted ancient styles of hairdressing. Rhinestones glittered in lieu of the real diamonds that once were worn by the queens of the mining camps. Dancing girls, newly rich cooks, poverty-stricken prospectors' wives suddenly beaming with wealth, nineteenth-century vamps, gambling hall habitues,--all were represented among the feminin-ity of Ohadi as they laughed and giggled at the outlandish costumes they wore and thoroughly enjoyed themselves.

Far at one side, making a brave effort with the "near" beer and "almost there" concoctions of a prohibition buried country, was the "old-fashioned bar" with its old-fashioned bartender behind it, roaring out his orders and serving drinks with one hand while he waved and pulled the trigger of a blank-cartridged revolver with the other. Farther on was the roulette wheel, and Fairchild strolled to it, watch-ing the others to catch the drift of the game before he essayed it, playing with pennies where, in the old days, men had gambled away fortunes; surrounded by a crowd that laughed and chattered and forgot its bets, around a place where once a "sleeper" might have meant a fortune. The spirit of the old times was abroad. The noise and clatter of a dance caller bellowed forth as he shouted for everybody to grab their "podners one an' all, do-se-do, promenade th' hall!" and Fairchild, as he watched, saw that his lack of dancing ability would not be a serious handicap. There were many others who did not know the old numbers. And those who did had worn their hobnailed boots, sufficient to take the spring out of any one's feet. The women were doing most of the leading, the men clattered along somewhere in the rear, laughing and shouting and inadvertently kicking one another on the shins. The old times had come back, boisterously, happily,--and every one was living in those days when the hills gushed wealth, and when poverty to-day might mean riches tomorrow.

Again and again Fairchild's eyes searched the crowds, the multicolored, over-dressed costumes of the women, the old-fashioned affairs with which many of the men had arrayed themselves, ranging all the way from high leather boots to frock suits and stovepipe beaver hats. From one face to another his gaze went; then he turned abstractedly to the long line of tables, with their devotees of keno, and bought a paddle.

From far away the drone of the caller sounded in a voice familiar, and Fairchild looked up to see the narrow-eyed, scarred face of Squint Rodaine, who was officiating at the wheel. He lost interest in the game; lackadaisically he placed the buttons on their squares as the numbers were shouted, finally to brush them all aside and desert the game. His hatred of the Rodaines had grown to a point where he could enjoy nothing with which they were connected, where he despised everything with which they had the remotest affiliation,--excepting, of course, one person. And as he rose, Fairchild saw that she was just entering the dance hall.

Quaint in an old-fashioned costume which represented more the Civil War days than it did those of the boom times of silver mining, she seemed prettier than ever to Robert Fairchild, more girlish, more entrancing. The big eyes appeared bigger now, peeping from the confines of a poke bonnet; the little hands seemed smaller with their half-length gloves and shielded by the enormous peacock feather fan they carried. Only a moment Fairchild hesitated. Maurice Rodaine, attired in a mauve frock suit and the inevitable accompanying beaver, had stopped to talk to some one at the door. She stood alone, looking about the hall, laughing and nodding,--and then she looked at him! Fairchild did not wait.

From the platform at the end of the big room the fiddles had begun to squeak, and the caller was shouting his announcements. Couples began to line up on the floor. The caller's voice grew louder:

"Two more couples--two more couples! Grab yo' podners!"

Fairchild was elbowing his way swiftly forward, apologizing as he went. A couple took its place beside the others. Once more the plea of the caller sounded:

"One more couple--then the dance starts. One more couple, lady an' a gent! One more--"

"Please!" Robert Fairchild had reached her and was holding forth his hand. She looked up in half surprise, then demurred.

"But I don't know these old dances."

"Neither do I--or any other, for that matter," he confessed with sudden boldness. "But does that make any difference? Please!"

She glanced quickly toward the door. Maurice Rodaine was still talking, and Fairchild saw a little gleam come into her eyes,--the gleam that shows when a woman decides to make some one pay for rudeness. Again he begged:

"Won't you--and then we 'll forget. I--I could n't take my payment in money!"

She eyed him quickly and saw the smile on his lips. From the platform the caller voiced another entreaty:

"One more cou-ple! Ain't there no lady an' gent that's goin' to fill out this here dance? One more couple--one more couple!"

Fairchild's hand was still extended. Again Anita Richmond glanced toward the door, chuckled to herself while Fairchild watched the dimples that the merriment caused, and then--Fairchild forgot the fact that he was wearing hobnailed shoes and that his clothes were worn and old. He was going forward to take his place on the dance floor, and she was beside him!

Some way, as through a haze, he saw her. Some way he realized that now and then his hand touched hers, and that once, as they whirled about the room, in obedience to the monarch on the fiddler's rostrum, his arm was about her waist, and her head touching his shoulder. It made little difference whether the dance calls were obeyed after that. Fairchild was making up for all the years he had plodded, all the years in which he had known nothing but a slow, grubbing life, living them all again and rightly, in the few swift moments of a dance.

The music ended, and laughing they returned to the side of the hall. Out of the haze he heard words, and knew indistinctly that they were his own:

"Will--will you dance with me again tonight?"

"Selfish!" she chided.

"But will you?"

For just a moment her eyes grew serious.

"Did you ever realize that we 've never been introduced?"

Fairchild was finding more conversation than he ever had believed possible.

"No--but I realize that I don't care--if you 'll forgive it. I--believe that I 'm a gentleman."

"So do I--or I would n't have danced with you."

"Then please--"

"Pardon me." She had laid a hand on his arm for just a moment, then hurried away. Fairchild saw that she was approaching young Rodaine, scowling in the background. That person shot an angry remark at her as she approached and followed it with streaming sentences. Fairchild knew the reason. Jealousy! Couples returning from the dance floor jostled against him, but he did not move. He was waiting--waiting for the outcome of the quarrel--and in a moment it came. Anita Richmond turned swiftly, her dark eyes ablaze, her pretty lips set and firm. She looked anxiously about her, sighted Fairchild, and then started toward him, while he advanced to meet her.

"I 've reconsidered," was her brief announcement. "I 'll dance the next one with you."

"And the next after that?"

Again: "Selfish!"

But Fairchild did not appear to hear.

"And the next and the next and the next!" he urged as the caller issued his inevitable invitations for couples. Anita smiled.

"Maybe--I 'll think about it."

"I 'll never know how to dance, unless you teach me." Fairchild pleaded, as they made their way to the center of the floor. "I 'll--"

"Don't work on my sympathies!"

"But it's the truth. I never will."

"S'lute yo' podners!" The dance was on. And while the music squealed from the rostrum, while the swaying forms some way made the rounds according to the caller's viewpoint of an old-time dance, Anita Richmond evidently "thought about it." When the next dance came, they went again on the floor together, Robert Fairchild and the brown-eyed girl whom he suddenly realized he loved, without reasoning the past or the future, without caring whom she might be or what her plans might contain; a man out of prison lives by impulse, and Fairchild was but lately released.

A third dance and a fourth, while in the intervals Fairchild's eyes sought out the sulky, sullen form of Maurice Rodaine, flattened against the wall, eyes evil, mouth a straight line, and the blackness of hate discoloring his face. It was as so much wine to Fairchild; he felt himself really young for the first time in his life. And as the music started again, he once more turned to his companion.

Only, however, to halt and whirl and stare in surprise. There had come a shout from the doorway, booming, commanding:

"'Ands up, everybody! And quick about it!"

Some one laughed and jabbed his hands into the air. Another, quickly sensing a staged surprise, followed the example. It was just the finishing touch necessary,-- the old-time hold-up of the old-time dance. The "bandit" strode forward.

"Out from be'ind that bar! Drop that gun!" he commanded of the white-aproned attendant. "Out from that roulette wheel. Everybody line up! Quick--and there ain't no time for foolin'."

Chattering and laughing, they obeyed, the sheriff, his star gleaming, standing out in front of them all, shivering in mock fright, his hands higher than any one's. The bandit, both revolvers leveled, stepped forward a foot or so, and again ordered speed. Fairchild, standing with his hands in the air, looked down toward Anita, standing beside him.

"Is n't it exciting," she exclaimed. "Just like a regular hold-up! I wonder who the bandit is. He certainly looks the part, does n't he?"

And Fairchild agreed that he did. A bandanna handkerchief was wrapped about his head, concealing his hair and ears. A mask was over his eyes, supplemented by another bandanna, which, beginning at the bridge of his nose, flowed over his chin, cutting off all possible chance of recognition. Only a second more he waited, then with a wave of the guns, shouted his command:

"All right, everybody! I'm a decent fellow. Don't want much, but I want it quick! This 'ere 's for the relief of widders and orphans. Make it sudden. Each one of you gents step out to the center of the room and leave five dollars. And step back when you 've put it there. Ladies stay where you 're at!"

Again a laugh. Fairchild turned to his companion, as she nudged him. "There, it's your turn."

Out to the center of the floor went Fairchild, the rest of the victims laughing and chiding him. Back he came in mock fear, his hands in the air. On down the line went the contributing men. Then the bandit rushed forward, gathered up the bills and gold pieces, shoved them in his pockets, and whirled toward the door.

"The purpose of this 'ere will be in the paper to-morrow," he announced. "And don't you follow me to find out! Back there!"

Two or three laughing men had started forward, among them a fiddler, who had joined the line, and who now rushed out in flaunting bravery, brandishing his violin as though to brain the intruder. Again the command: "Back there--get back!"

Then the crowd recoiled. Flashes had come from the masked man's guns, the popping of electric light globes above and the showering of glass testifying to the fact that they had contained something more than mere wadding. Somewhat dazed, the fiddler continued his rush, suddenly to crumple and fall, while men milled and women screamed. A door slammed, the lock clicked, and the crowd rushed for the windows. The hold-up had been real after all,--instead of a planned, joking affair. On the floor the fiddler lay gasping--and bleeding. And the bandit was gone.

All in a moment the dance hall seemed to have gone mad. Men were rushing about and shouting; panic-stricken women clawed at one another and fought their way toward a freedom they could not gain. Windows crashed as forms hurtled against them; screams sounded. Hurriedly, as the crowd massed thicker, Fairchild raised the small form of Anita in his arms and carried her to a chair, far at one side.

"It's all right now," he said, calming her. "Everything 's over--look, they 're helping the fiddler to his feet. Maybe he 's not badly hurt. Everything 's all right--"

And then he straightened. A man had unlocked the door from the outside and had rushed into the dance hall, excited, shouting. It was Maurice Rodaine.

"I know who it was," he almost screamed. "I got a good look at him--jumped out of the window and almost headed him off. He took off his mask outside--and I saw him."

"You saw him--?" A hundred voices shouted the question at once.

"Yes." Then Maurice Rodaine nodded straight toward Robert Fairchild. "The light was good, and I got a straight look at him. He was that fellow's partner--a Cornishman they call Harry!"

CHAPTER X

I don't believe it!" Anita Richmond exclaimed with conviction and clutched at Fairchild's arm. "I don't believe it!"

"I can't!" Robert answered. Then he turned to the accuser. "How could it be possible for Harry to be down here robbing a dance hall when he 's out working the mine?"

"Working the mine?" This time it was the sheriff. "What's the necessity for a day and night shift?"

The question was pertinent--and Fairchild knew it. But he did not hesitate.

"I know it sounds peculiar--but it's the truth. We agreed upon it yesterday afternoon."

"At whose suggestion?"

"I 'm not sure--but I think it was mine."

"Young fellow," the sheriff had approached him now, "you 'd better be certain about that. It looks to me like that might be a pretty good excuse to give when a man can't produce an alibi. Anyway, the identification seems pretty complete. Everybody in this room heard that man talk with a Cousin Jack accent. And Mr. Rodaine says that he saw his face. That seems conclusive."

"If Mr. Rodaine's word counts for anything."

The sheriff looked at him sharply.

"Evidently you have n't been around here long." Then he turned to the crowd. "I want a couple of good men to go along with me as deputies."

"I have a right to go." Fairchild had stepped forward.

"Certainly. But not as a deputy. Who wants to volunteer?"

Half a dozen men came forward, and from them the sheriff chose two. Fairchild turned to say good-by to Anita. In vain. Already Maurice Rodaine had escorted her, apparently against her will, to a far end of the dance hall, and there was quar-reling with her. Fairchild hurried to join the sheriff and his two deputies, just start-ing out of the dance hall. Five minutes later they were in a motor car, chugging up Kentucky Gulch.

The trip was made silently. There was nothing for Fairchild to say; he had told all he knew. Slowly, the motor car fighting against the grade, the trip was ac-complished. Then the four men leaped from the machine at the last rise before the tunnel was reached and three of them went forward afoot toward where a slight gleam of light came from the mouth of the Blue Poppy.

A consultation and then the creeping forms made the last fifty feet. The sheriff took the lead, at last to stop behind a boulder and to shout a command:

"Hey you, in there."

"'Ey yourself!" It was Harry's voice.

"Come out--and be quick about it. Hold your light in front of your face with both hands."

"The 'ell I will! And 'oo 's talking?"

"Sheriff Adams of Clear Creek County. You 've got one minute to come out--or I 'll shoot."

"I 'm coming on the run!"

And almost instantly the form of Harry, his acetylene lamp lighting up his bulbous, surprised countenance with its spraylike mustache, appeared at the mouth of the tunnel.

"What the bloody 'ell?" he gasped, as he looked into the muzzle of the revolver. From down the mountain side came the shout of one of the deputies:

"Sheriff! Looks like it's him, all right. I 've found a horse down here--all sweated up from running."

"That's about the answer." Sheriff Adams went forward and with a motion of his revolver sent Harry's hands into the air. "Let's see what you 've got on you."

A light gleamed below as an electric flash in the hands of one of the deputies began an investigation of the surroundings. The sheriff, finishing his search of 'Arry's pockets, stepped back.

"Well," he demanded, "what did you do with the proceeds?"

"The proceeds?" Harry stared blankly. "Of what?"

"Quit your kidding now. They 've found your horse down there."

"Would n't it be a good idea--" Fairchild had cut in acridly--"to save your accusations on this thing until you're a little surer of it? Harry has n't any horse. If he 's rented one, you ought to be able to find that out pretty shortly."

As if in answer, the sheriff turned and shouted a question down the mountain side. And back came the answer:

"It's Doc Mason's. Must have been stolen. Doc was at the dance."

"I guess that settles it." The officer reached for his hip pocket. "Stick out your hands, Harry, while I put the cuffs on them."

"But 'ow in bloody 'ell 'ave I been doing anything when I 've been up 'ere working on this chiv wheel? 'Ow--?"

"They say you held up the dance to-night and robbed us," Fairchild cut in. Harry's face lost its surprised look, to give way to a glance of keen questioning.

"And do you say it?"

"I most certainly do not. The identification was given by that honorable person known as Mr. Maurice Rodaine."

"Oh! One thief identifying another--"

"Just cut your remarks along those lines."

"Sheriff!" Again the voice from below.

"Yeh!"

"We 've found a cache down here. Must have been made in a hurry--two new revolvers, bullets, a mask, a couple of new handkerchiefs and the money."

Harry's eyes grew wide. Then he stuck out his hands.

"The evidence certainly is piling up!" he grunted. "I might as well save my talking for later."

"That's a good idea." The sheriff snapped the handcuffs into place. Then Fairchild shut off the pumps and they started toward the machine. Back in Ohadi more news awaited them. Harry, if Harry had been the highwayman, had gone to no expense for his outfit. The combined general store and hardware emporium of Gregg Brothers had been robbed of the articles necessary for a disguise,--also the revolvers and their bullets. Robert Fairchild watched Harry placed in the solitary cell of the county jail with a spirit that could not respond to the Cornishman's grin and his assurances that morning would bring a righting of affairs. Four charges hung heavy above him: that of horse-stealing, of burglary, of highway robbery, and worse, the final one of assault with attempt to kill. Fairchild turned wearily away; he could not find the optimism to join Harry's cheerful announcement that it would be "all right." The appearances were otherwise. Besides, up in the little hospital on the hill, Fairchild had seen lights gleaming as he entered the jail, and he knew that doctors were working there over the wounded body of the fiddler. Tired, heavy at heart, his earlier conquest of the night sodden and overshadowed now, he turned away from the cell and its optimistic occupant,--out into the night.

It was only a short walk to the hospital and Fairchild went there, to leave with at least a ray of hope. The probing operation had been completed; the fiddler would live, and at least the charge against Harry would not be one of murder. That was a thing for which to be thankful; but there was plenty to cause consternation, as Fairchild walked slowly down the dark, winding street toward the main thorough-fare. Without Harry, Fairchild now felt himself lost. Before the big, genial, eccentric Cornishman had come into his life, he had believed, with some sort of divine ignorance, that he could carry out his ambitions by himself, with no knowledge of the technical details necessary to mining, with no previous history of the Blue Poppy to guide him, and with no help against the enemies who seemed everywhere. Now he saw that it was impossible. More, the incidents of the night showed how swiftly those enemies were working, how sharp and stiletto-like their weapons.

That Harry was innocent was certain,--to Robert Fairchild. There was quite a difference between a joke which a whole town recognized as such and a deliberate robbery which threatened the life of at least one man. Fairchild knew in his heart that Harry was not built along those lines.

Looking back over it now, Fairchild could see how easily Fate had played into the hands of the Rodaines, if the Rodaines had not possessed a deeper concern than merely to seize upon a happening and turn it to their own account. The highwayman was big. The highwayman talked with a "Cousin-Jack" accent,--for all Cornishmen are "Cousin Jacks" in the mining country. Those two features in themselves, Fairchild thought, as he stumbled along in the darkness, were sufficient to start the scheming plot in the brain of Maurice Rodaine, already ugly and evil through the trick played by Harry on his father and the rebuke that had come from Anita Richmond. It was an easy matter for him to get the inspiration, leap out of the window, and then wait until the robber had gone, that he might flare forth with his accusation. And after that--.

Either Chance, or something stronger, had done the rest. The finding of the stolen horse and the carelessly made cache near the mouth of the Blue Poppy mine would be sufficient in the eyes of any jury. The evidence was both direct and circumstantial. To Fairchild's mind, there was small chance for escape by Harry, once his case went to trial. Nor did the pounding insistence of intuitive knowledge that the whole thing had been a deliberately staged plot on the part of the Rodaines, father and son, make the slightest difference in Fairchild's estimation. How could he prove it? By personal animosity? There was the whole town of Ohadi to testify that the highwayman was a big man, of the build of Harry, and that he spoke with a Cornish accent. There were the sworn members of the posse to show that they, without guidance, had discovered the horse and the cache,--and the Rodaines were nowhere about to help them. And experience already had told Fairchild that the Rodaines, by a deliberately constructed system, held a ruling power; that against their word, his would be as nothing. Besides, where would be Harry's alibi? He had none; he had been at the mine, alone. There was no one to testify for him, not even Fairchild.

The world was far from bright. Down the dark street the man wandered, his hands sunk deep in his pockets, his head low between his shoulders,--only to suddenly galvanize into intensity, and to stop short that he might hear again the voice which had come to him. At one side was a big house,--a house whose occupants he knew instinctively, for he had seen the shadow of a woman, hands outstretched, as she passed the light-strewn shade of a window on the second floor. More, he had heard her voice, supplemented by gruffer tones. And then it came again.

It was pleading, and at the same time angered with the passion of a person approaching hysteria. A barking sentence answered her, something that Fairchild could not understand. He left the old board sidewalk and crept to the porch that he might hear the better. Then every nerve within him jangled, and the black of the darkness changed to red. The Rodaines were within; he had heard first the cold voice of the father, then the rasping tones of the son, in upbraiding. More, there had come the sobbing of a woman; instinctively Fairchild knew that it was Anita Richmond. And then:

It was her voice, high, screaming. Hysteria had come,--the wild, racking hysteria of a person driven to the breaking point:

"Leave this house--hear me! Leave this house! Can't you see that you're killing him? Don't you dare touch me--leave this house! No--I won't be quiet--I won't-- you 're killing him, I tell you--!"

And Fairchild waited for nothing more. A lunge, and he was on the veranda. One more spring and he had reached the door, to find it unlocked, to throw it wide and to leap into the hall. Great steps, and he had cleared the stairs to the second floor.

A scream came from a doorway before him; dimly, as through a red screen, Fairchild saw the frightened face of Anita Richmond, and on the landing, fronting him angrily, stood the two Rodaines. For a moment, Fairchild disregarded them and turned to the sobbing, disheveled little being in the doorway.

"What's happened?"

"They were threatening me--and father!" she moaned. "But you shouldn't have come in--you should n't have--"

"I heard you scream. I could n't help it. I heard you say they were killing your father--"

The girl looked anxiously toward an inner room, where Fairchild could see faintly the still figure of a man outlined under the covers of an old-fashioned four-poster.

"They--they--got him excited. He had another stroke. I--I could n't stand it any longer."

"You 'd better get out," said Fairchild curtly to the Rodaines, with a suggestive motion toward the stairs. They hesitated a moment and Maurice seemed about to launch himself at Robert, but his father laid a restraining hand on his arm. A step and the elder Rodaine hesitated.

"I 'm only going because of your father," he said gruffly, with a glance toward Anita.

Fairchild knew differently, but he said nothing. The gray of Rodaine's countenance told where his courage lay; it was yellow gray, the dirty gray of a man who fights from cover, and from cover only.

"Oh, I know," Anita said. "It's--it's all right. I--I 'm sorry. I--did n't realize that I was screaming--please forgive me--and go, won't you? It means my father's life now."

"That's the only reason I am going; I 'm not going because--"

"Oh, I know. Mr. Fairchild should n't have come in here. He should n't have done it. I 'm sorry--please go."

Down the steps they went, the older man with his hand still on his son's arm; while, white-faced, Fairchild awaited Anita, who had suddenly sped past him into the sick room, then was wearily returning.

"Can I help you?" he asked at last.

"Yes," came her rather cold answer, only to be followed by a quickly whispered "Forgive me." And then the tones became louder--so that they could be heard at the bottom of the stairs: "You can help me greatly--simply by going and not creating any more of a disturbance."

"But--"

"Please go," came the direct answer. "And please do not vent your spite on Mr. Rodaine and his son. I 'm sure that they will act like gentlemen if you will. You should n't have rushed in here."

"I heard you screaming, Miss Richmond."

"I know," came her answer, as icily as ever. Then the door downstairs closed and the sound of steps came on the veranda. She leaned close to him. "I had to say that," came her whispered words. "Please don't try to understand anything I do in the future. Just go--please!"

And Fairchild obeyed.

CHAPTER XI

The Rodaines were on the sidewalk when Fairchild came forth from the Richmond home, and true to his instructions from the frightened girl, he brushed past them swiftly and went on down the street, not turning at the muttered invectives which came from the crooked lips of the older man, not seeming even to notice their presence as he hurried on toward Mother Howard's boarding house. Whether Fate had played with him or against him, he did not know,--nor could he summon the brain power to think. Happenings had come too thickly in the last few hours for him to differentiate calmly; everything depended upon what course the Rodaines might care to pursue. If theirs was to be a campaign of destruction, without a care whom it might involve, Fairchild could see easily that he too might soon be juggled into occupying the cell with Harry in the county jail. Wearily he turned the corner to the main street and made his plodding way, along it, his shoulders drooping, his brain fagged from the flaring heat of anger and the strain that the events of the night had put upon it. In his creaky bed in the old boarding house, he again sought to think, but in vain. He could only lie awake and stare into the darkness about him, while through his mind ran a muddled conglomeration of foreboding, waking dreams, revamps of the happenings of the last three weeks, memories which brought him nothing save sleeplessness and the knowledge that, so far, he fought a losing fight.

After hours, daylight began to streak the sky. Fairchild, dull, worn by excitement and fatigue, strove to rise, then laid his head on the pillow for just a moment of rest. And with that perversity which extreme weariness so often exerts, his eyes closed, and he slept,--to wake at last with the realization that it was late morning, and that some one was pounding on the door. Fairchild raised his head.

"Is that you, Mother Howard? I'm getting up, right away."

A slight chuckle answered him.

"But this is n't Mother Howard. May I see you a moment?"

"Who is it?"

"No one you know--yet. I 've come to talk to you about your partner. May I come in?"

"Yes." Fairchild was fully alive now to the activities that the day held before him. The door opened, and a young man, alert, almost cocky in manner, with black, snappy eyes showing behind horn-rimmed glasses, entered and reached for the sole chair that the room contained.

"My name 's Farrell," he announced. "Randolph P. Farrell. And to make a long story short, I 'm your lawyer."

"My lawyer?" Fairchild stared. "I haven't any lawyer in Ohadi. The only--"

"That does n't alter the fact. I 'm your lawyer, and I 'm at your service. And I don't mind telling you that it's just about my first case. Otherwise, I don't guess I 'd have gotten it."

"Why not?" The frankness had driven other queries from Fairchild's mind. Farrell, the attorney, grinned cheerily.

"Because I understand it concerns the Rodaines. Nobody but a fool out of college cares to buck up against them. Besides, nearly everybody has a little money stuck into their enterprises. And seeing I have no money at all, I 'm not financially interested. And not being interested, I 'm wholly just, fair and willing to fight 'em to a standstill. Now what's the trouble? Your partner 's in jail, as I understand it. Guilty or not guilty?"

"Wa--wait a minute!" The breeziness of the man had brought Fairchild to more wakefulness and to a certain amount of cheer. "Who hired you?" Then with a sudden inspiration: "Mother Howard did n't go and do this?"

"Mother Howard? You mean the woman who runs the boarding house? Not at all."

"But--"

"I 'm not exactly at liberty to state."

Suspicion began to assert itself. The smile of comradeship that the other man's manner instilled faded suddenly.

"Under those conditions, I don't believe--"

"Don't say it! Don't get started along those lines. I know what you 're think-ing. Knew that was what would happen from the start. And against the wishes of the person who hired me for this work, I--well, I brought the evidence. I might as well show it now as try to put over this secret stuff and lose a lot of time doing it. Here, take a glimpse and then throw it away, tear it up, swallow it, or do anything you want to with it, just so nobody else sees it. Ready? Look."

He drew forth a small visiting card. Fairchild glanced. Then he looked--and then he sat up straight in bed. For before him were the engraved words:

 Miss Anita Natalie Richmond.

While across the card was hastily written, in a hand distinctively feminine:

Mr. Fairchild: This is my good friend. He will help you. There is no fee at-tached. Please destroy.

Anita Richmond.

"Bu--but I don't understand."

"You know Miss--er--the writer of this card, don't you?"

"But why should she--?"

Mr. Farrell, barrister-at-law, grinned broadly.

"I see you don't know Miss--the writer of this card at all. That's her nature. Besides--well, I have a habit of making long stories short. All she 's got to do with me is crook her finger and I 'll jump through. I 'm--none of your business. But, anyway, here I am--"

Fairchild could not restrain a laugh. There was something about the man, about his nervous, yet boyish way of speaking, about his enthusiasm, that wiped out suspicion and invited confidence. The owner of the Blue Poppy mine leaned forward.

"But you did n't finish your sentence about--the writer of that card."

"You mean--oh--well, there 's nothing to that. I 'm in love with her. Been in love with her since I 've been knee-high to a duck. So 're you. So 's every other hu-man being that thinks he 's a regular man. So's Maurice Rodaine. Don't know about the rest of you--but I have n't got a chance. Don't even think of it any more--look on it as a necessary affliction, like wearing winter woolens and that sort of thing. Don't let it bother you. The problem right now is to get your partner out of jail. How much money have you got?"

"Only a little more than two thousand."

"Not enough. There 'll be bonds on four charges. At the least, they 'll be around a thousand dollars apiece. Probabilities are that they 'll run around ten thousand for the bunch. How about the Blue Poppy?"

Fairchild shrugged his shoulders.

"I don't know what it's worth."

"Neither do I. Neither does the judge. Neither does any one else. Therefore, it's worth at least ten thousand dollars. That 'll do the trick. Get out your deeds and that sort of thing--we 'll have to file them with the bond as security."

"But that will ruin us!"

"How so? A bond 's nothing more than a mortgage. It doesn't stop you from working on the mine. All it does is give evidence that your friend and partner will be on the job when the bailiff yells oyez, oyez, oyez. Otherwise, they 'll take the mine away from you and sell it at public sale for the price of the bond. But that's a happen-so of the future. And there 's no danger if our client--you will notice that I call him our client--is clothed with the dignity and the protecting mantle of innocence and stays here to see his trial out."

"He 'll do that, all right."

"Then we 're merely using the large and ample safe of the court of this judicial district as a deposit vault for some very valuable papers. I 'd suggest now that you get up, seize your deeds and accompany me to the palace of justice. Otherwise, that partner of yours will have to eat dinner in a place called in undignified language the hoosegow!"

It was like warm sunshine on a cold day, the chatter of this young man in horn-rimmed glasses. Soon Fairchild was dressed and walking hurriedly up the street with the voluble attorney. A half-hour more and they were before the court. Fairchild, the lawyer and the jail-worn Harry, his mustache fluttering in more directions than ever.

"Not guilty, Your Honor," said Randolph P. Farrell. "May I ask the extent of the bond?"

The judge adjusted his glasses and studied the information which the district attorney had laid before him.

"In view of the number of charges and the seriousness of each, I must fix an aggregate bond of five thousand dollars, or twelve hundred fifty dollars for each case."

"Thank you; we had come prepared for more. Mr. Fairchild, who is Mr. Harkins' partner, is here to appear as bondsman. The deeds are in his name alone, the partnership existing, as I understand it, upon their word of honor between them. I refer, Your Honor, to the deeds of the Blue Poppy mine. Would Your Honor care to examine them?"

His Honor would. His Honor did. For a long moment he studied them, and Fairchild, in looking about the courtroom, saw the bailiff in conversation with a tall, thin man, with squint eyes and a scar-marked forehead. A moment later, the judge looked over his glasses.

"Bailiff!"

"Yes, Your Honor."

"Have you any information regarding the value of the Blue Poppy mining claims?"

"Sir, I have just been talking to Mr. Rodaine. He says they 're well worth the value of the bond."

"How about that, Rodaine?" The judge peered down the court room. Squint Rodaine scratched his hawklike nose with his thumb and nodded.

"They 'll do," was his answer, and the judge passed the papers to the clerk of the court.

"Bond accepted. I 'll set this trial for--"

"If Your Honor please, I should like it at the very, very earliest possible moment," Randolph P. Farrell had cut in. "This is working a very great hardship upon an innocent man and--"

"Can't be done." The judge was scrawling on his docket. "Everything 's too crowded. Can't be reached before the November term. Set it for November 11th."

"Very well, Your Honor." Then he turned with a wide grin to his clients. "That's all until November."

Out they filed through the narrow aisle of the court room, Fairchild's knee brushing the trouser leg of Squint Rodaine as they passed. At the door, the attorney turned toward them, then put forth a hand.

"Drop in any day this week and we 'll go over things," he announced cheerfully. "We put one over on his royal joblots that time, anyway. Hates me from the ground up. Worst we can hope for is a conviction and then a Supreme Court reversal. I 'll get him so mad he 'll fill the case with errors. He used to be an instructor down at Boulder, and I stuck the pages of a lecture together on him one day. That's why I asked for an early trial. Knew he 'd give me a late one. That 'll let us have time to stir up a little favorable evidence, which right now we don't possess. Understand-- all money that comes from the mine is held in escrow until this case is decided. But I 'll explain that. Going to stick around here and bask in the effulgence of really possessing a case. S'long!"

And he turned back into the court room, while Fairchild, the dazed Harry stalking beside him, started down the street.

"'Ow do you figure it?" asked the Cornishman at last.

"What?"

"Rodaine. 'E 'elped us out!"

Fairchild stopped. It had not occurred to him before. But now he saw it: that if Rodaine, as an expert on mining, had condemned the Blue Poppy, it could have meant only one thing, the denial of bond by the judge and the lack of freedom for Harry. Fairchild rubbed a hand across his brow.

"I can't figure it," came at last. "And especially since his son is the accuser and since I got the best of them both last night!"

"Got the best of 'em? You?"

The story was brief in its telling. And it brought no explanation of the sudden amiability displayed by the crooked-faced Rodaine. They went on, striving vainly for a reason, at last to stop in front of the post-office, as the postmaster leaned out of the door.

"Your name's Fairchild, isn't it?" asked the person of letters, as he fastened a pair of gimlet eyes on the owner of the Blue Poppy.

"Yes."

"Thought so. Some of the fellows said you was. Better drop in here for your mail once in a while. There 's been a letter for you here for two days!"

"For me?" Vaguely Fairchild went within and received the missive, a plain, bond envelope without a return address. He turned it over and over in his hand before he opened it--then looked at the postmark,--Denver. At last:

"Open it, why don't you?"

Harry's mustache was tickling his ear, as the big miner stared over his shoulder. Fairchild obeyed. They gasped together. Before them were figures and sentences which blurred for a moment, finally to resolve into:

Mr. Robert Fairchild,   Ohadi, Colorado.

Dear Sir;

I am empowered by a client whose name I am not at liberty to state, to make you an offer of $50,000. for your property in Clear Creek County, known as the Blue Poppy mine. In replying, kindly address your letter to

Box 180, Denver, Colo.

Harry whistled long and thoughtfully.

"That's a 'ole lot of money!"

"An awful lot, Harry. But why was the offer made? There 's nothing to base it on. There 's--"

Then for a moment, as they stepped out of the post-office, he gave up the thought, even of comparative riches. Twenty feet away, a man and a girl were approaching, talking as though there never had been the slightest trouble between them. They crossed the slight alleyway, and she laid her hand on his arm, almost caressingly, Fairchild thought, and he stared hard as though in unbelief of their identity. But it was certain. It was Maurice Rodaine and Anita Richmond; they came closer, her eyes turned toward Fairchild, and then--

She went on, without speaking, without taking the trouble to notice, apparently, that he had been standing there.

CHAPTER XII

After this, there was little conversation until Harry and Fairchild had reached the boarding house. Then, with Mother Howard for an adviser, the three gathered in the old parlor, and Fairchild related the events of the night before, adding what had happened at the post-office, when Anita had passed him without speaking. Mother Howard, her arms folded as usual, bobbed her gray head.

"It's like her, Son," she announced at last. "She's a good girl. I've known her ever since she was a little tad not big enough to walk. And she loves her father."

"But--"

"She loves her father. Isn't that enough? The Rodaines have the money--and they have almost everything that Judge Richmond owns. It's easy enough to guess what they've done with it--tied it up so that he can't touch it until they're ready for him to do it. And they're not going to do that until they've gotten what they want."

"Which is--?"

"Anita! Any fool ought to be able to know that. Of course," she added with an acrid smile, "persons that are so head over heels in love themselves that they can't see ten feet in front of them wouldn't be able to understand it--but other people can. The Rodaines know they can't do anything directly with Anita. She wouldn't stand for it. She's not that kind of a girl. They know that money doesn't mean anything to her--and what's more, they've been forced to see that Anita ain't going to turn handsprings just for the back-action honor of marrying a Rodaine. Anita could marry a lot richer fellows than Maurice Rodaine ever dreamed of being, if she wanted to--and there wouldn't be any scoundrel of a father, or any graveyard wandering, crazy mother to go into the bargain. And they realize it. But they realize too, that there ain't a chance of them losing out as long as her father's happiness depends on doing what they want her to do. So, after all, ain't it easy to see the whole thing?"

"To you, possibly. But not to me."

Mother Howard pressed her lips in exasperation.

"Just go back over it," she recapitulated. "She got mad at him at the dance last night, did n't she? He 'd done something rude--from the way you tell it. Then you sashayed up and asked her to dance every dance with you. You don't suppose that was because you were so tall and handsome, do you?"

"Well--" Fairchild smiled ruefully--"I was hoping that it was because she rather liked me."

"Suppose it was? But she rather likes a lot of people. You understand women just like a pig understands Sunday--you don't know anything about 'em. She was mad at Maurice Rodaine and she wanted to give him a lesson. She never thought about the consequences. After the dance was over, just like the sniveling little coward he is, he got his father and went to the Richmond house. There they began laying out the old man because he had permitted his daughter to do such a disgraceful thing as to dance with a man she wanted to dance with instead of kowtowing and butting her head against the floor every time Maurice Rodaine crooked his finger. And they were n't gentle about it. What was the result? Poor old Judge Richmond got excited and had another stroke. And what did Anita do naturally--just like a woman? She got the high-strikes and then you came rushing in. After that, she calmed down and had a minute to think of what might be before her. That stroke last night was the second one for the Judge. There usually ain't any more after the third one. Now, can't you see why Anita is willing to do anything on earth just to keep peace and just to give her father a little rest and comfort and happiness in the last days of his life? You 've got to remember that he ain't like an ordinary father that you can go to and tell all your troubles. He 's laying next door to death, and Anita, just like any woman that's got a great, big, good heart in her, is willing to face worse than death to help him. It's as plain to me as the nose on Harry's face."

"Which is quite plain," agreed Fairchild ruefully. Harry rubbed the libeled proboscis, pawed at his mustache and fidgeted in his chair.

"I understand that, all right," he announced at last. "But why should anybody want to buy the mine?"

It brought Fairchild to the realization of a new development, and he brought forth the letter, once more to stare at it.

"Fifty thousand dollars is a lot of money," came at last. "It would pretty near pay us for coming out here, Harry."

"That it would."

"And what then?" Mother Howard, still looking through uncolored glasses, took the letter and scanned it. "You two ain't quitters, are you?"

"'Oo, us?" Harry bristled.

"Yes, you. If you are, get yourselves a piece of paper and write to Denver and take the offer. If you ain't--keep on fighting."

"I believe you 're right, Mother Howard."

Fairchild had reached for the letter again and was staring at it as though for inspiration. "That amount of money seems to be a great deal. Still, if a person will offer that much for a mine when there 's nothing in sight to show its value, it ought to mean that there's something dark in the woodpile and that the thing 's worth fighting out. And personally speaking, I 'm willing to fight!"

"I never quit in my life!" Harry straightened in his chair and his mustache stuck forth pugnaciously. Mother Howard looked down at him, pressed her lips, then smiled.

"No," she announced, "except to run away like a whipped pup after you 'd gotten a poor lonely boarding-house keeper in love with you!"

"Mother 'Oward, I 'll--"

But the laughing, gray-haired woman had scrambled through the doorway and slammed the door behind her, only to open it a second later and poke her head within.

"Need n't think because you can hold up a dance hall and get away with it, you can use cave-man stuff on me!" she admonished. And in that one sentence was all the conversation necessary regarding the charges against Harry, as far as Mother Howard was concerned. She did n't believe them, and Harry's face showed that the world had become bright and serene again. He swung his great arms as though to loosen the big muscles of his shoulders. He pecked at his mustache. Then he turned to Fairchild.

"Well," he asked, "what do we do? Go up to the mine--just like nothing 'ad ever 'appened?"

"Exactly. Wait until I change my clothes. Then we 'll be ready to start. I 'm not even going to dignify this letter by replying to it. And for one principal reason--" he added--"that I think the Rodaines have something to do with it."

"'Ow so?"

"I don't know. It's only a conjecture; I guess the connection comes from the fact that Squint put a good valuation on the mine this morning in court. And if it is any of his doings--then the best thing in the world is to forget it. I 'll be ready in a moment."

An hour later they entered the mouth of the Blue Poppy tunnel, once more to start the engines and to resume the pumping, meanwhile struggling back and forth with timbers from the mountain side, as they began the task of rehabilitating the tunnel where it had caved in just beyond the shaft. It was the beginning of a long task; well enough they knew that far below there would be much more of this to do, many days of back-breaking labor in which they must be the main participants, before they ever could hope to begin their real efforts in search of ore.

And so, while the iron-colored water gushed from the pump tubes. Harry and Fairchild made their trips, scrambling ones as they went outward, struggling ones as they came back, dragging the "stulls" or heavy timbers which would form the main supports, the mill-stakes, or lighter props, the laggs and spreaders, all found in the broken, well-seasoned timber of the mountain side, all necessary for the work which was before them. The timbering of a mine is not an easy task. One by one the heavy props must be put into place, each to its station, every one in a position which will furnish the greatest resistance against the tremendous weight from above, the constant inclination of the earth to sink and fill the man-made excavations. For the earth is a jealous thing; its own caverns it makes and preserves judiciously. Those made by the hand of humanity call forth the resistance of gravity and of disintegration, and it takes measures of strength and power to combat them. That day, Harry and Fairchild worked with all their strength at the beginning of a stint that would last--they did not, could not know how long. And they worked together. Their plan of a day and night shift had been abandoned; the trouble engendered by their first attempt had been enough to shelve that sort of program.

Hour after hour they toiled, until the gray mists hung low over the mountain tops, until the shadows lengthened and twilight fell. The engines ceased their chugging, the coughing swirl of the dirty water as it came from the drift, far below, stopped. Slowly two weary men jogged down the rutty road to the narrow, winding highway which led through Kentucky Gulch and into town. But they were happy with a new realization: that they were actively at work, that something had been accomplished by their labors, and progress made in spite of the machinations of malignant men, in spite of the malicious influences of the past and of the present, and in spite of the powers of Nature.

It was a new, a grateful life to Fairchild. It gave him something else to think about than the ponderings upon the mysterious events which seemed to whirl, like a maelstrom, about him. And more, it gave him little time to think at all, for that night he did not lie awake to stare about him in the darkness. Muscles were aching in spite of their inherent strength. His head pounded from the pressure of intensified heart action. His eyes closed wearily, yet with a wholesome fatigue. Nor did he wake until Harry was pounding on the door in the dawn of the morning.

Their meal came before the dining room was regularly open. Mother Howard herself flipping the flapjacks and frying the eggs which formed their breakfast, meanwhile finding the time to pack their lunch buckets. Then out into the crisp air of morning they went, and back to their labors.

Once more the pumps; once more the struggle against the heavy timbers; once more the "clunk" of the axe as it bit deep into wood, or the pounding of hammers as great spikes were driven into place. Late that afternoon they turned to a new duty,--that of mucking away the dirt and rotted logs from a place that once had been impassable. The timbering of the broken-down portion of the tunnel just behind the shaft had been repaired, and Harry flipped the sweat away from his broad forehead with an action of relief.

"Not that it does us any particular good," he announced. "There ain't nothing back there that we can get at. But it's room we 'll need when we start working down below, and we might as well 'ave it fixed up--"

He ceased suddenly and ran to the pumps. A peculiar gurgling sound had come from the ends of the hose, and the flow depreciated greatly; instead of the steady gush of water, a slimy silt was coming out now, spraying and splattering about on the sides of the drainage ditch. Wildly Harry waved a monstrous paw.

"Shut 'em off!" he yelled to Fairchild in the dimness of the tunnel. "It's sucking the muck out of the sump!"

"Out of the what?" Fairchild had killed the engines and run forward to where Harry, one big hand behind the carbide flare, was peering down the shaft.

"The sump--it's a little 'ole at the bottom of the shaft to 'old any water that 'appens to seep in. That means the 'ole drift is unwatered."

"Then the pumping job 's over?"

"Yeh." Harry rose. "You stay 'ere and dismantle the pumps, so we can send 'em back. I 'll go to town. We 've got to buy some stuff."

Then he started off down the trail, while Fairchild went to his work. And he sang as he dragged at the heavy hose, pulling it out of the shaft and coiling it at the entrance to the tunnel, as he put skids under the engines, and moved them, inch by inch, to the outer air. Work was before him, work which was progressing toward a goal that he had determined to seek, in spite of all obstacles. The mysterious offer which he had received gave evidence that something awaited him, that some one knew the real value of the Blue Poppy mine, and that if he could simply stick to his task, if he could hold to the unwavering purpose to win in spite of all the blocking pitfalls that were put in his path, some day, some time, the reward would be worth its price.

More, the conversation with Mother Howard on the previous morning had been comforting; it had given a woman's viewpoint upon another woman's actions. And Fairchild intuitively believed she was correct. True, she had talked of others who might have hopes in regard to Anita Richmond; in fact, Fairchild had met one of those persons in the lawyer, Randolph Farrell. But just the same it all was cheering. It is man's supreme privilege to hope.

And so Fairchild was happy and somewhat at ease for the first time in weeks. Out at the edge of the mine, as he made his trips, he stopped now and then to look at something he had disregarded previously,--the valley stretching out beneath him, the three hummocks of the far-away range, named Father, Mother and Child by some romantic mountaineer; the blue-gray of the hills as they stretched on, farther and farther into the distance, gradually whitening until they resolved themselves into the snowy range, with the gaunt, high-peaked summit of Mount Evans scratching the sky in the distance.

There was a shimmer in the air, through which the trees were turned into a bluer green, and the crags of the mountains made softer, the gaping scars of prospect holes less lonely and less mournful with their ever-present story of lost hopes. On a great boulder far at one side a chipmunk chattered. Far down the road an ore train clattered along on the way to the Sampler,--that great middleman institution which is a part of every mining camp, and which, like the creamery station at the cross roads, receives the products of the mines, assays them by its technically correct system of four samples and four assayers to every shipment, and buys them, with its allowances for freight, smelting charges and the innumerable expenditures which must be made before money can become money in reality. Fairchild sang louder than ever, a wordless tune, an old tune, engendered in his brain upon a paradoxically happy and unhappy night,--that of the dance when he had held Anita Richmond in his arms, and she had laughed up at him as, by her companionship, she had paid the debt of the Denver road. Fairchild had almost forgotten that. Now, with memory, his brow puckered, and his song died slowly away.

"What the dickens was she doing?" he asked himself at last. "And why should she have wanted so terribly to get away from that sheriff?"

There was no answer. Besides, he had promised to ask for none. And further, a shout from the road, accompanied by the roaring of a motor truck, announced the fact that Harry was making his return.

Five men were with him, to help him carry in ropes, heavy pulleys, weights and a large metal shaft bucket, then to move out the smaller of the pumps and trundle away with them, leaving the larger one and the larger engine for a single load. At last Harry turned to his paraphernalia and rolled up his sleeves.

"'Ere 's where we work!" he announced. "It's us for a pulley and bucket arrangement until we can get the 'oist to working and the skip to running. 'Elp me 'eave a few timbers."

It was the beginning of a three-days' job, the building of a heavy staging over the top of the shaft, the affixing of the great pulley and then the attachment of the bucket at one end, and the skip, loaded with pig iron, on the other. Altogether, it formed a sort of crude, counterbalanced elevator, by which they might lower themselves into the shaft, with various bumpings and delays,--but which worked successfully, nevertheless. Together they piled into the big, iron bucket. Harry lugging along spikes and timbers and sledges and ropes. Then, pulling away at the cable which held the weights, they furnished the necessary gravity to travel downward.

An eerie journey, faced on one side by the crawling rope of the skip as it traveled along the rusty old track on its watersoaked ties, on the others by the still dripping timbers of the aged shaft and its broken, rotting ladder, while the carbide lanterns cast shadows about, while the pulley above creaked and the eroded wheels of the skip squeaked and protested! Downward--a hundred feet--and they collided with the upward-bound skip, to fend off from it and start on again. The air grew colder, more moist. The carbides spluttered and flared. Then a slight bump, and they were at the bottom. Fairchild started to crawl out from the bucket, only to resume his old position as Harry yelled with fright.

"Don't do it!" gulped the Cornishman. "Do you want me to go up like a skyrocket? Them weights is all at the top. We 've got to fix a plug down 'ere to 'old this blooming bucket or it 'll go up and we 'll stay down!"

Working from the side of the bucket, still held down by the weight of the two men, they fashioned a catch, or lock, out of a loop of rope attached to heavy spikes, and fastened it taut.

"That 'll 'old," announced the big Cornishman. "Out we go!"

Fairchild obeyed with alacrity. He felt now that he was really coming to something, that he was at the true beginning of his labors. Before him the drift tunnel, damp and dripping and dark, awaited, seeming to throw back the flare of the carbides as though to shield the treasures which might lie beyond. Harry started forward a step, then pausing, shifted his carbide and laid a hand on his companion's shoulder.

"Boy," he said slowly, "we 're starting at something now--and I don't know where it's going to lead us. There's a cave-in up 'ere, and if we 're ever going to get anywhere in this mine, we 'll 'ave to go past it. And I 'm afraid of what we 're going to find when we cut our wye through!"

Clouds of the past seemed to rise and float past Fairchild. Clouds which carried visions of a white, broken old man sitting by a window, waiting for death, visions of an old safe and a letter it contained. For a long, long moment, there was silence. Then came Harry's voice again.

"I 'm afraid it ain't going to be good news, Boy. But there ain't no wye to get around it. It's got to come out sometime--things like that won't stay 'idden forever. And your father 's gone now--gone where it can't 'urt 'im."

"I know," answered Fairchild in a queer, husky voice. "He must have known, Harry--he must have been willing that it come, now that he is gone. He wrote me as much."

"It's that or nothing. If we sell the mine, some one else will find it. And we can't 'it the vein without following the drift to the stope. But you're the one to make the decision."

Again, a long moment; again, in memory, Fairchild was standing in a gloomy, old-fashioned room, reading a letter he had taken from a dusty safe. Finally his answer came:

"He told me to go ahead, if necessary. And we 'll go, Harry."

CHAPTER XIII

They started forward then, making their way through the slime and silt of the drift flooring, slippery and wet from years of flooding. From above them the water dripped from the seep-soaked hanging-wall, which showed rough and splotchy in the gleam of the carbides and seemed to absorb the light until they could see only a few feet before them as they clambered over water-soaked timbers, disjointed rails of the little tram track which once had existed there, and floundered in and out of the greasy pockets of mud which the floating ties of the track had left behind. On--on--they stopped.

Progress had become impossible. Before them, twisted and torn and piled about in muddy confusion, the timbers of the mine suddenly showed in a perfect barricade, supplanted from behind by piles of muck and rocky refuse which left no opening to the chamber of the stope beyond. Harry's carbide went high in the air, and he slid forward, to stand a moment in thought before the obstacle. At place after place he surveyed it, finally to turn with a shrug of his shoulders.

"It's going to mean more 'n a month of the 'ardest kind of work, Boy," came his final announcement. "'Ow it could 'ave caved in like that is more than I know. I 'm sure we timbered it good."

"And look--" Fairchild was beside him now, with his carbide--"how every-thing's torn, as though from an explosion."

"It seems that wye. But you can't tell. Rock 'as an awful way of churning up things when it decides to turn loose. All I know is we 've got a job cut out for us."

There was only one thing to do,--turn back. Fifteen minutes more and they were on the surface, making their plans; projects which entailed work from morn-ing until night for many a day to come. There was a track to lay, an extra skip to be lowered, that they might haul the muck and broken timbers from the cave-in to the shaft and on out to the dump. There were stulls and mill-stakes and laggs to cut and to be taken into the shaft. And there was good, hard work of muscle and brawn and pick and shovel, that muck might be torn away from the cave-in, and good timbers put in place, to hold the hanging wall from repeating its escapade of eighteen years before. Harry reached for a new axe and indicated another.

"We 'll cut ties first," he announced.

And thus began the weeks of effort, weeks in which they worked with crude appliances; weeks in which they dragged the heavy stulls and other timbers into the tunnel and then lowered them down the shaft to the drift, two hundred feet below, only to follow them in their counter-balanced bucket and laboriously pile them along the sides of the drift, there to await use later on. Weeks in which they worked in mud and slime, as they shoveled out the muck and with their gad hooks tore down loose portions of the hanging wall to form a roadbed for their new tram. Weeks in which they cut ties, in which they crawled from their beds even before dawn, nor returned to Mother Howard's boarding house until long after dark; weeks in which they seemed to lose all touch with the outside world. Their whole universe had turned into a tunnel far beneath the surface of the earth, a drift leading to a cave-in, which they had not yet begun to even indent with excavations.

It was a slow, galling progress, but they kept at it. Gradually the tram line began to take shape, pieced together from old portions of the track which still lay in the drift and supplemented by others bought cheaply at that graveyard of miner's hopes,--the junk yard in Ohadi. At last it was finished; the work of moving the heavy timbers became easier now as they were shunted on to the small tram truck from which the body had been dismantled and trundled along the rails to the cave-in, there to be piled in readiness for their use. And finally--

A pick swung in the air, to give forth a chunky, smacking sound, as it struck water-softened, spongy wood. The attack against the cave-in had begun, to progress with seeming rapidity for a few hours, then to cease, until the two men could remove the debris which they had dug out and haul it by slow, laborious effort to the surface. But it was a beginning, and they kept at it.

A foot at a time they tore away the old, broken, splintered timbers and the rocky refuse which lay piled behind each shivered beam; only to stop, carry away the muck, and then rebuild. And it was effort,--effort which strained every muscle of two strong men, as with pulleys and handmade, crude cranes, they raised the big logs and propped them in place against further encroachment of the hanging wall. Cold and damp, in the moist air of the tunnel they labored, but there was a joy in it all. Down here they could forget Squint Rodaine and his chalky-faced son; down here they could feel that they were working toward a goal and lay aside the handicap which humans might put in their path.

Day after day of labor and the indentation upon the cave-in grew from a matter of feet to one of yards. A week. Two. Then, as Harry swung his pick, he lurched forward and went to his knees. "I 've gone through!" he announced in happy surprise. "I 've gone through. We 're at the end of it!"

Up went Fairchild's carbide. Where the pick still hung in the rocky mass, a tiny hole showed, darker than the surrounding refuse. He put forth a hand and clawed at the earth about the tool; it gave way beneath his touch, and there was only vacancy beyond. Again Harry raised his pick and swung it with force. Fairchild joined him. A moment more and they were staring at a hole which led to darkness, and there was joy in Harry's voice as he made a momentary survey.

"It's fairly dry be'ind there," he announced. "Otherwise we 'd have been scrambling around in water up to our necks. We 're lucky there, any'ow."

Again the attack and again the hole widened. At last Harry straightened.

"We can go in now," came finally. "Are you willing to go with me?"

"Of course. Why not?"

The Cornishman's hand went to his mustache.

"I ain't tickled about what we 're liable to find."

"You mean--?"

But Harry stopped him.

"Let's don't talk about it till we 'ave to. Come on."

Silently they crawled through the opening, the silt and fine rock rattling about them as they did so, to come upon fairly dry earth on the other side, and to start forward. Under the rays of the carbides, they could see that the track here was in fairly good condition; the only moisture being that of a natural seepage which counted for little. The timbers still stood dry and firm, except where dripping water in a few cases had caused the blocks to become spongy and great holes to be pressed in them by the larger timbers which held back the tremendous weight from above.

Suddenly, as they walked along. Harry took the lead, holding his lantern far ahead of him, with one big hand behind it, as though for a reflector. Then, just as suddenly, he turned.

"Let's go out," came shortly.

"Why?"

"It's there!" In the light of the lantern,

Harry's face was white, his big lips livid. "Let's go--"

But Fairchild stopped him.

"Harry," he said, and there was determination in his voice, "if it's there--we 've got to face it. I 'll be the one who will suffer. My father is gone. There are no accusations where he rests now; I 'm sure of that. If--if he ever did anything in his life that wasn't right, he paid for it. We don't know what happened, Harry--all we are sure of is that if it's what we 're--we 're afraid of, we 've gone too far now to turn back. Don't you think that certain people would make an investigation if we should happen to quit the mine now?"

"The Rodaines!"

"Exactly. They would scent something, and within an hour they 'd be down in here, snooping around. And how much worse would it be for them to tell the news--than for us!"

"Nobody 'as to tell it--" Harry was staring at his carbide flare--"there 's a wye."

"But we can't take it, Harry. In my father's letter was the statement that he made only one mistake--that of fear. I 'm going to believe him--and in spite of what I find here, I 'm going to hold him innocent, and I 'm going to be fair and square and aboveboard about it all. The world can think what it pleases--about him and about me. There 's nothing on my conscience--and I know that if my father had not made the mistake of running away when he did, there would have been nothing on his."

Harry shook his head.

"'E could n't do much else, Boy. Rodaine was stronger in some ways then than he is now. That was in different days. That was in times when Squint Rodaine could 'ave gotten a 'undred men together quicker 'n a cat's wink and lynched a man without 'im 'aving a trial or anything. And if I 'd been your father, I 'd 'ave done the same as 'e did. I 'd 'ave run too--'e 'd 'ave paid for it with 'is life if 'e didn't, guilty or not guilty. And--" he looked sharply toward the younger man--"you say to go on?"

"Go on," said Fairchild, and he spoke the words between tightly clenched teeth. Harry turned his light before him, and once more shielded it with his big hand. A step--two, then:

"Look--there--over by the footwall!"

Fairchild forced his eyes in the direction designated and stared intently. At first it appeared only like a succession of disjointed, broken stones, lying in straggly fashion along the footwall of the drift where it widened into the stope, or upward slant on the vein. Then, it came forth clearer, the thin outlines of something which clutched at the heart of Robert Fairchild, which sickened him, which caused him to fight down a sudden, panicky desire to shield his eyes and to run,--a heap of age-denuded bones, the scraps of a miner's costume still clinging to them, the heavy shoes protruding in comically tragic fashion over bony feet; a huddled, cramped skeleton of a human being!

They could only stand and stare at it,--this reminder of a tragedy of a quarter of a century agone. Their lips refused to utter the words that strove to travel past them; they were two men dumb, dumb through a discovery which they had forced themselves to face, through a fact which they had hoped against, each more or less silently, yet felt sure must, sooner or later, come before them. And now it was here.

And this was the reason that twenty years before Thornton Fairchild, white, grim, had sought the aid of Harry and of Mother Howard. This was the reason that a woman had played the part of a man, singing in maudlin fashion as they traveled down the center of the street at night, to all appearances only three disappointed miners seeking a new field. And yet--

"I know what you 're thinking." It was Harry's voice, strangely hoarse and weak. "I 'm thinking the same thing. But it must n't be. Dead men don't alwyes mean they 've died--in a wye to cast reflections on the man that was with 'em. Do you get what I mean? You've said--" and he looked hard into the cramped, suffering face of Robert Fairchild--"that you were going to 'old your father innocent. So 'm I. We don't know, Boy, what went on 'ere. And we 've got to 'ope for the best."

Then, while Fairchild stood motionless and silent, the big Cornishman forced himself forward, to stoop by the side of the heap of bones which once had represented a man, to touch gingerly the clothing, and then to bend nearer and hold his carbide close to some object which Fairchild could not see. At last he rose and with old, white features, approached his partner.

"The appearances are against us," came quietly. "There 's a 'ole in 'is skull that a jury 'll say was made by a single jack. It 'll seem like some one 'ad killed 'im, and then caved in the mine with a box of powder. But 'e 's gone, Boy--your father--I mean. 'E can't defend 'imself. We 've got to take 'is part."

"Maybe--" Fairchild was grasping at the final straw--"maybe it's not the person we believe it to be at all. It might be somebody else--who had come in here and set off a charge of powder by accident and--"

But the shaking of Harry's head stifled the momentary ray of hope.

"No. I looked. There was a watch--all covered with mold and mildewed. I pried it open. It's got Larsen's name inside!"

CHAPTER XIV

Again there was a long moment of silence, while Harry stood pawing at his mustache and while Robert Fairchild sought to summon the strength to do the thing which was before him. It had been comparatively easy to make resolutions while there still was hope. It was a far different matter now. All the soddenness of the old days had come back to him, ghosts which would not be driven away; memories of a time when he was the grubbing, though willing slave of a victim of fear,--of a man whose life had been wrecked through terror of the day when intruders would break their way through the debris, and when the discovery would be made. And it had remained for Robert Fairchild, the son, to find the hidden secret, for him to come upon the thing which had caused the agony of nearly thirty years of suffering, for him to face the alternative of again placing that gruesome find into hiding, or to square his shoulders before the world and take the consequences. Murder is not an easy word to hear, whether it rests upon one's own shoulders, or upon the memory of a person beloved. And right now Robert Fairchild felt himself sagging beneath the weight of the accusation.

But there was no time to lose in making his decision. Beside him stood Harry, silent, morose. Before him,--Fairchild closed his eyes in an attempt to shut out the sight of it. But still it was there, the crumpled heap of tattered clothing and human remains, the awry, heavy shoes still shielding the fleshless bones of the feet. He turned blindly, his hands groping before him.

"Harry," he called, "Harry! Get me out of here--I--can't stand it!"

Wordlessly the big man came to his side. Wordlessly they made the trip back to the hole in the cave-in and then followed the trail of new-laid track to the shaft. Up--up--the trip seemed endless as they jerked and pulled on the weighted rope, that their shaft bucket might travel to the surface. Then, at the mouth of the tunnel, Robert Fairchild stood for a long time staring out over the soft hills and the radiance of the snowy range, far away. It gave him a new strength, a new determination. The light, the sunshine, the soft outlines of the scrub pines in the distance, the freedom and openness of the mountains seemed to instill into him a courage he could not feel down there in the dampness and darkness of the tunnel. His shoulders surged, as though to shake off a great weight. His eyes brightened with resolution. Then he turned to the faithful Harry, waiting in the background.

"There's no use trying to evade anything, Harry. We 've got to face the music. Will you go with me to notify the coroner--or would you rather stay here?"

"I 'll go."

Silently they trudged into town and to the little undertaking shop which also served as the office of the coroner. They made their report, then accompanied the officer, together with the sheriff, back to the mine and into the drift. There once more they clambered through the hole in the cave-in and on toward the beginning of the stope. And there they pointed out their discovery.

A wait for the remainder of that day,--a day that seemed ages long, a day in which Robert Fairchild found himself facing the editor of the *Bugle*, and telling his story, Harry beside him. But he told only what he had found, nothing of the past, nothing of the white-haired man who had waited by the window, cringing at the slightest sound on the old, vine-clad veranda, nothing of the letter which he had found in the dusty safe. Nothing was asked regarding that; nothing could be gained by telling it. In the heart of Robert Fairchild was the conviction that somehow, some way, his father was innocent, and in his brain was a determination to fight for that innocence as long as it was humanly possible. But gossip told what he did not.

There were those who remembered the departure of Thornton Fairchild from Ohadi. There were others who recollected perfectly that in the center of the rig was a singing, maudlin man, apparently "Sissie" Larsen. And they asked questions. They cornered Harry, they shot their queries at him one after another. But Harry was adamant.

"I ain't got anything to sye! And there's an end to it!"

Then, forcing his way past them, he crossed the street and went up the worn steps to the little office of Randolph P. Farrell, with his grinning smile and his horn-rimmed glasses, there to tell what he knew,--and to ask advice. And with the information the happy-go-lucky look faded, while Fairchild, entering behind Harry, heard a verdict which momentarily seemed to stop his heart.

"It means, Harry, that you were accessory to a crime--if this was a murder. You knew that something had happened. You helped without asking questions. And if it can be proved a murder--well," and he drummed on his desk with the end of his pencil--"there 's no statute of limitations when the end of a human life is concerned!"

Only a moment Harry hesitated. Then:

"I 'll tell the truth--if they ask me."

"When?" The lawyer was bending forward.

"At the inquest. Ain't that what you call it?"

"You'll tell nothing. Understand? You'll tell nothing, other than that you, with Robert Fairchild, found that skeleton. An inquest is n't a trial. And that can't come without knowledge and evidence that this man was murdered. So, remember--you tell the coroner's jury that you found this body and nothing more!"

"But--"

"It's a case for the grand jury after that, to study the findings of the coroner's jury and to sift out what evidence comes to it."

"You mean--" This time it was Fairchild cutting in--"that if the coroner's jury cannot find evidence that this man was murdered, or something more than mere supposition to base a charge on--there 'll be no trouble for Harry?"

"It's very improbable. So tell what happened on this day of this year of our Lord and nothing more! You people almost had me scared myself for a minute. Now, get out of here and let a legal light shine without any more clouds for a few minutes."

They departed then and traveled down the stairs with far more spring in their step than when they had entered. Late that night, as they were engaged at their usual occupation of relating the varied happenings of the day to Mother Howard, there came a knock at the door. Instinctively, Fairchild bent toward her:

"Your name 's out of this--as long as possible."

She smiled in her mothering, knowing way. Then she opened the door, there to find a deputy from the sheriff's office.

"They 've impaneled a jury up at the courthouse," he announced. "The coroner wants Mr. Fairchild and Mr. Harkins to come up there and tell what they know about this here skeleton they found."

It was the expected. The two men went forth, to find the street about the courthouse thronged, for already the news of the finding of the skeleton had traveled far, even into the little mining camps which skirted the town. It was a mystery of years long agone, and as such it fascinated and lured, in far greater measure perhaps, than some murder of a present day. Everywhere were black crowds under the faint street lamps. The basement of the courthouse was illuminated; and there were clusters of curious persons about the stairways. Through the throngs started Harry and Fairchild, only to be drawn aside by Farrell, the attorney.

"I 'm not going to take a part in this unless I have to," he told them. "It will look better for you if it is n't necessary for me to make an appearance. Whatever you do," and he addressed Harry, "say nothing about what you were telling me this afternoon. In the first place, you yourself have no actual knowledge of what happened. How do you know but what Thornton Fairchild was attacked by this man and forced to kill in self-defense? It's a penitentiary offense for a man to strike another, without sufficient justification, beneath ground. And had Sissie Larsen even so much as slapped Thornton Fairchild, that man would have been perfectly justified in killing him to protect himself. I 'm simply telling you that so that you will have no qualms in keeping concealed facts which, at this time, have no bearing. Guide yourselves accordingly--and as I say, I will be there only as a spectator, unless events should necessitate something else."

They promised and went on, somewhat calmer in mind, to edge their way to the steps and to enter the basement of the courthouse. The coroner and his jury, composed of six miners picked up haphazard along the street--according to the custom of coroners in general--were already present. So was every person who possibly could cram through the doors of the big room. To them all Fairchild paid little attention,--all but three.

They were on a back seat in the long courtroom,--Squint Rodaine and his son, chalkier, yet blacker than ever, while between them sat an old woman with white hair which straggled about her cheeks, a woman with deep-set eyes, whose hands wandered now and then vaguely before her; a wrinkled woman, fidgeting about on her seat, watching with craned neck those who stuffed their way within the already crammed room, her eyes never still, her lips moving constantly, as though mumbling some never-ending rote. Fairchild stared at her, then turned to Harry.

"Who 's that with the Rodaines?"

Harry looked furtively. "Crazy Laura--his wife."

"But--"

"And she ain't 'ere for anything good!"

Harry's voice bore a tone of nervousness. "Squint Rodaine don't even recognize 'er on the street--much less appear in company with 'er. Something's 'appening!"

"But what could she testify to?"

"'Ow should I know?" Harry said it almost petulantly. "I did n't even know she--"

"Oyez, oyez, oyez!" It was the bailiff, using a regular district-court introduction of the fact that an inquest was about to be held. The crowded room sighed and settled. The windows became frames for human faces, staring from without. The coroner stepped forward.

"We are gathered here to-night to inquire into the death of a man supposed to be L. A. Larsen, commonly called 'Sissie', whose skeleton was found to-day in the Blue Poppy mine. What this inquest will bring forth, I do not know, but as sworn and true members of the coroner's jury, I charge and command you in the great name of the sovereign State of Colorado, to do your full duty in arriving at your verdict."

The jury, half risen from its chair, some with their left hands held high above them, some with their right, swore in mumbling tones to do their duty, whatever that might be. The coroner surveyed the assemblage.

"First witness," he called out; "Harry Harkins!"

Harry went forward, clumsily seeking the witness chair. A moment later he had been sworn, and in five minutes more, he was back beside Fairchild, staring in a relieved manner about him. He had been questioned regarding nothing more than the mere finding of the body, the identification by means of the watch, and the notification of the coroner. Fairchild was called, to suffer no more from the queries of the investigator than Harry. There was a pause. It seemed that the inquest was over. A few people began to move toward the door--only to halt. The coroner's voice had sounded again:

"Mrs. Laura Rodaine!"

Prodded to her feet by the squint-eyed man beside her, she rose, and laughing in silly fashion, stumbled to the aisle, her straying hair, her ragged clothing, her big shoes and shuffling gait all blending with the wild, eerie look of her eyes, the constant munching of the almost toothless mouth. Again she laughed, in a vacant, embarrassed manner, as she reached the stand and held up her hand for the administration of the oath. Fairchild leaned close to his partner.

"At least she knows enough for that."

Harry nodded.

"She knows a lot, that ole girl. They say she writes down in a book everything she does every day. But what can she be 'ere to testify to?"

The answer seemed to come in the questioning voice of the coroner.

"Your name, please?"

"Laura Rodaine. Least, that's the name I go by. My real maiden name is Laura Masterson, and--"

"Rodaine will be sufficient. Your age?"

"I think it's sixty-four. If I had my book I could tell. I--"

"Your book?"

"Yes, I keep everything in a book. But it is n't here. I could n't bring it."

"The guess will be sufficient in this case. You 've lived here a good many years, Mrs. Rodaine?"

"Yes. Around thirty-five. Let's see--yes, I 'm sure it's thirty-five. My boy was born here--he 's about thirty and we came here five years before that."

"I believe you told me to-night that you have a habit of wandering around the hills?"

"Yes, I 've done that--I do it right along--I 've done it ever since my husband and I split up--that was just a little while after the boy was born--"

"Sufficient. I merely wanted to establish that fact. In wandering about, did you ever see anything, twenty-three or four years ago or so, that would lead you to believe you know something about the death of this man whose demise we are inquiring?"

The big hand of Harry caught at Fairchild's arm. The old woman had raised her head, craning her neck and allowing her mouth to fall open, as she strove for words. At last:

"I know something. I know a lot. But I 've never figured it was anybody's business but my own. So I have n't told it. But I remember--"

"What, Mrs. Rodaine?"

"The day Sissie Larsen was supposed to leave town--that was the day he got killed."

"Do you remember the date?"

"No--I don't remember that."

"Would it be in your book?"

She seemed to become suddenly excited. She half rose in her chair and looked down the line of benches to where her husband sat, the scar showing plainly in the rather brilliant light, his eyes narrowed until they were nearly closed. Again the question, and again a moment of nervousness before she answered:

"No--no--it would n't be in my book. I looked."

"But you remember?"

"Just like as if it was yesterday."

"And what you saw--did it give you any idea--"

"I know what I saw."

"And did it lead to any conclusion?"

"Yes."

"What, may I ask?"

"That somebody had been murdered!"

"Who--and by whom?"

Crazy Laura munched at her toothless gums for a moment and looked again toward her husband. Then, her watery, almost colorless eyes searching, she began a survey of the big room, looking intently from one figure to another. On and on--finally to reach the spot where stood Robert Fairchild and Harry, and there they stopped. A lean finger, knotted by rheumatism, darkened by sun and wind, stretched out.

"Yes, I know who did it, and I know who got killed. It was 'Sissie' Larsen--he was murdered. The man who did it was a fellow named Thornton Fairchild who owned the mine--if I ain't mistaken, he was the father of this young man--"

"I object!" Farrell, the attorney, was on his feet and struggling forward, jamming his horn-rimmed glasses into a pocket as he did so. "This has ceased to be an inquest; it has resolved itself into some sort of an inquisition!"

"I fail to see why." The coroner had stepped down and was facing him.

"Why? Why--you 're inquiring into a death that happened more than twenty years ago--and you 're basing that inquiry upon the word of a woman who is not legally able to give testimony in any kind of a court or on any kind of a case! It's not judicial, it's not within the confines of a legitimate, honorable practice, and it certainly is not just to stain the name of any man with the crime of murder upon the word of an insane person, especially when that man is dead and unable to defend himself!"

"Are n't you presuming?"

"I certainly am not. Have you any further evidence upon the lines that she is going to give?"

"Not directly."

"Then I demand that all the testimony which this woman has given be stricken out and the jury instructed to disregard it."

The official smiled.

"I think otherwise. Besides, this is merely a coroner's inquest and not a court action. The jury is entitled to all the evidence that has any bearing on the case."

"But this woman is crazy!"

"Has she ever been adjudged so, or committed to any asylum for the insane?"

"No--but nevertheless, there are a hundred persons in this court room who will testify to the fact that she is mentally unbalanced and not a fit person to fasten a crime upon any man's head by her testimony. And referring even to yourself, Coroner, have you within the last twenty-five years, in fact, since a short time after the birth of her son, called her anything else but Crazy Laura? Has any one else in this town called her any other name? Man, I appeal to your--"

"What you say may be true. It may not. I don't know. I only am sure of one thing--that a person is sane in the eyes of the law until adjudged otherwise. Therefore, her evidence at this time is perfectly legal and proper."

"It won't be as soon as I can bring an action before a lunacy court and cause her examination by a board of alienists."

"That's something for the future. In that case, things might be different. But I can only follow the law, with the members of the jury instructed, of course, to accept the evidence for what they deem it is worth. You will proceed, Mrs. Rodaine. What did you see that caused you to come to this conclusion?"

"Can't you even stick to the rules and ethics of testimony?" It was the final plea of the defeated Farrell. The coroner eyed him slowly.

"Mr. Farrell," came his answer, "I must confess to a deviation from regular court procedure in this inquiry. It is customary in an inquest of this character; certain departures from the usual rules must be made that the truth and the whole truth be learned. Proceed, Mrs. Rodaine, what was it you saw?"

Transfixed, horrified, Fairchild watched the mumbling, munching mouth, the staring eyes and straying white hair, the bony, crooked hands as they weaved before her. From those toothless jaws a story was about to come, true or untrue, a story that would stain the name of his father with murder! And that story now was at its beginning.

"I saw them together that afternoon early," the old woman was saying. "I came up the road just behind them, and they were fussing. Both of 'em acted like they were mad at each other, but Fairchild seemed to be the maddest.

"I did n't pay much attention to them because I just thought they were fighting about some little thing and that it wouldn't amount to much. I went on up the gulch--I was gathering flowers. After awhile, the earth shook and I heard a big explosion, from way down underneath me--like thunder when it's far away. Then, pretty soon, I saw Fairchild come rushing out of the mine, and his hands were all bloody. He ran to the creek and washed them, looking around to see if anybody was watching him--but he did n't notice me. Then when he 'd washed the blood from his hands, he got up on the road and went down into town. Later on, I thought I saw all three of 'em leave town, Fairchild, Sissie and a fellow named Harkins. So I never paid any more attention to it until to-day. That's all I know."

She stepped down then and went back to her seat with Squint Rodaine and the son, fidgeting there again, craning her neck as before, while Fairchild, son of a man just accused of murder, watched her with eyes fascinated from horror. The coroner looked at a slip of paper in his hand.

"William Barton," he called. A miner came forward, to go through the usual formalities, and then to be asked the question:

"Did you see Thornton Fairchild on the night he left Ohadi?"

"Yes, a lot of us saw him. He drove out of town with Harry Harkins, and a fellow who we all thought was Sissie Larsen. The person we believed to be Sissie was singing like the Swede did when he was drunk."

"That's all. Mr. Harkins, will you please take the stand again?"

"I object!" again it was Farrell. "In the first place, if this crazy woman's story is the result of a distorted imagination, then Mr. Harkins can add nothing to it. If it is not, Mr. Harkins is cloaked by the protection of the law which fully applies to such cases and which, Mr. Coroner, you cannot deny."

The coroner nodded.

"I agree with you this time, Mr. Farrell. I wish to work no hardship on any one. If Mrs. Rodaine's story is true, this is a matter for a special session of the grand jury. If it is not true--well, then there has been a miscarriage of justice and it is a matter to be rectified in the future. But at the present, there is no way of determining that matter. Gentlemen of the jury," he turned his back on the crowded room and faced the small, worried appearing group on the row of kitchen chairs, "you have heard the evidence. You will find a room at the right in which to conduct your deliberations. Your first official act will be to select a foreman and then to attempt to determine from the evidence as submitted the cause of death of the corpse over whom this inquest has been held. You will now retire."

Shuffling forms faded through the door at the right. Then followed long moments of waiting, in which Robert Fairchild's eyes went to the floor, in which he strove to avoid the gaze of every one in the crowded court room. He knew what they were thinking, that his father had been a murderer, and that he--well, that he was blood of his father's blood. He could hear the buzzing of tongues, the shifting of the court room on the unstable chairs, and he knew fingers were pointing at him. For once in his life he had not the strength to face his fellow men. A quarter of an hour--a knock on the door--then the six men clattered forth again, to hand a piece of paper to the coroner. And he, adjusting his glasses, turned to the court room and read:

"We, the jury, find that the deceased came to his death from injuries sustained at the hands of Thornton Fairchild, in or about the month of June, 1892."

That was all, but it was enough. The stain had been placed; the thing which the white-haired man who had sat by a window back in Indianapolis had feared all his life had come after death. And it was as though he were living again in the body of his son, his son who now stood beside the big form of Harry, striving to force his eyes upward and finally succeeding,--standing there facing the morbid, staring crowd as they turned and jostled that they might look at him, the son of a murderer!

How long it lasted he did not, could not know. The moments were dazed, bleared things which consisted to him only of a succession of eyes, of persons who pointed him out, who seemed to edge away from him as they passed him. It seemed hours before the court room cleared. Then, the attorney at one side, Harry at the other, he started out of the court room.

The crowd still was on the street, milling, circling, dividing into little groups to discuss the verdict. Through them shot scrambling forms of newsboys, seeking, in imitation of metropolitan methods, to enhance the circulation of the *Bugle* with an edition of a paper already hours old. Dazedly, simply for the sake of something to take his mind from the throngs and the gossip about him, Fairchild bought a paper and stepped to the light to glance over the first page. There, emblazoned under the "Extra" heading, was the story of the finding of the skeleton in the Blue Poppy mine, while beside it was something which caused Robert Fairchild to almost forget, for the moment, the horrors of the ordeal which he was undergoing. It was a paragraph leading the "personal" column of the small, amateurish sheet, announcing the engagement of Miss Anita Natalie Richmond to Mr. Maurice Rodaine, the wedding to come "probably in the late fall!"

CHAPTER XV

Fairchild did not show the item to Harry. There was little that it could accomplish, and besides, he felt that his comrade had enough to think about. The unexpected turn of the coroner's inquest had added to the heavy weight of Harry's troubles; it meant the probability in the future of a grand jury investigation and the possible indictment as accessory after the fact in the murder of "Sissie" Larsen. Not that Fairchild had been influenced in the slightest by the testimony of Crazy Laura; the presence of Squint Rodaine and his son had shown too plainly that they were connected in some way with it, that, in fact, they were responsible. An opportunity had arisen for them, and they had seized upon it. More, there came the shrewd opinion of old Mother Howard, once Fairchild and Harry had reached the boarding house and gathered in the parlor for their consultation:

"Ain't it what I said right in the beginning?" the gray-haired woman asked. "She 'll kill for that man, if necessary. It was n't as hard as you think--all Squint Rodaine had to do was to act nice to her and promise her a few things that he 'll squirm out of later on, and she went on the stand and lied her head off."

"But for a crazy woman--"

"Laura's crazy--and she ain't crazy. I 've seen that woman as sensible and as shrewd as any sane woman who ever drew breath. Then again, I 've seen her when I would n't get within fifty miles of her. Sometimes she 's pitiful to me; and then again I 've got to remember the fact that she 's a dangerous woman. Goodness only knows what would happen to a person who fell into her clutches when she 's got one of those immortality streaks on."

"One of those what?" Harry looked up in surprise.

"Immortality. That's why you 'll find her sneaking around graveyards at night, gathering herbs and taking them to that old house on the Georgeville Road, where she lives, and brewing them into some sort of concoction that she sprinkles on the graves. She believes that it's a sure system of bringing immortality to a person. Poison--that's about what it is."

Harry shrugged his shoulders.

"Poison 's what she is!" he exclaimed. "Ain't it enough that I 'm accused of every crime in the calendar without 'er getting me mixed up in a murder? And--" this time he looked at Fairchild with dolorous eyes--"'ow 're we going to furnish bond this time, if the grand jury indicts me?"

"I 'm afraid there won't be any."

Mother Howard set her lips for a minute, then straightened proudly.

"Well, I guess there will! They can't charge you a million dollars on a thing like that. It's bondable--and I guess I 've got a few things that are worth something--and a few friends that I can go to. I don't see why I should be left out of everything, just because I 'm a woman!"

"Lor' love you!" Harry grinned, his eyes showing plainly that the world was again good for him and that his troubles, as far as a few slight charges of penitentiary offenses were concerned, amounted to very little in his estimation. Harry had a habit of living just for the day. And the support of Mother Howard had wiped out all future difficulties for him. The fact that convictions might await him and that the heavy doors at Canon City might yawn for him made little difference right now. Behind the great bulwark of his mustache, his big lips spread in a happy announcement of joy, and the world was good.

Silently, Robert Fairchild rose and left the parlor for his own room. Some way he could not force himself to shed his difficulties in the same light, airy way as Harry. He wanted to be alone, alone where he could take stock of the obstacles which had arisen in his path, of the unexplainable difficulties and tribulations which had come upon him, one trailing the other, ever since he had read the letter left for him by his father. And it was a stock-taking of disappointing proportions.

Looking back, Fairchild could see now that his dreams had led only to catastrophes. The bright vista which had been his that day he sat swinging his legs over the tailboard of the truck as it ground up Mount Lookout had changed to a thing of gloomy clouds and of ominous futures. Nothing had gone right. From the very beginning, there had been only trouble, only fighting, fighting, fighting against insurmountable odds, which seemed to throw him ever deeper into the mire of defeat, with every onslaught. He had met a girl whom he had instinctively liked, only to find a mystery about her which could not be fathomed. He had furthered his acquaintance with her, only to bring about a condition where now she passed him on the street without speaking and which, he felt, had instigated that tiny notice in the *Bugle*, telling of her probable marriage in the late autumn to a man he detested as a cad and as an enemy. He had tried his best to follow the lure of silver; if silver existed in the Blue Poppy mine, he had labored against the powers of Nature, only to be the unwilling cause of a charge of murder against his father. And more, it was clear, cruelly clear, that if it had not been for his own efforts and those of a man who had come to help him, the skeleton of Sissie Larsen never would have been discovered, and the name of Thornton Fairchild might have gone on in the peace which the white-haired, frightened man had sought.

But now there was no choosing. Robert was the son of a murderer. Six men had stamped that upon him in the basement of the courthouse that night. His funds were low, growing lower every day, and there was little possibility of rehabilitating them until the trial of Harry should come, and Fate should be kind enough to order an acquittal, releasing the products from escrow. In case of a conviction, Fairchild could see only disaster. True, the optimistic Farrell had spoken of a Supreme Court reversal of any verdict against his partner, but that would avail little as far as the mine was concerned. It must still remain in escrow as the bond of Harry until the case was decided, and that might mean years. And one cannot borrow money upon a thing that is mortgaged in its entirety to a commonwealth. In the aggregate, the outlook was far from pleasant. The Rodaines had played with stacked cards, and so far every hand had been theirs. Fairchild's credit, and his standing, was ruined. He had been stamped by the coroner's jury as the son of a murderer, and that mark must remain upon him until it could be cleared by forces now imperceptible to Fairchild. His partner was under bond, accused of four crimes. The Rodaines had won a victory, perhaps greater than they knew. They had succeeded in soiling the reputations of the two men they called enemies, damaging them to such an extent that they must henceforth fight at a disadvantage, without the benefit of a solid ground of character upon which to stand. Fairchild suddenly realized that he was all but whipped, that the psychological advantage was all on the side of Squint Rodaine, his son, and the crazy woman who did their bidding. More, another hope had gone glimmering; even had the announcement not come forth that Anita Richmond had given her promise to marry Maurice Rodaine, the action of a coroner's jury that night had removed her from hope forever. A son of a man who has been called a slayer has little right to love a woman, even if that woman has a bit of mystery about her. All things can be explained--but murder!

It was growing late, but Fairchild did not seek bed. Instead he sat by the window, staring out at the shadows of the mountains, out at the free, pure night, and yet at nothing. After a long time, the door opened, and a big form entered--Harry--to stand silent a moment, then to come forward and lay a hand on the other man's shoulder.

"Don't let it get you, Boy," he said softly--for him. "It's going to come out all right. Everything comes out all right--if you ain't wrong yourself."

"I know, Harry. But it's an awful tangle right now."

"Sure it is. But it ain't as if a sane person 'ad said it against you. There 'll never be anything more to that; Farrell 'll 'ave 'er adjudged insane if it ever comes to anything like that. She 'll never give no more testimony. I 've been talking with 'im--'e stopped in just after you came upstairs. It's only a crazy woman."

"But they took her word for it, Harry. They believed her. And they gave the verdict--against my father!"

"I know. I was there, right beside you. I 'eard it. But it 'll come out right, some way."

There was a moment of silence, then a gripping fear at the heart of Fairchild.

"Just how crazy is she, Harry?"

"'Er? Plumb daft! Of course, as Mother 'Oward says, there 's times when she 's straight--but they don't last long. And, if she 'd given 'er testimony in writing, Mother 'Oward says it all might 'ave been different, and we 'd not 'ave 'ad anything to worry about."

"In writing?"

"Yes, she 's 'arfway sane then. It seems 'er mind 's disconnected, some wye. I don't know 'ow--Mother 'Oward 's got the 'ole lingo, and everybody in town knows about it. Whenever anybody wants to get anything real straight from Crazy Laura, they make 'er write it. That part of 'er brain seems all right. She remembers everything she does then and 'ow crazy it is, and tells you all about it."

"But why did n't Farrell insist upon that tonight?"

"'E could n't have gotten 'er to do it. And nobody can get 'er to do it as long has Squint's around--so Mother 'Oward says. 'E 's got a influence about 'im. And she does exactly what 'e 'll sye--all 'e 's got to do is to look at 'er. Notice 'ow flustered up she got when the coroner asked 'er about that book?"

"I wonder what it would really tell?"

Harry chuckled.

"Nobody knows. Nobody 's ever seen it. Not even Squint Rodaine. That's the one thing she 's got the strength to keep from 'im--I guess it's a part of 'er right brain that tells 'er to keep it a secret! I 'm going to bed now. So 're you. And you 're going to sleep. Good night."

He went out of the room then, and Fairchild, obedient to the big Cornishman's command, sought rest. But it was a hard struggle. Morning came, and he joined Harry at breakfast, facing the curious glances of the other boarders, staving off their inquiries and their illy couched consolations. For, in spite of the fact that it was not voiced in so many words, the conviction was present that Crazy Laura had told at least a semblance of the truth, and that the dovetailing incidents of the past fitted into a well-connected story for which there must be some foundation. Moreover, in the corner were Blindeye Bozeman and Taylor Bill, hurrying through their breakfast that they might go to their work in the Silver Queen, Squint Rodaine's mine, less than a furlong from the ill-boding Blue Poppy. Fairchild could see that they were talking about him, their eyes turned often in his direction; once Taylor Bill nodded and sneered as he answered some remark of his companion. The blood went hot in Fairchild's brain. He rose from the table, hands clenched, muscles tensed, only to find himself drawn back by the strong grasp of Harry. The big Cornishman whispered to him as he took his seat again:

"It 'll only make more trouble. I know 'ow you feel--but 'old in. 'Old in!"

It was an admonition which Fairchild was forced to repeat to himself more than once that morning as he walked uptown with Harry, to face the gaze of the street loafers, to be plied with questions, and to strive his best to fence away from them. There were those who were plainly curious; there were others who professed not to believe the testimony and who talked loudly of action against the coroner for having introduced the evidence of a woman known by every one to be lacking in balanced mentality. There were others who, by their remarks, showed that they were concealing the real truth of their thoughts and only using a cloak of interest to guide them to other food for the carrion proclivities of their minds. To all of them Fairchild and Harry made the same reply: that they had nothing to say, that they had given all the information possible on the witness stand during the inquest, and that there was nothing further forthcoming.

And it was while he made this statement for the hundredth time that Fairchild saw Anita Richmond going to the post-office with the rest of the usual crowd, following the arrival of the morning train. Again she passed him without speaking, but her glance did not seem so cold as it had been on the morning that he had seen her with Rodaine, nor did the lack of recognition appear as easily simulated. That she knew what had happened and the charge that had been made against his father, Fairchild did not doubt. That she knew he had read the "personal" in the *Bugle* was as easily determined. Between them was a gulf--caused by what Fairchild could only guess--a gulf which he could not essay to cross, and which she, for some reason, would not. But there was nothing that could stop him from watching her, with hungry eyes which followed her until she had disappeared in the doorway of the post-office, eyes which believed they detected a listlessness in her walk and a slight droop to the usually erect little shoulders, eyes which were sure of one thing: that the smile was gone from the lips, that upon her features were the lines and hollows of sleeplessness, and the unmistakable lack of luster and color which told him that she was not happy. Even the masculine mentality of Fairchild could discern that. But it could not answer the question which the decision brought. She had become engaged to a man whom she had given evidence of hating. She had refused to recognize Fairchild, whom she had appeared to like. She had cast her lot with the Rodaines--and she was unhappy. Beyond that, everything was blank to Fairchild.

An hour later Harry, wandering by the younger man's side, strove for words and at last uttered them.

"I know it's disagreeable," came finally. "But it's necessary. You 'ave n't quit?"

"Quit what?"

"The mine. You 're going to keep on, ain't you?"

Fairchild gritted his teeth and was silent. The answer needed strength. Finally it came.

"Harry, are you with me?"

"I ain't stopped yet!"

"Then that's the answer. As long as there 's a bit of fight left in us, we 'll keep at that mine. I don't know where it's going to lead us--but from appearances as they stand now, the only outlook seems to be ruin. But if you 're willing, I 'm willing, and we 'll make the scrap together."

Harry hitched at his trousers.

"They 've got that blooming skeleton out by this time. I 'm willing to start--any time you say."

The breath went over Fairchild's teeth in a long, slow intake. He clenched his hands and held them trembling before him for a lengthy moment. Then he turned to his partner.

"Give me an hour," he begged. "I 'll go then--but it takes a little grit to--"

"Who's Fairchild here?" A messenger boy was making his way along the curb with a telegram. Robert stretched forth a hand in surprise.

"I am. Why?"

The answer came as the boy shoved forth the yellow envelope and the delivery sheet. Fairchild signed, then somewhat dazedly ran a finger under the slit of the envelope. Then, wondering, he read:

Please come to Denver at once. Have most important information for you.

R. V. Barnham,   H & R Building.

A moment of staring, then Fairchild passed the telegram over to Harry for his opinion. There was none. Together they went across the street and to the office of Farrell, their attorney. He studied the telegram long. Then:

"I can't see what on earth it means, unless there is some information about this skeleton or the inquest. If I were you, I 'd go."

"But supposing it's some sort of a trap?"

"No matter what it is, go and let the other fellow do all the talking. Listen to what he has to say and tell him nothing. That's the only safe system. I 'd go down on the noon train--that 'll get you there about two. You can be back by 10:30 to-morrow."

"No 'e can't," it was Harry's interruption as he grasped a pencil and paper. "I 've got a list of things a mile long for 'im to get. We're going after this mine 'ammer and tongs now!"

When noon came, Robert Fairchild, with his mysterious telegram, boarded the train for Denver, while in his pocket was a list demanding the outlay of nearly a thousand dollars: supplies of fuses, of dynamite, of drills, of a forge, of single and double jack sledges, of fulminate caps,--a little of everything that would be needed in the months to come, if he and 'Arry were to work the mine. It was only a beginning, a small quantity of each article needed, part of which could be picked up in the junk yards at a reasonable figure, other things that would eat quickly into the estimate placed upon the total. And with a capital already dwindling, it meant an expenditure which hurt, but which was necessary, nevertheless.

Slow, puffing and wheezing, the train made its way along Clear Creek canon, crawled across the newly built trestle which had been erected to take the place of that which had gone out with the spring flood of the milky creek, then jangled into Denver. Fairchild hurried uptown, found the old building to which he had been directed by the telegram, and made the upward trip in the ancient elevator, at last to knock upon a door. A half-whining voice answered him, and he went within.

A greasy man was there, greasy in his fat, uninviting features, in his seemingly well-oiled hands as they circled in constant kneading, in his long, straggling hair, in his old, spotted Prince Albert--and in his manners. Fairchild turned to peer at the glass panel of the door. It bore the name he sought. Then he looked again at the oily being who awaited him.

"Mr. Barnham?"

"That's what I 'm called." He wheezed with the self-implied humor of his remark and motioned toward a chair. "May I ask what you 've come to see me about?"

"I have n't the slightest idea. You sent for me." Fairchild produced the telegram, and the greasy person who had taken a position on the other side of a worn, walnut table became immediately obsequious.

"Of course! Of course! Mr. Fairchild! Why did n't you say so when you came in? Of course--I 've been looking for you all day. May I offer you a cigar?"

He dragged a box of domestic perfectos from a drawer of the table and struck a match to light one for Fairchild. He hastily summoned an ash tray from the little room which adjoined the main, more barren office. Then with a bustling air of urgent business he hurried to both doors and locked them.

"So that we may not be disturbed," he confided in that high, whining voice. "I am hoping that this is very important."

"I also." Fairchild puffed dubiously upon the more dubious cigar. The greasy individual returned to his table, dragged the chair nearer it, then, seating himself, leaned toward Fairchild.

"If I 'm not mistaken, you 're the owner of the Blue Poppy mine."

"I 'm supposed to be."

"Of course--of course. One never knows in these days what he owns or when he owns it. Very good, I 'd say, Mr. Fairchild, very good. Could you possibly do me the favor of telling me how you 're getting along?"

Fairchild's eyes narrowed.

"I thought you had information--for me!"

"Very good again." Mr. Barnham raised a fat hand and wheezed in an effort at intense enjoyment of the reply. "So I have--so I have. I merely asked that to be asking. Now, to be serious, have n't you some enemies, Mr. Fairchild?"

"Have I?"

"I was merely asking."

"And I judged from your question that you seemed to know."

"So I do. And one friend." Barnham pursed his heavy lips and nodded in an authoritative manner. "One, very, very good friend."

"I was hoping that I had more than that."

"Ah, perhaps so. But I speak only from what I know. There is one person who is very anxious about your welfare."

"So?"

Mr. Barnham leaned forward in an exceedingly friendly manner.

"Well, is n't there?"

Fairchild squared away from the table.

"Mr. Barnham," came coldly; the inherent distrust for the greasy, uninviting individual having swerved to the surface. "You wired me that you had some very important news for me. I came down here expressly because of that wire. Now that I 'm here, your mission seems to be wholly taken up in drawing from me any information that I happen to possess about myself. Plainly and frankly, I don't like it, and I don't like you--and unless you can produce a great deal more than you have already, I 'll have to chalk up the expense to a piece of bad judgment and go on about my business."

He started to rise, and Barnham scrambled to his feet.

"Please don't," he begged, thrusting forth a fat hand, "please, please don't. This is a very important matter. One--one has to be careful in going about a thing as important as this is. The person is in a very peculiar position."

"But I 'm tired of the way you beat around the bush. You tell me some meager scrap of filmy news and then ask me a dozen questions. As I told you before, I don't like it--and I 'm just about at the point where I don't care what information you have!"

"But just be patient a moment--I 'm coming to it. Suppose--" then he cupped his hands and stared hard at the ceiling, "Suppose that I told you that there was some one who was willing to see you through all your troubles, who had arranged everything for you, and all you had to do would be to say the word to find yourself in the midst of comfort and riches?"

CHAPTER XVI

Fairchild blinked in surprise at this and sank back into his chair. Finally he laughed uneasily and puffed again on the dubious cigar.

"I 'd say," came finally, "that there is n't any such animal."

"But there is. She has--" Then he stopped, as though to cover the slip. Fairchild leaned forward.

"She?"

Mr. Barnham gave the appearance of a very flustered man.

"My tongue got away from me; I should n't have said it. I really should n't have said it. If she ever finds it out, it will mean trouble for me. But truly," and he beamed, "you are such a tough customer to deal with and so suspicious--no offense meant, of course--that I really was forced to it. I--feel sure she will forgive me."

"Whom do you mean by 'she'?"

Mr. Barnham smiled in a knowing manner.

"You and I both know," came his cryptic answer. "She is your one great, good friend. She thinks a great deal of you, and you have done several things to cause that admiration. Now, Mr. Fairchild, coming to the point, suppose she should point a way out of your troubles?"

"How?"

"In the first place, you and your partner are in very great difficulties."

"Are we?" Fairchild said it sarcastically.

"Indeed you are, and there is no need of attempting to conceal the fact. Your friend, whose name must remain a secret, does not love you--don't ever think that--but--"

Then he hesitated as though to watch the effect on Fairchild's face. There was none; Robert had masked it. In time the words went on: "But she does think enough of you to want to make you happy. She has recently done a thing which gives her a great deal of power in one direction. In another, she has connections who possess vast money powers and who are looking for an opening here in the west. Now,--" he made a church steeple out of his fingers and leaned back in his chair, staring vacuously at the ceiling, "if you will say the word and do a thing which will relieve her of a great deal of embarrassment, I am sure that she can so arrange things that life will be very easy for you henceforth."

"I 'm becoming interested."

"In the first place, she is engaged to be married to a very fine young man. You, of course, may say differently, and I do not know--I am only taking her word for it. But--if I understand it, your presence in Ohadi has caused a few disagreements between them and--well, you know how willful and headstrong girls will be. I believe she has committed a few--er--indiscretions with you."

"That's a lie!" Fairchild's temper got away from him and his fist banged on the table. "That's a lie and you know it!"

"Pardon me--er--pardon me! I made use of a word that can have many meanings, and I am sure that in using it, I did n't place the same construction that you did in hearing it. But let that pass. I apologize. What I should have said was that, if you will pardon me, she used you, as young women will do, as a foil against her fiance in a time of petty quarreling between them. Is that plainer?"

It was too plain to Fairchild. It hurt. But he nodded his head and the other man went on.

"Now the thing has progressed to a place where you may be--well--what one might call the thorn in the side of their happiness. You are the 'other man', as it were, to cause quarrels and that sort of thing. And she feels that she has not done rightly by you, and, through her friendship and a desire to see peace all around, believes she can arrange matters to suit all concerned. To be plain and blunt, Mr. Fairchild, you are not in an enviable position. I said that I had information for you, and I 'm going to give it. You are trying to work a mine. That demands capital. You have n't got it and there is no way for you to procure it. To get capital, one must have standing--and you must admit that you are lacking to a great extent in that very necessary ingredient. In the first place, your mine is in escrow, being held in court in lieu of five thousand dollars bond on--"

"You seem to have been making a few inquiries?"

"Not at all. I never heard of the proposition before she brought it to me. As I say, the deeds to your mine are held in escrow. Your partner now is accused of four crimes and will go to trial on them in the fall. It is almost certain that he will be convicted on at least one of the charges. That would mean that the deeds to the mine must remain in jurisdiction of the court in lieu of a cash bond while the case goes to the Supreme Court. Otherwise, you must yield over your partner to go to jail. In either event, the result would not be satisfactory. For yourself, I dare say that a person whose father is supposed to have committed a murder--not that I say he did it, understand--hardly could establish sufficient standing to borrow the money to proceed on an undertaking which requires capital. Therefore, I should say that you were in somewhat of a predicament. Now--" a long wait and then, "please take this as only coming from a spokesman: My client is in a position to use her good offices to change the viewpoint of the man who is the chief witness against your partner. She also is in a position to use those same good offices in another direction, so that there might never be a grand jury investigation of the finding of a certain body or skeleton, or something of the kind, in your mine--which, if you will remember, brought about a very disagreeable situation. And through her very good connections in another way, she is able to relieve you of all your financial embarrassment and procure for you from a certain eastern syndicate, the members of which I am not at liberty to name, an offer of $200,000 for your mine. All that is necessary for you to do is to say the word."

Fairchild leaned forward.

"And of course," he said caustically, "the name of this mysterious feminine friend must be a secret?"

"Certainly. No mention of this transaction must be made to her directly, or indirectly. Those are my specific instructions. Now, Mr. Fairchild, that seems to me to be a wonderful offer. And it--"

"Do you want my answer now?"

"At any time when you have given the matter sufficient thought."

"That's been accomplished already. And there 's no need of waiting. I want to thank you exceedingly for your offer, and to tell you--that you can go straight to hell!"

And without looking back to see the result of his ultimatum, Fairchild rose, strode to the door, unlocked it, and stamped down the hall. He had taken snap judgment, but in his heart, he felt that he was right. What was more, he was as sure as he was sure of life itself that Anita Richmond had not arranged the interview and did not even know of it. One streaking name was flitting through Fairchild's brain and causing it to seethe with anger. Cleverly concealed though the plan might have been, nicely arranged and carefully planted, to Robert Fairchild it all stood out plainly and clearly--the Rodaines!

And yet why? That one little word halted Fairchild as he left the elevator. Why should the Rodaines be willing to free him from all the troubles into which his mining ventures had taken him, start him out into the world and give him a fortune with which to make his way forward? Why? What did they know about the Blue Poppy mine, when neither he nor Harry had any idea of what the future might hold for them there? Certainly they could not have investigated in the years that were gone; the cave-in precluded that. There was no other tunnel, no other means of determining the riches which might be hidden within the confines of the Blue Poppy claims, yet it was evident. That day in court Rodaine had said that the Blue Poppy was a good property and that it was worth every cent of the value which had been placed on it. How did he know? And why--?

At least one answer to Rodaine's action came to him. It was simple now to see why the scar-faced man had put a good valuation on the mine during the court procedure and apparently helped Fairchild out in a difficulty. In fact, there were several reasons for it. In the first place, the tying up of the mine by placing it in the care of a court would mean just that many more difficulties for Fairchild, and it would mean that the mine would be placed in a position where work could be hampered for years if a first conviction could be obtained. Further, Rodaine could see that if by any chance the bond should be forfeited, it would be an easy matter for the claims to be purchased cheap at a public sale by any one who desired them and who had the inside information of what they were worth. And evidently Rodaine and Rodaine alone possessed that knowledge.

It was late now. Fairchild went to a junk yard or two, searching for the materials which Harry had ordered, and failed to find them. Then he sought a hotel, once more to struggle with the problems which the interview with Barnham had created and to cringe at a thought which arose like a ghost before him:

Suppose that it had been Anita Richmond after all who had arranged this? It was logical in a way. Maurice Rodaine was the one man who could give direct evidence against Harry as the man who had held up the Old Times Dance, and Anita now was engaged to marry him. Judge Richmond had been a friend of Thornton Fairchild; could it have been possible that this friendship might have entailed the telling of secrets which had not been related to any one else? The matter of the finding of the skeleton could be handled easily, Fairchild saw, through Maurice Rodaine. One word from him to his father could change the story of Crazy Laura and make it, on the second telling, only the maundering tale of an insane, herb-gathering woman. Anita could have arranged it, and Anita might have arranged it. Fairchild wished now that he could recall his words, that he could have held his temper and by some sort of strategy arranged matters so that the offer might have come more directly--from Anita herself.

Yet, why should she have gone through this procedure to reach him? Why had she not gone to Farrell with the proposition--to a man whom she knew Fairchild trusted, instead of to a greasy, hand rubbing shyster? And besides--

But the question was past answering now. Fairchild had made his decision, and he had told the lawyer where to go. If, at the same time, he had relegated the woman who had awakened affection in his heart, only to have circumstances do their best to stamp it out again, to the same place,--well, that had been done, too, and there was no recalling of it now. But one thing was certain: the Blue Poppy mine was worth money. Somewhere in that beetling hill awaited wealth, and if determination counted for anything, if force of will and force of muscle were worth only a part of their accepted value, Fairchild meant to find it. Once before an offer had come, and now that he thought of it, Fairchild felt almost certain that it had been from the same source. That was for fifty thousand dollars. Why should the value have now jumped to four times its original figures? It was more than the adventurer could encompass; he sought to dismiss it all, went to a picture show, then trudged back to his hotel and to sleep.

The next day found him still striving to put the problem away from him as he went about the various errands outlined by Harry. A day after that, then the puffing, snorting, narrow-gauged train took him again through Clear Creek canon and back to Ohadi. The station was strangely deserted.

None of the usual loungers were there. None of the loiterers who, watch in hand, awaited the arrival and departure of the puffing train as though it were a matter of personal concern. Only the bawling 'bus man for the hotel, the station agent wrestling with a trunk or two,--that was all. Fairchild looked about him in surprise, then approached the agent.

"What's happened? Where 's everybody?"

"Up on the hill."

"Something happened?"

"A lot. From what I hear it's a strike that's going to put Ohadi on the map again."

"Who made it?"

"Don't know. Some fellow came running down here an hour or so ago and said there 'd been a tremendous strike made on the hill, and everybody beat it up there."

Fairchild went on, to turn into a deserted street,--a street where the doors of the stores had been left open and the owners gone. Everywhere it was the same; it was as if Ohadi suddenly had been struck by some catastrophe which had wiped out the whole population. Only now and then a human being appeared, a few persons left behind at the banks, but that was about all. Then from far away, up the street leading from Kentucky Gulch, came the sound of cheering and shouting. Soon a crowd appeared, led by gesticulating, vociferous men, who veered suddenly into the Ohadi Bank at the corner, leaving the multitude without for a moment, only to return, their hands full of gold certificates, which they stuck into their hats, punched through their buttonholes, stuffed into their pockets, allowing them to hang half out, and even jammed down the collars of their rough shirts, making outstanding decorations of currency about their necks. On they came, closer--closer, and then Fairchild gritted his teeth. There were four of them leading the parade, displaying the wealth that stood for the bonanza of the silver strike they had just made, four men whose names were gall and wormwood to Robert Fairchild.

Blindeye Bozeman and Taylor Bill were two of them. The others were Squint and Maurice Rodaine!

CHAPTER XVII

Had it been any one else, Fairchild would have shouted for happiness and joined the parade. As it was, he stood far at one side, a silent, grim figure, watching the miners and townspeople passing before him, leaping about in their happiness, calling to him the news that he did not want to hear:

The Silver Queen had "hit." The faith of Squint Rodaine, maintained through the years, had shown his perspicacity. It was there; he always had said it was there, and now the strike had been made at last, lead-silver ore, running as high as two hundred dollars a ton. And just like Squint--so some one informed Fairchild--he had kept it a secret until the assays all had been made and the first shipments started to Denver. It meant everything for Ohadi; it meant that mining would boom now, that soon the hills would be clustered with prospectors, and that the little town would blossom as a result of possessing one of the rich silver mines of the State. Some one tossed to Fairchild a small piece of ore which had been taken from a car at the mouth of the mine; and even to his uninitiated eyes it was apparent,--the heavy lead, bearing in spots the thin filagree of white metal--and silver ore must be more than rich to make a showing in any kind of sample.

He felt cheap. He felt defeated. He felt small and mean not to be able to join the celebration. Squint and Maurice Rodaine possessed the Silver Queen; that they, of all persons, should be the fortunate ones was bitter and hard to accept. Why should they, of every one in Ohadi, be the lucky men to find a silver bonanza, that they might flaunt it before him, that they might increase their standing in the community, that they might raise themselves to a pedestal in the eyes of every one and thereby rally about them the whole town in any difficulty which might arise in the future? It hurt Fairchild, it sickened him. He saw now that his enemies were more powerful than ever. And for a moment he almost wished that he had yielded down there in Denver, that he had not given the ultimatum to the greasy Barnham, that he had accepted the offer made him,--and gone on, out of the fight forever.

Anita! What would it mean to her? Already engaged, already having given her answer to Maurice Rodaine, this now would be an added incentive for her to follow her promise. It would mean a possibility of further argument with her father, already too weak from illness to find the means of evading the insidious pleas of the two men who had taken his money and made him virtually their slave. Could they not demonstrate to him now that they always had worked for his best interests? And could not that plea go even farther--to Anita herself--to persuade her that they were always laboring for her, that they had striven for this thing that it might mean happiness for her and for her father? And then, could they not content themselves with promises, holding before her a rainbow of the far-away, to lead her into their power, just as they had led the stricken, bedridden man she called "father"? The future looked black for Robert Fairchild. Slowly he walked past the happy, shouting crowd and turned up Kentucky Gulch toward the ill-fated Blue Poppy.

The tunnel opening looked more forlorn than ever when he sighted it, a bleak, staring, single eye which seemed to brood over its own misfortunes, a dead, hopeless thing which never had brought anything but disappointment. A choking came into Fairchild's throat. He entered the tunnel slowly, ploddingly; with lagging muscles he hauled up the bucket which told of Harry's presence below, then slowly lowered himself into the recesses of the shaft and to the drift leading to the stope, where only a few days before they had found that gaunt, whitened, haunting thing which had brought with it a new misfortune.

A light gleamed ahead, and the sound of a single jack hammering on the end of a drill could be heard. Fairchild called and went forward, to find Harry, grimy and sweating, pounding away at a narrow streak of black formation which centered in the top of the stope.

"It's the vein," he announced, after he had greeted Fairchild, "and it don't look like it's going to amount to much!"

"No?"

Harry withdrew the drill from the hole he was making and mopped his forehead.

"It ain't a world-beater," came disconsolately. "I doubt whether it 'll run more 'n twenty dollars to the ton, the wye smelting prices 'ave gone up! And there ain't much money in that. What 'appened in Denver?"

"Another frame-up by the Rodaines to get the mine away from us. It was a lawyer. He stalled that the offer had been made to us by Miss Richmond."

"How much?"

"Two hundred thousand dollars and us to get out of all the troubles we are in."

"And you took it, of course?"

"I did not!"

"No?" Harry mopped his forehead again. "Well, maybe you 're right. Maybe you 're wrong. But whatever you did--well, that's just the thing I would 'ave done."

"Thanks, Harry."

"Only--" and Harry was staring lugubriously at the vein above him, "it's going to take us a long time to get two hundred thousand dollars out of things the wye they stand now."

"But--"

"I know what you're thinking--that there's silver 'ere and that we 're going to find it. Maybe so. I know your father wrote some pretty glowing accounts back to Beamish in St. Louis. It looked awful good then. Then it started to pinch out, and now--well, it don't look so good."

"But this is the same vein, is n't it?"

"I don't know. I guess it is. But it's pinching fast. It was about this wye when we first started on it. It was n't worth much and it was n't very wide. Then, all of a sudden, it broadened out, and there was a lot more silver in it. We thought we 'd found a bonanza. But it narrowed down again, and the old standard came back. I don't know what it's going to do now--it may quit altogether."

"But we 're going to keep at it, Harry, sink or swim."

"You know it!"

"The Rodaines have hit--maybe we can have some good luck too."

"The Rodaines?" Harry stared. "'It what?"

"Two hundred dollar a ton ore!"

A long whistle. Then Harry, who had been balancing a single jack, preparatory to going back to his work, threw it aside and began to roll down his sleeves.

"We 're going to 'ave a look at it."

"A look? What good would it--?"

"A cat can look at a king," said Harry. "They can't arrest us for going up there like everybody else."

"But to go there and ask them to look at their riches--"

"There ain't no law against it!"

He reached for his carbide lamp, hooked to a small chink of the hanging wall, and then pulled his hat over his bulging forehead. Carefully he attempted to smooth his straying mustache, and failing, as always, gave up the job.

"I 'd be 'appy, just to look at it," he announced. "Come on. Let's forget 'oo they are and just be lookers-on."

Fairchild agreed against his will. Out of the shaft they went and on up the hill to where the townspeople again were gathering about the opening of the Silver Queen. A few were going in. Fairchild and 'Arry joined them.

A long walk, stooping most of the way, as the progress was made through the narrow, low-roofed tunnel; then a slight raise which traveled for a fair distance at an easy grade--at last to stop; and there before them, jammed between the rock, was the strike, a great, heavy streaking vein, nearly six feet wide, in which the ore stuck forth in tremendous chunks, embedded in a black background. Harry eyed it studiously.

"You can see the silver sticking out!" he announced at last. "It's wonderful-- even if the Rodaines did do it."

A form brushed past them, Blindeye Bozeman, returning from the celebration. Picking up a drill, he studied it with care, finally to lay it aside and reach for a gad, a sort of sharp, pointed prod, with which to tear away the loose matter that he might prepare the way for the biting drive of the drill beneath the five-pound hammer, or single jack. His weak, watery eyes centered on Harry, and he grinned.

"Didn't believe it, huh?" came his query.

Harry pawed his mustache.

"I believed it, all right, but anybody likes to look at the United States Mint!"

"You 've said it. She 's going to be more than that when we get a few portable air compressors in here and start at this thing in earnest with pneumatic drills. What's more, the old man has declared Taylor Bill and me in on it--for a ten per cent. bonus. How's that sound to you?"

"Like 'eaven," answered Harry truthfully. "Come on, Boy, let's us get out of 'ere. I 'll be getting the blind staggers if I stay much longer."

Fairchild accompanied him wordlessly. It was as though Fate had played a deliberate trick, that it might laugh at him. And as he walked along, he wondered more than ever about the mysterious telegram and the mysterious conversation of the greasy Barnham in Denver. That--as he saw it now--had been only an attempt at another trick. Suppose that he had accepted; suppose that he had signified his willingness to sell his mine and accept the good offices of the "secret friend" to end his difficulties. What would have been the result?

For once a ray of cheer came to him. The Rodaines had known of this strike long before he ever went to that office in Denver. They had waited long enough to have their assays made and had completed their first shipment to the smelter. There was no necessity that they buy the Blue Poppy mine. Therefore, was it simply another trick to break him, to lead him up to a point of high expectations, then, with a laugh at his disappointment, throw him down again? His shoulders straightened as they reached the outside air, and he moved close to Harry as he told him his conjectures. The Cornishman bobbed his head.

"I never thought of it that way!" he agreed. "But it could explain a lot of things. They 're working on our--what-you-call-it?"

"Psychological resistance."

"That's it. Psych--that's it. They want to beat us and they don't care 'ow. It 'urts a person to be disappointed. That's it. I alwyes said you 'ad a good 'ead on you! That's it. Let's go back to the Blue Poppy."

Back they went, once more to descend the shaft, once more to follow the trail along the drift toward the opening of the stope. And there, where loose earth covered the place where a skeleton once had rested, Fairchild took off his coat and rolled up his sleeves.

"Harry," he said, with a new determination, "this vein does n't look like much, and the mine looks worse. From the viewpoint we 've got now of the Rodaine plans, there may not be a cent in it. But if you're game, I'm game, and we'll work the thing until it breaks us."

"You 've said it. If we 'it anything, fine and well--if we can turn out five thousand dollars' worth of stuff before the trial comes up, then we can sell hit under the direction of the court, turn over that money for a cash bond, and get the deeds back. If we can't, and if the mine peters out, then we ain't lost anything but a lot of 'opes and time. But 'ere goes. We 'll double-jack. I 've got a big 'ammer 'ere. You 'old the drill for awhile and turn it, while I sling th' sledge. Then you take th' 'ammer and Lor' 'ave mercy on my 'ands if you miss."

Fairchild obeyed. They began the drilling of the first indentation into the six-inch vein which lay before them. Hour after hour they worked, changing positions, sending hole after hole into the narrow discoloration which showed their only prospect of returns for the investments which they had put into the mine. Then, as the afternoon grew late, Harry disappeared far down the drift to return with a handful of greasy, candle-like things, wrapped in waxed paper.

"I knew that dynamite of yours could n't be shipped in time, so I bought a little up 'ere," he explained, as he cut one of the sticks in two with a pocketknife and laid the pieces to one side. Then out came a coil of fuse, to be cut to its regular lengths and inserted in the copper-covered caps of fulminate of mercury, Harry showing his contempt for the dangerous things by crimping them about the fuse with his teeth, while Fairchild, sitting on a small pile of muck near by, begged for caution. But Harry only grinned behind his big mustache and went on.

Out came his pocketknife again as he slit the waxed paper of the gelatinous sticks, then inserted the cap in the dynamite. One after another the charges were shoved into the holes, Harry tamping them into place with a steel rod, instead of with the usual wooden affair, his mustache brushing his shoulder as he turned to explain the virtues of dynamite when handled by an expert.

"It's all in the wye you do it," he announced. "If you don't strike fire with a steel rod, it's fine."

"But if you do?"

"Oh, then!" Harry laughed. "Then it's flowers and a funeral--after they 've finished picking you up." One after another he pressed the dynamite charges tight into the drill holes and tamped them with muck wrapped in a newspaper that he dragged from his hip pocket. Then he lit the fuses from his lamp and stood a second in assurance that they all were spluttering.

"Now we run!" he announced, and they hurried, side by side, down the drift tunnel until they reached the shaft. "Far enough," said Harry.

A long moment of waiting. Then the earth quivered and a muffled, booming roar came from the distance. Harry stared at his carbide lamp.

"One," he announced. Then, "Two."

Three, four and five followed, all counted seriously, carefully by Harry. Finally they turned back along the drift toward the stope, the acrid odor of dynamite smoke-cutting at their nostrils as they approached the spot where the explosions had occurred. There Harry stood in silent contemplation for a long time, holding his carbide over the pile of ore that had been torn from the vein above.

"It ain't much," came at last. "Not more 'n 'arf a ton. We won't get rich at that rate. And besides--" he looked upward--"we ain't even going to be getting that pretty soon. It's pinching out."

Fairchild followed his gaze, to see in the torn rock above him only a narrow streak now, fully an inch and a half narrower than the vein had been before the powder holes had been drilled. It could mean only one thing: that the bet had been played and lost, that the vein had been one of those freak affairs that start out with much promise, seem to give hope of eternal riches, and then gradually dwindle to nothing. Harry shook his head.

"It won't last."

"Not more than two or three more shots," Fairchild agreed.

"You can't tell about that. It may run that way all through the mountain--but what's a four-inch vein? You can go up 'ere in the Argonaut tunnel and find 'arf a dozen of them things that they don't even take the trouble to mine. That is, unless they run 'igh in silver--" he picked up a chunk of the ore from the muck pile where it had been deposited and studied it intently--"but I don't see any pure silver sticking out in this stuff."

"But it must be here somewhere. I don't know anything about mining--but don't veins sometimes pinch off and then show up later on?"

"Sure they do--sometimes. But it's a gamble."

"That's all we 've had from the beginning, Harry."

"And it's about all we 're going to 'ave any time unless something bobs up sudden like."

Then, by common consent, they laid away their working clothes and left the mine, to wander dejectedly down the gulch and to the boarding house. After dinner they chatted a moment with Mother Howard, neglecting to tell her, however, of the downfall of their hopes, then went upstairs, each to his room. An hour later Harry knocked at Fairchild's door, and entered, the evening paper in his hand.

"'Ere 's something more that's nice," he announced, pointing to an item on the front page. It was the announcement that a general grand jury was to be convened late in the summer and that one of its tasks probably would be to seek to unravel the mystery of the murder of Sissie Larsen!

Fairchild read it with morbidity. Trouble seemed to have become more than occasional, and further than that, it appeared to descend upon him at just the times when he could least resist it. He made no comment; there was little that he could say. Again he read the item and again, finally to turn the page and breathe sharply. Before him was a six-column advertisement, announcing the strike in the Silver Queen mine and also spreading the word that a two-million-dollar company would be formed, one million in stock to represent the mine itself, the other to be subscribed to exploit this new find as it should be exploited. Glowing words told of the possibilities of the Silver Queen, the assayer's report was reproduced on a special cut which evidently had been made in Denver and sent to Ohadi by rush delivery. Offices had been opened; everything had been planned in advance and the advertisement written before the town was aware of the big discovery up Kentucky Gulch. All of it Fairchild read with a feeling he could not down,--a feeling that Fate, somehow, was dealing the cards from the bottom, and that trickery and treachery and a venomous nature were the necessary ingredients, after all, to success. The advertisement seemed to sneer at him, to jibe at him, calling as it did for every upstanding citizen of Ohadi to join in on the stock-buying bonanza that would make the Silver Queen one of the biggest mines in the district and Ohadi the big silver center of Colorado. The words appeared to be just so many daggers thrust into his very vitals. But Fairchild read them all, in spite of the pain they caused. He finished the last line, looked at the list of officers, and gasped.

For there, following one another, were three names, two of which Fairchild had expected. But the other-- They were, president and general manager, R. B. (Squint) Rodaine; secretary-treasurer, Maurice Rodaine; and first vice-president-- Miss Anita Natalie Richmond!

CHAPTER XVIII

After that, Fairchild heard little that Harry said as he rambled on about the plans for the future. He answered the big Cornishman's questions with monosyllables, volunteering no information. He did not even show him the advertisement--he knew that it would be as galling to Harry as it was to him. And so he sat and stared, until finally his partner said good night and left the room.

That name could mean only one thing: that she had consented to become a partner with them, that they had won her over, after all. Now, even a different light came upon the meeting with Barnham in Denver and a different view to Fairchild. What if she had been playing their game all along? What if she had been merely a tool for them; what if she had sent Farrell at their direction, to learn everything he and Harry knew? What--?

Fairchild sought to put the thought from him and failed. Now that he looked at it in retrospect, everything seemed to have a sinister meaning. He had met the girl under circumstances which never had been explained. The first time she ever had seen him after that she pretended not to recognize him. Yet, following a conversation with Maurice Rodaine, she took advantage of an opportunity to talk to him and freely admitted to him that she had been the person he believed her to be. True, Fairchild was looking now at his idol through blue glasses, and they gave to her a dark, mysterious tone that he could not fathom. There were too many things to explain; too many things which seemed to connect her directly with the Rodaines; too many things which appeared to show that her sympathies were there and that she might only be a trickster in their hands, a trickster to trap him! Even the episode of the lawyer could be turned to this account. Had not another lawyer played the friendship racket, in an effort to buy the Blue Poppy mine?

And here Fairchild smiled grimly. From the present prospects, it would seem that the gain would have been all on his side, for certainly there was little to show now toward a possibility of the Blue Poppy ever being worth anything near the figure which he had been offered for it. And yet, if that offer had not been made as some sort of stiletto jest, why had it been made at all? Was it because Rodaine knew that wealth did lie concealed there? Was it because Squint Rodaine had better information even than the faithful, hard-working, unfortunate Harry? Fairchild suddenly took hope. He clenched his hands and he spoke, to himself, to the darkness and to the spirits of discouragement that were all about him:

"If it's there, we 'll find it--if we have to work our fingers to the bone, if we have to starve and die there--we'll find it!"

With that determination, he went to bed, to awake in the morning filled with a desire to reach the mine, to claw at its vitals with the sharp-edged drills, to swing the heavy sledge until his shoulders and back ached, to send the roaring charges of dynamite digging deeper and deeper into that thinning vein. And Harry was beside him every step of the way.

A day's work, the booming charges, and they returned to the stope to find that the vein had neither lessened nor grown greater. Another day--and one after that. The vein remained the same, and the two men turned to mucking that they might fill their ore car with the proceeds of the various blasts, haul it to the surface by the laborious, slow process of the man-power elevator, then return once more to their drilling, begrudging every minute that they were forced to give to the other work of tearing away the muck and refuse that they might gain the necessary room to follow the vein.

The days grew to a week, and a week to a fortnight. Once a truck made its slow way up the tortuous road, chortled away with a load of ore, returned again and took the remainder from the old, half-rotted ore bins, to the Sampler, there to be laid aside while more valuable ore was crushed and sifted for its assays, and readier money taken in. The Blue Poppy had nothing in its favor. Ten or twenty dollar ore looked small beside the occasional shipments from the Silver Queen, where Blindeye Bozeman and Taylor Bill formed the entire working staff until the much-sought million dollars should flow in and a shaft-house, portable air pumps, machine drills and all the other attributes of modern mining methods should be put into operation.

And it appeared that the million dollars would not be slow in coming. Squint Rodaine had established his office in a small, vacant store building on the main street, and Fairchild could see, as he went to and from his work, a constant stream of townspeople as they made that their goal--there to give their money into the keeping of the be-scarred man and to trust to the future for wealth. It galled Fairchild, it made his hate stronger than ever; yet within him there could not live the hope that the Silver Queen might share the fate of the Blue Poppy. Other persons besides the Rodaines were interested now, persons who were putting their entire savings into the investment; and Fairchild could only grit his teeth and hope--for them--that it would be an everlasting bonanza. As for the girl who was named as vice-president--

He saw her, day after day, riding through town in the same automobile that he had helped re-tire on the Denver road. But now she did not look at him; now she pretended that she did not see him. Before,--well, before, her eyes had at least met his, and there had been some light of recognition, even though her carefully masked face had belied it. Now it was different. She had gone over to the Rodaines, she was engaged to marry the chalky-faced, hook-nosed son and she was vice-president of their two-million-dollar mining corporation. Fairchild did not even strive to find a meaning for it all; women are women, and men do well sometimes if they diagnose themselves.

The summer began to grow old, and Fairchild felt that he was aging with it. The long days beneath the ground had taught him many things about mining now, all to no advantage. Soon they would be worth nothing, save as five-dollar-a-day single-jackers, working for some one else. The bank deposits were thinning, and the vein was thinning with it. Slowly but surely, as they fought, the strip of pay ore in the rocks was pinching out. Soon would come the time when they could work it no longer. And then,--but Fairchild did not like to think about that.

September came, and with it the grand jury. But here for once was a slight ray of hope. The inquisitorial body dragged through its various functionings, while Farrell stood ready with his appeal to the court for a lunacy board at the first hint of an investigation into Crazy Laura's story. Three weeks of prying into "vice conditions", gambling, profiteering and the usual petty nonsense with which so many grand juries have managed to fritter away time under the misapprehension of ap-plying some weighty sort of superhuman reasoning to ordinary things, and then good news. The body of twelve good men and true had worn themselves out with other matters and adjourned without even taking up the mystery of the Blue Poppy mine. But the joy of Fairchild and Harry was short-lived. In the long, legal phrase-ology of the jury's report was the recommendation that this important subject be the first for inquiry by the next grand inquisitorial body to be convened,--and the threat still remained.

But before the two men were now realities which were worse even than threats, and Harry turned from his staging late one afternoon to voice the most important.

"We 'll start single-jacking to-morrow," he announced with a little sigh. "In the 'anging wall."

"You mean--?"

"We can't do much more up 'ere. It ain't worth it. The vein 's pinched down until we ain't even getting day laborer's wages out of it--and it's October now."

October! October--and winter on the way. October--and only a month until the time when Harry must face a jury on four separate charges, any one of which might send him to Canon City for the rest of his days; Harry was young no longer. October--and in the dreamy days of summer, Fairchild had believed that October would see him rich. But now the hills were brown with the killing touch of frost; the white of the snowy range was creeping farther and farther over the mountains; the air was crisp with the hint of zero soon to come; the summer was dead, and Fairchild's hopes lay inert beside it. He was only working now because he had determined to work. He was only laboring because a great, strong, big-shouldered man had come from Cornwall to help him and was willing to fight it out to the end. October--and the announcement had said that a certain girl would be married in the late fall, a girl who never looked in his direction any more, who had allowed her name to become affiliated with that of the Rodaines, now nearing the task of completing their two million. October--month of falling leaves and dying dreams, month of fragrant beauties gone to dust, the month of the last, failing fight against the clutch of grim, all-destroying winter. And Fairchild was sagging in defeat just as the leaves were falling from the shaking aspens, as the moss tendrils were curling into brittle, brown things of death. October!

For a long moment, Fairchild said nothing, then as Harry came from the staging, he moved to the older man's side.

"I--I did n't quite catch the idea," came at last. Harry pointed with his sledge.

"I 've been noticing the vein. It keeps turning to the left. It struck me that it might 'ave branched off from the main body and that there 's a bigger vein over there some'eres. We 'll just 'ave to make a try for it. It's our only chance."

"And if we fail to find it there?"

"We 'll put a couple of 'oles in the foot wall and see what we strike. And then--"

"Yes--?"

"If it ain't there--we 're whipped!"

It was the first time that Harry had said the word seriously. Fairchild pretended not to hear. Instead, he picked up a drill, looked at its point, then started toward the small forge which they had erected just at the foot of the little raise leading to the stope. There Harry joined him; together they heated the long pieces of steel and pounded their biting faces to the sharpness necessary to drilling in the hard rock of the hanging wall, tempering them in the bucket of water near by, working silently, slowly,--hampered by the weight of defeat. They were being whipped; they felt it in every atom of their beings. But they had not given up their fight. Two blows were left in the struggle, and two blows they meant to strike before the end came. The next morning they started at their new task, each drilling holes at points five feet apart in the hanging wall, to send them in as far as possible, then at the end of the day to blast them out, tearing away the rock and stopping their work at drilling that they might muck away the refuse. The stope began to take on the appearance of a vast chamber, as day after day, banging away at their drill holes, stopping only to sharpen the bits or to rest their aching muscles, they pursued into the entrails of the hills the vagrant vein which had escaped them. And day after day, each, without mentioning it to the other, was tortured by the thought of that offer of riches, that mysterious proffer of wealth for the Blue Poppy mine,--tortured like men who are chained in the sight of gold and cannot reach it. For the offer carried always the hint that wealth was there, somewhere, that Squint Rodaine knew it, but that they could not find it. Either that--or flat failure. Either wealth that would yield Squint a hundredfold for his purchase, or a sneer that would answer their offer to sell. And each man gritted his teeth and said nothing. But they worked on.

October gave up its fight. The first day of November came, to find the chamber a wide, vacuous thing now, sheltering stone and refuse and two struggling men,-- nothing more. Fairchild ceased his labors and mopped his forehead, dripping from the heat engendered by frenzied labor; without the tunnel opening, the snow lay deep upon the mountain sides, for it had been more than a week since the first of the white blasts had scurried over the hills to begin the placid, cold enwrapment of the winter. A long moment, then:

"Harry."

"Aye."

"I 'm going after the other side. We 've been playing a half-horsed game here."

"I 've been thinking that, Boy."

"Then I 'm going to tackle the foot wall. You stay where you are, for a few more shots; it can't do much good, the way things are going, and it can't do much harm. I was at the bank to-day."

"Yeh."

"My balance is just two hundred."

"Counting what we borrowed from Mother 'Oward?"

"Yes."

Harry clawed at his mustache. His nose, already red from the pressure of blood, turned purplish.

"We 're nearing the end, Boy. Tackle the foot wall."

They said no more. Fairchild withdrew his drill from the "swimmer" or straightforward powder hole and turned far to the other side of the chamber, where the sloping foot wall showed for a few feet before it dived under the muck and refuse. There, gad in hand, he pecked about the surface, seeking a spot where the rock had splintered, thereby affording a softer entrance for the biting surface of the drill. Spot after spot he prospected, suddenly to stop and bend forward. At last came an exclamation, surprised, wondering:

"Harry!"

"Yeh."

"Come here."

The Cornishman left his work and walked to Fairchild's side. The younger man pointed.

"Do you ever fill up drill holes with cement?" he asked.

"Not as I know of. Why?"

"There 's one." Fairchild raised his gad and chipped away the softer surface of the rock, leaving a tubular protuberance of cement extending. Harry stared.

"What the bloody 'ell?" he conjectured. "D' you suppose--" Then, with a sudden resolution: "Drill there! Gad a 'ole off to one side a bit and drill there. It seems to me Sissie Larsen put a 'ole there or something--I can't remember. But drill. It can't do any 'arm."

The gad chipped away the rock. Soon the drill was biting into the surface of the foot wall. Quitting time came; the drill was in two feet, and in the morning, Fairchild went at his task again. Harry watched him over a shoulder.

"If it don't bring out anything in six feet--it ain't there," he announced. Fairchild found the humor to smile.

"You 're almost as cheerful as I am." Noon came and they stopped for lunch. Fairchild finished the remark begun hours before. "I 'm in four feet now--and all I get is rock."

"Sure now?"

"Look."

They went to the foot wall and with a scraper brought out some of the muggy mass caused by the pouring of water into the "down-hole" to make the sittings capable of removal. Harry rubbed it with a thumb and forefinger.

"That's all," he announced, as he went back to his dinner pail. Together, silently, they finished their luncheon. Once more Fairchild took up his work, dully, almost lackadaisically, pounding away at the long, six-foot drill with strokes that had behind them only muscles, not the intense driving power of hope. A foot he progressed into the foot wall and changed drills. Three inches more. Then--

"Harry!"

"What's 'appened?" The tone of Fairchild's voice had caused the Cornishman to lean from his staging and run to Fairchild's side. That person had cupped his hand and was holding it beneath the drill hole, while into it he was pulling the muck with the scraper and staring at it.

"This stuff's changed color!" he exclaimed. "It looks like--"

"Let me see!" The older man took a portion of the blackish, gritty mass and held it close to his carbide. "It looks like something--it looks like something!" His voice was high, excited. "I 'll finish the 'ole and jam enough dynamite in there to tear the insides out of it. I 'll give 'er 'ell. But in the meantime, you take that down to the assayer!"

CHAPTER XIX

Fairchild did not hesitate. Scraping the watery conglomeration into a tobacco can, he threw on his coat and ran for the shaft. Then he pulled himself up, singing, and dived into the fresh-made drifts of a new storm as he started toward town; nor did he stop to investigate the fast fading footprints of some one who evidently had passed the mine a short time before. Fairchild was too happy to notice such things just now; in a tin can in his side pocket was a blackish, muggy mixture which might mean worlds to him; he was hurrying to receive the verdict, which could come only from the retorts and tests of one man, the assayer.

Into town and through it to the scrambling buildings of the Sampler, where the main products of the mines of Ohadi found their way before going to the smelter. There he swung wide the door and turned to the little room on the left, the sanctum of a white-haired, almost tottering old man who wandered about among his test tubes and "buttons" as he figured out the various weights and values of the ores as the samples were brought to him from the dirty, dusty, bin-filled rooms of the Sampler proper. A queer light came into the old fellow's eyes as he looked into those of Robert Fairchild.

"Don't get 'em too high!" he admonished.

Fairchild stared.

"What?"

"Hopes. I 've seen many a fellow come in just like you. I 've been here thirty year. They call me Old Undertaker Chastine!"

Fairchild laughed.

"But I'm hoping--"

"Yep, Son." Undertaker Chastine looked over his glasses. "You 're just like all the rest. You 're hoping. That's what they all do; they come in here with their eyes blazing like a grate fire and their faces all lighted up as bright as an Italian cathedral. And they tell me they 've got the world by the tail. Then I take their specimens and I put 'em over the hurdles,--and half the time they go out wishing there was n't any such person in the world as an assayer. Boy," and he pursed his lips, "I 've buried more fortunes than you could shake a stick at. I 've seen men come in here millionaires and go out paupers--just because I 've had to tell 'em the truth. And I 'm soft-hearted. I would n't kill a flea--not even if it was eatin' up the best bird dog that ever set a pa'tridge. And just because o' that, I 've adopted the system of taking all hope out of a fellow right in the beginning. Then if you 've really got something, it's a joyful surprise. If you ain't, the disappointment don't hurt so much. So trot 'er out and let the old Undertaker have a look at 'er. But I 'm telling you right at the start that it won't amount to much."

Sobered now, Fairchild reached for his tobacco can, which had been stuffed full of every scrap of slime that he and 'Arry had been able to drag from the powder hole. Evidently, his drill had been in the ore, whatever it was, for some time before he realized it; the can was heavy, exceedingly heavy, giving evidence of purity of something at least. But Undertaker Chastine shook his head.

"Can't tell," he announced. "Feels heavy, looks black and all that. But it might not be anything but straight lead with a sprinkling of silver. I 've seen stuff that looked a lot better than this not run more 'n fifteen dollars to the ton. And then again--"

He began to tinker about with his pottery. He dragged out a scoop from somewhere and prepared various white powders. Then he turned to the furnace, with its high-chimneyed draft, and filled a container with the contents of the tobacco can.

"Let 'er roast, Son," he announced. "That's the only way. Let 'er roast--and while it's getting hot, well, you just cool your heels."

Long waiting--while the eccentric old assayer told doleful tales of other days, tales of other men who had rushed in, just like Fairchild, with their sample of ore, only to depart with the knowledge that they were no richer than before, days when the news of the demonetization of silver swooped down upon the little town like some black tornado, closing down the mines, shutting up the gambling halls and great saloons, nailing up the doors, even of the Sampler, for years to come.

"Them was the times when there was a lot of undertakers around here besides me," Chastine went on. "Everybody was an undertaker then. Lor', Boy, how that thing hit. We 'd been getting along pretty well at ninety-five cents and a dollar an ounce for silver, and there was men around here wearing hats that was the biggest in the shop, but that did n't come anywhere near fittin' 'em. And then, all of a sudden, it hit! We used to get in all our quotations in those days over the telephone, and every morning I 'd phone down to Old Man Saxby that owned the Sampler then to find out how the New York market stood. The treasury, you know, had been buying up three or four million ounces of silver a month for minting. Then some high-falutin' Congressman got the idea they didn't want to do that any more, and he began to talk. Well, one morning, I telephoned down, and silver 'd dropped to eighty-five. The next morning it went to seventy. The House or the Senate, I 've forgotten which, had passed the demonetization bill. After that, things dragged along and then--I telephoned down again.

"'What's the quotation on silver?' I asked him."

"'Hell,' says Old Man Saxby, 'there ain't any quotation! Close 'er up--close up everything. They 've passed the demonetization bill, the president 's going to sign it, and you ain't got a job.'

"And young feller--" Old Undertaker Chastine looked over his glasses again, "that was some real disappointment. And it's a lot worse than you 're liable to get in a minute."

He turned to the furnace and took out the pottery dish in which the sample had been smelting, white-hot now. He cooled it and tinkered with his chemicals. He fussed with his scales, he adjusted his glasses, he coughed once or twice in an embarrassed manner; finally to turn to Fairchild.

"Young man," he queried, "it ain't any of my business, but where 'd you get this ore?"

"Out of my mine, the Blue Poppy!"

"Sure you ain't been visiting?"

"What do you mean?" Fairchild was staring at him in wonderment.

Old Undertaker Chastine rubbed his hands on his big apron and continued to look over his glasses.

"What 'll you take for the Blue Poppy mine, Son?"

"Why--it's not for sale."

"Sure it ain't going to be--soon?"

"Absolutely not." Then Fairchild caught the queer look in the man's eyes. "What do you mean by all these questions? Is that good ore--or is n't it?"

"Son, just one more question--and I hope you won't get mad at me. I 'm a funny old fellow, and I do a lot of things that don't seem right at the beginning. But I 've saved a few young bloods like you from trouble more than once. You ain't been high-grading?"

"You mean--"

"Just exactly what I said--wandering around somebody else's property and picking up a few samples, as it were, to mix in with your own product? Or planting them where they can be found easily by a prospective buyer?"

Fairchild's chin set, and his arms moved slowly. Then he laughed--laughed at the small, white-haired, eccentric old man who through his very weakness had the strength to ask insulting questions.

"No--I 'll give you my word I have n't been high-grading," he said at last. "My partner and I drilled a hole in the foot wall of the stope where we were working, hoping to find the rest of a vein that was pinching out on us. And we got this stuff. Is it any good?"

"Is it good?" Again Old Undertaker Chastine looked over his glasses. "That's just the trouble. It's too good--it's so good that it seems there's something funny about it. Son, that stuff assays within a gram, almost, of the ore they 're taking out of the Silver Queen!"

"What's that?" Fairchild had leaped forward and grasped the other man by the shoulders, his eyes agleam, his whole being trembling with excitement. "You're not kidding me about it? You're sure--you 're sure?"

"Absolutely! That's why I was so careful for a minute. I thought maybe you had been doing a little high-grading or had been up there and sneaked away some of the ore for a salting proposition. Boy, you 've got a bonanza, if this holds out."

"And it really--"

"It's almost identical. I never saw two samples of ore that were more alike. Let's see, the Blue Poppy's right up Kentucky Gulch, not so very far away from the Silver Queen, is n't it? Then there must be a tremendous big vein concealed around there somewhere that splits, one half of it running through the mountain in one direction and the other cutting through on the opposite side. It looks like peaches and cream for you, Son. How thick is it?"

"I don't know. We just happened to put a drill in there and this is some of the scrapings."

"You have n't cut into it at all, then?"

"Not unless Harry, my partner, has put in a shot since I 've been gone. As soon as we saw that we were into ore, I hurried away to come down here to get an assay."

"Well, Son, now you can hurry back and begin cutting into a fortune. If that vein's only four inches wide, you 've got plenty to keep you for the rest of your life."

"It must be more than that--the drill must have been into it several inches before I ever noticed it. I 'd been scraping the muck out of there without paying much attention. It looked so hopeless."

Undertaker Chastine turned to his work.

"Then hurry along, Son. I suppose," he asked, as he looked over his glasses for the last time, "that you don't want me to say anything about it?"

"Not until--"

"You 're sure. I know. Well, good news is awful hard to keep--but I 'll do my best. Run along."

And Fairchild "ran." Whistling and happy, he turned out of the office of the Sampler and into the street, his coat open, his big cap high on his head, regardless of the sweep of the cold wind and the fine snow that it carried on its icy breath. Through town he went, bumping into pedestrians now and then, and apologizing in a vacant, absent manner. The waiting of months was over, and Fairchild at last was beginning to see his dreams come true. Like a boy, he turned up Kentucky Gulch, bucking the big drifts and kicking the snow before him in flying, splattering spray, stopping his whistling now and then to sing,--foolish songs without words or rhyme or rhythm, the songs of a heart too much engrossed with the joy of living to take cognizance of mere rules of melody!

So this was the reason that Rodaine had acknowledged the value of the mine that day in court! This was the reason for the mysterious offer of fifty thousand dollars and for the later one of nearly a quarter of a million! Rodaine had known; Rodaine had information, and Rodaine had been willing to pay to gain possession of what now appeared to be a bonanza. But Rodaine had failed. And Fairchild had won!

Won! But suddenly he realized that there was a blankness about it all. He had won money, it is true. But all the money in the world could not free him from the taint that had been left upon him by a coroner's investigation, from the hint that still remained in the recommendation of the grand jury that the murder of Sissie Larsen be looked into further. Nor could it remove the stigma of the four charges against Harry, which soon were to come to trial, and without a bit of evidence to combat them. Riches could do much--but they could not aid in that particular, and somewhat sobered by the knowledge, Fairchild turned from the main road and on up through the high-piled snow to the mouth of the Blue Poppy mine.

A faint acrid odor struck his nostrils as he started to descend the shaft, the "perfume" of exploded dynamite, and it sent anew into Fairchild's heart the excitement and intensity of the strike. Evidently Harry had shot the deep hole, and now, there in the chamber, was examining the result, which must, by this time, give some idea of the extent of the ore and the width of the vein. Fairchild pulled on the rope with enthusiastic strength, while the bucket bumped and swirled about the shaft in descent. A moment more and he had reached the bottom, to leap from the carrier, light his carbide lamp which hung where he had left it on the timbers, and start forward.

The odor grew heavier. Fairchild held his light before him and looked far ahead, wondering why he could not see the gleam from Harry's lamp. He shouted. There was no answer, and he went on.

Fifty feet! Seventy-five! Then he stopped short with a gasp. Twisted and torn before him were the timbers of the tunnel, while muck and refuse lay everywhere. A cave-in--another cave-in--at almost the exact spot where the one had occurred years before, shutting off the chamber from communication with the shaft, tearing and rending the new timbers which had been placed there and imprisoning Harry behind them!

Fairchild shouted again and again, only gaining for his answer the ghostlike echoes of his own voice as they traveled to the shaft and were thrown back again. He tore off his coat and cap, and attacked the timbers like the fear-maddened man he was, dragging them by superhuman force out of the way and clearing a path to the refuse. Then, running along the little track, he searched first on one side, then the other, until, nearly at the shaft, he came upon a miner's pick and a shovel. With these, he returned to the task before him.

Hours passed, while the sweat poured from his forehead and while his muscles seemed to tear themselves loose from their fastenings with the exertion that was placed upon them. Foot after foot, the muck was torn away, as Fairchild, with pick and shovel, forced a tunnel through the great mass of rocky debris which choked the drift. Onward--onward--at last to make a small opening in the barricade, and to lean close to it that he might shout again. But still there was no answer.

Feverish now, Fairchild worked with all the reserve strength that was in him. He seized great chunks of rock that he could not even have budged at an ordinary time and threw them far behind him. His pick struck again and again with a vicious, clanging reverberation; the hole widened. Once more Fairchild leaned toward it.

"Harry!" he called. "Harry!"

But there was no answer. Again he shouted, then he returned to his work, his heart aching in unison with his muscles. Behind that broken mass, Fairchild felt sure, was his partner, torn, bleeding through the effects of some accident, he did not know what, past answering his calls, perhaps dead. Greater became the hole in the cave-in; soon it was large enough to admit his body. Seizing his carbide lamp, Fairchild made for the opening and crawled through, hurrying onward toward the chamber where the stope began, calling Harry's name at every step, in vain. The shadows before him lengthened, as the chamber gave greater play to the range of light. Fairchild rushed within, held high his carbide and looked about him. But no crumpled form of a man lay there, no bruised, torn human being. The place was empty, except for the pile of stone and refuse which had been torn away by dynamite explosions in the hanging wall, where Harry evidently had shot away the remaining refuse in a last effort to see what lay in that direction,--stones and muck which told nothing. On the other side--

Fairchild stared blankly. The hole that he had made into the foot wall had been filled with dynamite and tamped, as though ready for shooting. But the charge had not been exploded. Instead--on the ground lay the remainder of the tamping paper and a short foot and a half of fuse, with its fulminate of mercury cap attached, where it had been pulled from its berth by some great force and hastily stamped out. And Harry--Harry was gone!

CHAPTER XX

It was as though the shades of the past had come to life again, to repeat in the twentieth century a happening of the nineteenth. There was only one difference--no form of a dead man now lay against the foot wall, to rest there more than a score of years until it should come to light, a pile of bones in time-shredded clothing. And as he thought of it, Fairchild remembered that the earthly remains of "Sissie" Larsen had lain within almost a few feet of the spot where he had drilled the prospect hole into the foot wall, there to discover the ore that promised bonanza.

But this time there was nothing and no clue to the mystery of Harry's disappearance. Fairchild suddenly strengthened with an idea. Perhaps, after all, he had been on the other side of the cave-in and had hurried on out of the mine. But in that event, would he not have waited for his return, to tell him of the accident? Or would he not have proceeded down to the Sampler to bring the news if he had not cared to remain at the tunnel opening? However, it was a chance, and Fairchild took it. Once more he crawled through the hole that he had made in the cave-in and sought the outward world. Then he hurried down Kentucky Gulch and to the Sampler. But Harry had not been there. He went through town, asking questions, striving his best to shield his anxiety, cloaking his queries under the cover of cursory remarks. Harry had not been seen. At last, with the coming of night, he turned toward the boarding house, and on his arrival. Mother Howard, sighting his white face, hurried to him.

"Have you seen Harry?" he asked.

"No--he has n't been here."

It was the last chance. Clutching fear at his heart, he told Mother Howard of the happenings at the mine, quickly, as plainly as possible. Then once more he went forth, to retrace his steps to the Blue Poppy, to buck the wind and the fine snow and the high, piled drifts, and to go below. But the surroundings were the same: still the cave-in, with its small hole where he had torn through it, still the ragged hanging wall where Harry had fired the last shots of dynamite in his investigations, still the trampled bit of fuse with its cap attached. Nothing more. Gingerly Fairchild picked up the cap and placed it where a chance kick could not explode it. Then he returned to the shaft.

Back into the black night, with the winds whistling through the pines. Back to wandering about through the hills, hurrying forward at the sight of every faint, dark object against the snow, in the hope that Harry, crippled by the cave-in, might have some way gotten out of the shaft. But they were only boulders or logs or stumps of trees. At midnight, Fairchild turned once more toward town and to the boarding house. But Harry had not appeared. There was only one thing left to do.

This time, when Fairchild left Mother Howard's, his steps did not lead him toward Kentucky Gulch. Instead he kept straight on up the street, past the little line of store buildings and to the courthouse, where he sought out the sole remaining light in the bleak, black building,--Sheriff Bardwell's office. That personage was nodding in his chair, but removed his feet from the desk and turned drowsily as Fairchild entered.

"Well?" he questioned, "what's up?"

"My partner has disappeared. I want to report to you--and see if I can get some help."

"Disappeared? Who?"

"Harry Harkins. He 's a big Cornishman, with a large mustache, very red face, about sixty years old, I should judge--"

"Wait a minute," Bardwell's eyes narrowed. "Ain't he the fellow I arrested in the Blue Poppy mine the night of the Old Times dance?"

"Yes."

"And you say he 's disappeared?"

"I think you heard me!" Fairchild spoke with some asperity. "I said that he had disappeared, and I want some help in hunting for him. He may be injured, for all I know, and if he 's out here in the mountains anywhere, it's almost sure death for him unless he can get some aid soon. I--"

But the sheriff's eyes still remained suspiciously narrow.

"When does his trial come up?"

"A week from to-morrow."

"And he 's disappeared." A slow smile came over the other man's lips. "I don't think it will help much to start any relief expedition for him. The thing to do is to get a picture and a general description and send it around to the police in the various parts of the country! That 'll be the best way to find him!"

Fairchild's teeth gritted, but he could not escape the force of the argument, from the sheriff's standpoint. For a moment there was silence, then the miner came closer to the desk.

"Sheriff," he said as calmly as possible, "you have a perfect right to give that sort of view. That's your business--to suspect people. However, I happen to feel sure that my partner would stand trial, no matter what the charge, and that he would not seek to evade it in any way. Some sort of an accident happened at the mine this afternoon--a cave-in or an explosion that tore out the roof of the tunnel--and I am sure that my partner is injured, has made his way out of the mine, and is wandering among the hills. Will you help me to find him?"

The sheriff wheeled about in his chair and studied a moment. Then he rose.

"Guess I will," he announced. "It can't do any harm to look for him, anyway."

Half an hour later, aided by two deputies who had been summoned from their homes, Fairchild and the sheriff left for the hills to begin the search for the missing Harry. Late the next afternoon, they returned to town, tired, their horses almost crawling in their dragging pace after sixteen hours of travel through the drifts of the hills and gullies. Harry had not been found, and so Fairchild reported when, with drooping shoulders, he returned to the boarding house and to the waiting Mother Howard. And both knew that this time Harry's disappearance was no joke, as it had been before. They realized that back of it all was some sinister reason, some mystery which they could not solve,--for the present at least. That night, Fairchild faced the future and made his resolve.

There was only a week now until Harry's case should come to trial. Only a week until the failure of the defendant to appear should throw the deeds of the Blue Poppy mine into the hands of the court, to be sold for the amount of the bail. And in spite of the fact that Fairchild now felt his mine to be a bonanza, unless some sort of a miracle could happen before that time, the mine was the same as lost. True, it would go to the highest bidder at a public sale and any money brought in above the amount of bail would be returned to him. But who would be that bidder? Who would get the mine--perhaps for twenty or twenty-five thousand dollars, when it now was worth millions? Certainly not he. Already he and Harry had borrowed from Mother Howard all that she could lend them. True she had friends; but none could produce from twenty to two hundred thousand dollars for a mine, simply on his word. And unless something should happen to intervene, unless Harry should return, or in some way Fairchild could raise the necessary five thousand dollars to furnish a cash bond and again recover the deeds of the Blue Poppy, he was no better off than before the strike was made. Long he thought, finally to come to his conclusion, and then, with the air of a gambler who has placed his last bet to win or lose, he went to bed.

But morning found him awake long before the rest of the house was stirring. Downtown he hurried, to eat a hasty breakfast in the all-night restaurant, then to start on a search for men. The first workers on the street that morning found Fairchild offering them six dollars a day. And by eight o'clock, ten of them were at work in the drift of the Blue Poppy mine, working against time that they might repair the damage which had been caused by the cave-in.

It was not an easy task. That day and the next and the next after that, they labored. Then Fairchild glanced at the progress that was being made and sought out the pseudo-foreman.

"Will it be finished by night?" he asked.

"Easily."

"Very well. I may need these men to work on a day and night shift, I 'm not sure. I 'll be back in an hour."

Away he went and up the shaft, to travel as swiftly as possible through the drift-piled road down Kentucky Gulch and to the Sampler. There he sought out old Undertaker Chastine, and with him went to the proprietor.

"My name is Fairchild, and I 'm in trouble," he said candidly. "I 've brought Mr. Chastine in with me because he assayed some of my ore a few days ago and believes he knows what it's worth. I 'm working against time to get five thousand dollars. If I can produce ore that runs two hundred dollars to the ton, and if I 'll sell it to you for one hundred seventy-five dollars a ton until I can get the money I need, provided I can get the permission of the court,--will you put it through for me?"

The Sampler owner smiled.

"If you 'll let me see where you 're getting the ore." Then he figured a moment. "That 'd be thirty or forty ton," came at last. "We could handle that as fast as you could bring it in here."

But a new thought had struck Fairchild,--a new necessity for money.

"I 'll give it to you for one hundred fifty dollars a ton, providing you do the hauling and lend me enough after the first day or so to pay my men."

"But why all the excitement--and the rush?"

"My partner 's Harry Harkins. He 's due for trial Friday, and he 's disappeared. The mine is up as security. You can see what will happen unless I can substitute a cash bond for the amount due before that time. Is n't that sufficient?"

"It ought to be. But as I said, I want to see where the ore comes from."

"You 'll see in the morning--if I 've got it," answered Fairchild with a new hope thrilling in his voice. "All that I have so far is an assay of some drill scrapings. I don't know how thick the vein is or whether it's going to pinch out in ten minutes after we strike it. But I 'll know mighty soon."

Every cent that Robert Fairchild possessed in the world was in his pockets,-- two hundred dollars. After he had paid his men for their three days of labor, there would be exactly twenty dollars left. But Fairchild did not hesitate. To Farrell's office he went and with him to an interview, in chambers, with the judge. Then, the necessary permission having been granted, he hurried back to the mine and into the drift, there to find the last of the muck being scraped away from beneath the site of the cave-in. Fairchild paid off. Then he turned to the foreman.

"How many of these men are game to take a chance?"

"Pretty near all of 'em--if there 's any kind of a gamble to it."

"There 's a lot of gamble. I 've got just twenty dollars in my pocket--enough to pay each man one dollar apiece for a night's work if my hunch doesn't pan out. If it does pan, the wages are twenty dollars a day for three days, with everybody, including myself, working like hell! Who's game?"

The answer came in unison. Fairchild led the way to the chamber, seized a hammer and took his place.

"There 's two-hundred-dollar ore back of this foot wall if we can break in and start a new stope," he announced. "It takes a six-foot hole to reach it, and we can have the whole story by morning. Let's go!"

Along the great length of the foot wall, extending all the distance of the big chamber, the men began their work, five men to the drills and as many to the sledges, as they started their double-jacking. Hour after hour the clanging of steel against steel sounded in the big underground room, as the drills bit deeper and deeper into the hard formation of the foot wall, driving steadily forward until their contact should have a different sound, and the muggy scrapings bear a darker hue than that of mere wall-rock. Hour after hour passed, while the drill-turners took their places with the sledges, and the sledgers went to the drills--the turnabout system of "double-jacking"--with Fairchild, the eleventh man, filling in along the line as an extra sledger, that the miners might be the more relieved in their strenuous, frenzied work. Midnight came. The first of the six-foot drills sank to its ultimate depth. Then the second and third and fourth: finally the fifth. They moved on. Hours more of work, and the operation had been repeated. The workmen hurried for the powder house, far down the drift, by the shaft, lugging back in their pockets the yellow, candle-like sticks of dynamite, with their waxy wrappers and their gelatinous contents together with fuses and caps. Crimping nippers--the inevitable accompaniment of a miner--came forth from the pockets of the men. Careful tamping, then the men took their places at the fuses.

"Give the word!" one of them announced crisply as he turned to Fairchild. "Each of us 'll light one of these things, and then I say we 'll run! Because this is going to be some explosion!"

Fairchild smiled the smile of a man whose heart is thumping at its maximum speed. Before him in the long line of the foot wall were ten holes, "up-holes", "downs" and "swimmers", attacking the hidden ore in every direction. Ten holes drilled six feet into the rock and tamped with double charges of dynamite. He straightened.

"All right, men! Ready?"

"Ready!"

"Touch 'em off!"

The carbide lamps were held close to the fuses for a second. Soon they were all going, spitting like so many venomous, angry serpents--but neither Fairchild nor the miners had stopped to watch. They were running as hard as possible for the shaft and for the protection that distance might give. A wait that seemed ages. Then:

"One!"

"And two--and three!"

"There goes four and five--they went together!"

"Six--seven--eight--nine--"

Again a wait, while they looked at one another with vacuous eyes. A long interval until the tenth.

"Two went together then! I thought we 'd counted nine?" The foreman stared, and Fairchild studied. Then his face lighted.

"Eleven 's right. One of them must have set off the charge that Harry left in there. All the better--it gives us just that much more of a chance."

Back they went along the drift tunnel now, coughing slightly as the sharp smoke of the dynamite cut their lungs. A long journey that seemed as many miles instead of feet. Then with a shout, Fairchild sprang forward, and went to his hands and knees.

It was there before him--all about him--the black, heavy masses of lead-silver ore, a great, heaping, five-ton pile of it where it had been thrown out by the tremendous force of the explosion. It seemed that the whole great floor of the cavern was covered with it, and the workmen shouted with Fairchild as they seized bits of the precious black stuff and held it to the light for closer examination.

"Look!" The voice of one of them was high and excited. "You can see the fine streaks of silver sticking out! It's high-grade and plenty of it!"

But Fairchild paid little attention. He was playing in the stuff, throwing it in the air and letting it fall to the floor of the cavern again, like a boy with a new sack of marbles, or a child with its building blocks. Five tons and the night was not yet over! Five tons, and the vein had not yet shown its other side!

Back to work they went now, six of the men drilling, Fairchild and the other four mucking out the refuse, hauling it up the shaft, and then turning to the ore that they might get it to the old, rotting bins and into position for loading as soon as the owner of the Sampler could be notified in the morning and the trucks could fight their way through the snowdrifts of Kentucky Gulch to the mine for loading. Again through the hours the drills bit into the rock walls, while the ore car clattered along the tram line and while the creaking of the block and tackle at the shaft seemed endless. In three days, approximately forty tons of ore must come out of that mine,--and work must not cease.

Morning, and in spite of the sleep-laden eyes, the heavy aching in his head, the tired drooping of the shoulders, Fairchild tramped to the boarding house to notify Mother Howard and ask for news of Harry. There had been none. Then he went on, to wait by the door of the Sampler until Bittson, the owner, should appear, and drag him away up the hill, even before he could open up for the morning.

"There it is!" he exclaimed, as he led him to the entrance of the chamber. "There it is; take all you want of it and assay it!"

Bittson went forward into the cross-cut, where the men were drilling even at new holes, and examined the vein. Already it was three feet thick, and there was still ore ahead. One of the miners looked up.

"Just finishing up on the cross-cut," he announced, as he nodded toward his drill. "I 've just bitten into the foot wall on the other side. Looks to me like the vein 's about five feet thick--as near as I can measure it."

"And--" Bittson picked up a few samples, examined them by the light of the carbides and tossed them away--"you can see the silver sticking out. I caught sight of a couple of pencil threads of it in one or two of those samples. All right, Boy!" he turned to Fairchild. "What was that bargain we made?"

"It was based on two hundred dollars a ton ore. This may run above--or below. But whatever it is, I 'll sell you all you can handle for the next three days at fifty dollars a ton under the assay price."

"You 've said the word. The trucks will be here in an hour if we have to shovel a path all the way up Kentucky Gulch."

He hurried away then, while Fairchild and the men followed him into town and to their breakfast. Then, recruiting a new gang on the promise of payment at the end of their three-day shift, Fairchild went back to the mine. But the word had spread, and others were there before him.

Already a wide path showed up Kentucky Gulch. Already fifteen or twenty miners were assembled about the opening of the Blue Poppy tunnel, awaiting permission to enter, the usual rush upon a lucky mine to view its riches. Behind him, Fairchild could see others coming from Ohadi to take a look at the new strike, and his heart bounded with happiness tinged with sorrow. Harry was not there to enjoy it all; Harry was gone, and in spite of his every effort, Fairchild had failed to find him.

All that morning they thronged down the shaft of the Blue Poppy. The old method of locomotion grew too slow; willing hands repaired the hoist and sent volunteers for a gasoline engine to run it, while in the meantime officials of curiosity labored on the broken old ladder that once had encompassed the distance from the bottom of the shaft to the top, rehabilitating it to such an extent that it might be used again. The drift was crowded with persons bearing candles and carbides. The big chamber was filled, leaving barely room for the men to work with their drills at the final holes that would be needed to clear the vein to the foot wall on the other side and enable the miners to start upward on their new stope. Fairchild looked about him proudly, happily; it was his, his and Harry's--if Harry ever should come back again--the thing he had worked for, the thing he had dreamed of, planned for.

Some one brushed against him, and there came a slight tug at his coat. Fairchild looked downward to see passing the form of Anita Richmond. A moment later she looked toward him, but in her eyes there was no light of recognition, nothing to indicate that she had just given him a signal of greeting and congratulation. And yet Fairchild felt that she had. Uneasily he walked away, following her with his eyes as she made her way into the blackness of the tunnel and toward the shaft. Then, absently, he put his hand into his pocket.

Something there caused his heart to halt momentarily,--a piece of paper. He crumpled it in his hand, he rubbed his fingers over it wonderingly; it had not been in his pocket before she had passed him. Hurriedly he walked to the far side of the chamber and there, pretending to examine a bit of ore, brought the missive from its place of secretion, to unfold it with trembling fingers, then to stare at the words which showed before him: "Squint Rodaine is terribly worried about something. Has been on an awful rampage all morning. Something critical is brewing, but I don't know what. Suggest you keep watch on him. Please destroy this."

That was all. There was no signature. But Robert Fairchild had seen the writing of Anita Richmond once before!

CHAPTER XXI

So she was his friend! So all these days of waiting had not been in vain; all the cutting hopelessness of seeing her, only to have her turn away her head and fail to recognize him, had been for their purpose after all. And yet Fairchild remembered that she was engaged to Maurice Rodaine, and that the time of the wedding must be fast approaching. Perhaps there had been a quarrel, perhaps-- Then he smiled. There was no perhaps about it! Anita Richmond was his friend; she had been forced into the promise of marriage to Maurice Rodaine, but she had not been forced into a relinquishment of her desire to reward him somehow, some way, for the attention that he had shown her and the liking that she knew existed in his heart.

Hastily Fairchild folded the paper and stuffed it into an inside pocket. Then, seeking out one of the workmen, he appointed him foreman of the gang, to take charge in his absence. Following which, he made his way out of the mine and into town, there to hire men of Mother Howard's suggestion and send them to the Blue Poppy, to take their stations every few feet along the tunnel, to appear mere spectators, but in reality to be guards who were constantly on the watch for anything untoward that might occur. Fairchild was taking no chances now. An hour more found him at the Sampler, watching the ore as it ran through the great crusher hoppers, to come forth finely crumbled powder and be sampled, ton by ton, for the assays by old Undertaker Chastine and the three other men of his type, without which no sampler pays for ore. Bittson approached, grinning.

"You guessed just about right," he announced. "That stuff 's running right around two hundred dollars a ton. Need any money now?"

"All you can let me have!"

"Four or five hundred? We 've gotten in eight tons of that stuff already; don't guess I 'd be taking any risk on that!" he chuckled. Fairchild reached for the currency eagerly. All but a hundred dollars of it would go to Mother Howard,--for that debt must be paid off first. And, that accomplished, denying himself the invitation of rest that his bed held forth for him, he started out into town, apparently to loiter about the streets and receive the congratulations of the towns-people, but in reality to watch for one person and one alone,--Squint Rodaine!

He saw him late in the afternoon, shambling along, his eyes glaring, his lips moving wordlessly, and he took up the trail. But it led only to the office of the Silver Queen Development Company, where the scar-faced man doubled at his desk, and, stuffing a cigar into his mouth, chewed on it angrily. Instinctively Fairchild knew that the greatest part of his mean temper was due to the strike in the Blue Poppy; instinctively also he felt that Squint Rodaine had known of the value all along, that now he was cursing himself for the failure of his schemes to obtain possession of what had appeared until only a day before to be nothing more than a disappointing, unlucky, ill-omened hole in the ground. Fairchild resumed his loitering, but evening found him near the Silver Queen office.

Squint Rodaine did not leave for dinner. The light burned long in the little room, far past the usual closing time and until after the picture-show crowds had come and gone, while the man of the blue-white scar remained at his desk, staring at papers, making row after row of figures, and while outside, facing the chill and the cold of winter, Fairchild trod the opposite side of the street, careful that no one caught the import of his steady, sentry-like pace, yet equally careful that he did not get beyond a range of vision where he could watch the gleam of light from the office of the Silver Queen. Anita's note had told him little, yet had implied much. Something was fermenting in the seething brain of Squint Rodaine, and if the past counted for anything, it was something that concerned him.

An hour more, then Fairchild suddenly slunk into the shadows of a doorway. Squint had snapped out the light and was locking the door. A moment later he had passed him, his form bent, his shoulders hunched forward, his lips muttering some unintelligible jargon. Fifty feet more, then Fairchild stepped from the doorway and took up the trail.

It was not a hard one to follow. The night wind had brought more snow with it, to make a silent pad upon the sidewalks and to outline to Fairchild more easily

the figure which slouched before him. Gradually Robert dropped farther and farther in the rear; it gave him that much more protection, that much more surety in
trailing his quarry to wherever he might be bound.

And it was a certainty that the destination was not home. Squint Rodaine
passed the street leading to his house without even looking up. Two blocks more,
and they reached the city limits. But Squint kept on, and far in the rear, watching
carefully every move, Fairchild followed his quarry's shadow.

A mile, and they were in the open country, crossing and recrossing the ice-dot-
ted Clear Creek. A furlong more, then Fairchild went to his knees that he might use
the snow for a better background. Squint Rodaine had turned up the lane which
led to a great, shambling, old, white building that, in the rosy days of the mining
game, had been a roadhouse with its roulette wheels, its bar, its dining tables and its
champagne, but which now, barely furnished in only a few of its rooms, inhabited
by mountain rats and fluttering bats and general decay for the most part, formed the
uncomfortable abode of Crazy Laura!

And Fairchild followed. It could mean only one thing when Rodaine sought
the white-haired, mumbling old hag whom once he had called his wife. It could
mean but one outcome, and that of disaster for some one. Mother Howard had said
that Crazy Laura would kill for Squint. Fairchild felt sure that once, at least, she
had lied for him, so that the name of Thornton Fairchild might be branded as that
of a murderer and that his son might be set down in the community as a person of
ill-intent and one not to be trusted. And now that Squint Rodaine was seeking her
once more, Fairchild meant to follow, and to hear--if such a thing were within the
range of human possibility--the evil drippings of his crooked lips.

He crossed to the side of the road where ran the inevitable gully and taking
advantage of the shelter, hurried forward, smiling grimly in the darkness at the
memory of the fact that things were now reversed; that he was following Squint
Rodaine as Rodaine once had followed him. Swiftly he moved, closer--closer; the
scar-faced man went through the tumble-down gate and approached the house, not
knowing that his pursuer was less than fifty yards away!

A moment of cautious waiting then, in which Fairchild did not move. Finally a
light showed in an upstairs room of the house, and Fairchild, masking his own footprints in those made by Rodaine, crept to the porch. Swiftly, silently, protected by

the pad of snow on the soles of his shoes, he made the doorway and softly tried the lock. It gave beneath his pressure, and he glided within the dark hallway, musty and dusty in its odor, forbidding, evil and dark. A mountain rat, already disturbed by the entrance of Rodaine, scampered across his feet, and Fairchild shrunk into a corner, hiding himself as best he could in case the noise should cause an investigation from above. But it did not. Now Fairchild could hear voices, and in a moment more they became louder, as a door opened.

"It don't make any difference! I ain't going to stand for it! I tell you to do something and you go and make a mess of it! Why did n't you wait until they were both there?"

"I--I thought they were, Roady!" The woman's voice was whining, pleading. "Ain't you going to kiss me?"

"No, I ain't going to kiss you. You went and made a mess of things."

"You kissed me the night our boy was born. Remember that, Roady? Don't you remember how you kissed me then?"

"That was a long time ago, and you were a different woman then. You 'd do what I 'd tell you."

"But I do now, Roady. Honest, I do. I 'll do anything you tell me to--if you 'll just be good to me. Why don't you hold me in your arms any more--?"

A scuffling sound came from above. Fairchild knew that she had made an effort to clasp him to her, and that he had thrust her away. The voices came closer.

"You know what you got us into, don't you? They made a strike there to-day--same value as in the Silver Queen. If it had n't been for you--"

"But they get out someway--they always get out." The voice was high and weird now. "They 're immortal. That's what they are--they 're immortal. They have the gift--they can get out--"

"Bosh! Course they get out when you wait until after they 're gone. Why, one of 'em was downtown at the assayer's, so I understand, when you went in there."

"But the other--he 's immortal. He got out--"

"You're crazy!"

"Yes, crazy!" She suddenly shrieked at the word. "That's what they all call me--Crazy Laura. And you call me Crazy Laura too, when my back 's turned. But I ain't--hear me--I ain't! I know--they're immortal, just like the others were immortal! I can't hold 'em when they 've got the spirit that rises above--I 've tried, ain't I--and I 've only got one!"

"One?" Squint's voice became suddenly excited. "One--what one?"

"I 'm not going to tell. But I know--Crazy Laura--that's what they call me--and they give me a sulphur pillow to sleep on. But I know--I know!"

There was silence then for a moment, and Fairchild, huddled in the darkness below, felt the creeping, crawling chill of horror pass over him as he listened. Above were a rogue and a lunatic, discussing between them what, at times, seemed to concern him and his partner; more, it seemed to go back to other days, when other men had worked the Blue Poppy and met misfortunes. A bat fluttered about, just passing his face, its vermin-covered wings sending the musty air close against his cringing flesh. Far at the other side of the big hall a mountain rat resumed its gnawing. Then it ceased. Squint Rodaine was talking again.

"So you 're not going to tell me about 'the one', eh? What have you got this door shut for?"

"No door 's shut."

"It is--don't you think I can see? This door leading into the front room."

The sound of heavy shoes, followed by a lighter tread. Then a scream above which could be heard the jangling of a rusty lock and the bumping of a shoulder against wood. High and strident came Crazy Laura's voice:

"Stay out of there--I tell you, Roady! Stay out of there! It's something that mortals should n't see--it's something--stay out--stay out!"

"I won't--unlock this door!"

"I can't do it--the time has n't come yet--I must n't--"

"You won't--well, there 's another way." A crash, the sudden, stumbling feet of a man, then the scratching of a match and an exclamation: "So this is your immortal, eh?"

Only a moaning answered, moaning intermingled with some vague form of a weird chant, the words of which Fairchild in the musty, dark hall below could not distinguish. At last came Squint's voice again, this time in softened tones:

"Laura--Laura, honey."

"Yes, Squint."

"Why did n't you tell your sweetheart about this?"

"I must n't--you 've spoiled it now, Roady."

"No--Honey. I can show you the way. He 's nearly gone. What were you going to do when he went--?"

"He 'd have dissolved in air, Roady--I know. The spirits have told me."

"Perhaps so." The voice of the scar-faced, mean-visaged Squint Rodaine was still honeyed, still cajoling. "Perhaps so--but not at once. Is n't there a barrel of lime in the basement?"

"Yes."

"Come downstairs with me."

They started downward then, and Fairchild, creeping as swiftly as he could, hurried under the protection of the rotten casing, where the wainscoting had dropped away with the decay of years. There he watched them pass, Rodaine in the lead, carrying a smoking lamp with its half-broken chimney careening on the base. Crazy Laura, mumbling her toothless gums, her hag-like hands extended before her, shuffling along in the rear. He heard them go far to the rear of the house, then descend more stairs. And he went flat to his stomach on the floor, with his ear against a tiny chink that he might hear the better. Squint still was talking in his loving tones.

"See, Honey," he was saying. "I 've--I 've broken the spell by going in upstairs. You should have told me. I did n't know--I just thought--well, I thought there was some one in there you liked, and I got jealous."

"Did you, Roady?" She cackled. "Did you?"

"Yes--I did n't know you had **him** there. And you were making him immortal?"

"I found him, Roady. His eyes were shut, and he was bleeding. It was at dusk, and nobody saw him when I carried him in here. Then I started giving him the herbs--"

"That you 've gathered around at night?"

"Yes--where the dead sleep. I get the red berries most. That's the blood of the dead, come to life again."

The quaking, crazy voice from below caused Fairchild to shiver with a sudden cold that no warmth could eradicate. Still, however, he lay there listening, fearful that every move from below might bring a cessation of their conversation. But

Rodaine talked on.

"Of course, I know. But I 've spoiled that now. There's another way, Laura. Get that spade. See, the dirt's soft here. Dig a hole about four feet deep and six or seven feet long. Then put half that lime from the barrel in there. Understand?"

"What for?"

"It's the only way now; we 'll have to do that. It's the other way to immortality. You 've given him the herbs?"

"Yes."

"Then this is the end. See? Now do that, won't you, Honey?"

"You'll kiss me, Roady?"

"There!" The faint sound of a kiss came from below. "And there's another one. And another!"

"Just like the night our boy was born. Don't you remember how you bent over and kissed me then and held me in your arms?"

"I 'm holding you that way now, Honey--just the same way that I held you the night our boy was born. And I 'll help you with this. You dig the hole and put half the lime in there--don't put it all. We 'll need the rest to put on top of him. You 'll have it done in about two hours. There 's something else needed--some acid that I 've got to get. It 'll make it all the quicker. I 'll be back, Honey. Kiss me."

Fairchild, seeking to still the horror-laden quiver of his body, heard the sound of a kiss and then the clatter of a man's heavy shoes on the stairs, accompanied by a slight clink from below. He knew that sound,--the scraping of the steel of a spade against the earth as it was dragged into use. A moment more and Rodaine, mumbling to himself, passed out the door. But the woman did not come upstairs. Fairchild knew why: her crazed mind was following the instructions of the man who knew how to lead the lunatic intellect into the channels he desired; she was digging, digging a grave for some one, a grave to be lined with quicklime!

Now she was talking again and chanting, but Fairchild did not attempt to determine the meaning of it all. Upstairs was some one who had been found by this woman in an unconscious state and evidently kept in that condition through the potations of the ugly poison-laden drugs she brewed,--some one who now was doomed to die and to lie in a quicklime grave! Carefully Fairchild gained his feet; then, as silently as possible, he made for the rickety stairs, stopping now and again to listen for discovery from below. But it did not come; the insane woman was chanting louder than ever now. Fairchild went on.

He felt his way up the remaining stairs, a rat scampering before him; he sneaked along the wall, hands extended, groping for that broken door, finally to find it. Cautiously he peered within, striving in vain to pierce the darkness. At last, listening intently for the singing from below, he drew a match from his pocket and scratched it noiselessly on his trousers. Then, holding it high above his head, he looked toward the bed--and stared in horror!

A blood-encrusted face showed on the slipless pillow, while across the forehead was a jagged, red, untended wound. The mouth was open, the breathing was heavy and labored. The form was quite still, the eyes closed. And the face was that of Harry!

CHAPTER XXII

S o this explained, after a fashion, Harry's disappearance. This revealed why the search through the mountains had failed. This--

But Fairchild suddenly realized that now was not a time for conjecturing upon the past. The man on the bed was unconscious, incapable of helping himself. Far below, a white-haired woman, her toothless jaws uttering one weird chant after another, was digging for him a quicklime grave, in the insane belief that she was aiding in accomplishing some miracle of immortality. In time--and Fairchild did not know how long--an evil-visaged, scar-faced man would return to help her carry the inert frame of the unconscious man below and bury it. Nor could Fairchild tell from the conversation whether he even intended to perform the merciful act of killing the poor, broken being before he covered it with acids and quick-eating lime in a grave that soon would remove all vestige of human identity forever. Certainly now was not a time for thought; it was one for action!

And for caution. Instinct told Fairchild that for the present, at least, Rodaine must believe that Harry had escaped unaided. There were too many other things in which Robert felt sure Rodaine had played a part, too many other mysterious happenings which must be met and coped with, before the man of the blue-white scar could know that finally the underling was beginning to show fight, that at last the crushed had begun to rise. Fairchild bent and unlaced his shoes, taking off also the heavy woolen socks which protected his feet from the biting cold. Steeling himself to the ordeal which he must undergo, he tied the laces together and slung the footgear over a shoulder. Then he went to the bed.

As carefully as possible, he wrapped Harry in the blankets, seeking to protect him in every way against the cold. With a great effort, he lifted him, the sick man's frame huddled in his arms like some gigantic baby, and started out of the eerie, darkened house.

The stairs--the landing--the hall! Then a query from below:

"Is that you, Roady?"

The breath pulled sharp into Fairchild's lungs. He answered in the best imitation he could give of the voice of Squint Rodaine:

"Yes. Go on with your digging, Honey. I 'll be there soon."

"And you'll kiss me?"

"Yes. Just like I kissed you the night our boy was born."

It was sufficient. The chanting began again, accompanied by the swish of the spade as it sank into the earth and the cludding roll of the clods as they were thrown to one side. Fairchild gained the door. A moment more and he staggered with his burden into the protecting darkness of the night.

The snow crept about his ankles, seeming to freeze them at every touch, but Fairchild did not desist. His original purpose must be carried out if Rodaine were not to know,--the appearance that Harry had aroused himself sufficiently to wrap the blankets about him and wander off by himself. And this could be accomplished only by the pain and cold and torture of a barefoot trip.

Some way, by shifting the big frame of his unconscious partner now and then, Fairchild made the trip to the main road and veered toward the pumphouse of the Diamond J. mine, running as it often did without attendance while the engineer made a trip with the electric motor into the hill. Cautiously he peered through the windows. No one was there. Beyond lay warmth and comfort--and a telephone. Fairchild went within and placed Harry on the floor. Then he reached for the 'phone and called the hospital.

"Hello!" he announced in a husky, disguised voice. "This is Jeb Gresham of Georgeville. I 've just found a man lying by the side of the Diamond J. pumphouse, unconscious, with a big cut in his head. I 've brought him inside. You 'll find him there; I 've got to go on. Looks like he 's liable to die unless you can send the ambulance for him."

"We 'll make it a rush trip," came the answer, and Fairchild hung up the 'phone, to rub his half-frozen, aching feet a moment, then to reclothe them in the socks and shoes, watching the entrance of the Diamond J. tunnel as he did so. A long minute--then he left the pumphouse, made a few tracks in the snow around the entrance, and walked swiftly down the road. Fifteen minutes later, from a hiding place at the side of the Clear Creek bridge, he saw the lights of the ambulance as it swerved to the pumphouse. Out came the stretcher. The attendants went in search of the injured man. When they came forth again, they bore the form of Harry Harkins, and the heart of Fairchild began to beat once more with something resembling regularity. His partner--at least such was his hope and his prayer--was on the way to aid and to recovery, while Squint Rodaine would know nothing other than that he had wandered away! Grateful, lighter in heart than he had been for days. Fairchild plodded along the road in the tracks of the ambulance, as it headed back for town.

The news already had spread by the time he reached there; news travels fast in a small mining camp. Fairchild went to the hospital, and to the side of the cot where Harry had been taken, to find the doctor there before him, already bandaging the wound on Harry's head and looking with concern now and then at the pupils of the unconscious man's eyes.

"Are you going to stay here with him?" the physician asked, after he had finished the dressing of the laceration.

"Yes," Fairchild said, in spite of aching fatigue and heavy eyes. The doctor nodded.

"Good. I don't know whether he 's going to pull through or not. Of course, I can't say--but it looks to me from his breathing and his heart action that he 's not suffering as much from this wound as he is from some sort of poisoning.

"We 've given him apomorphine and it should begin to take effect soon. We 're using the batteries too. You say that you 're going to be here? That's a help. They 're shy a nurse on this floor to-night, and I 'm having a pretty busy time of it. I 'm very much afraid that poor old Judge Richmond 's going to lay down his cross before morning."

"He 's dying?" Fairchild said it with a clutching sensation at his throat. The physician nodded.

"There 's hardly a chance for him."

"You 're going there?"

"Yes."

"Will you please give--?"

The physician waited. Finally Fairchild shook his head.

"Never mind," he finished. "I thought I would ask you something--but it would be too much of a favor. Thank you just the same. Is there anything I can do here?"

"Nothing except to keep watch on his general condition. If he seems to be getting worse, call the interne. I 've left instructions with him."

"Very good."

The physician went on, and Fairchild took his place beside the bed of the unconscious Harry, his mind divided between concern for his faithful partner and the girl who, some time in the night, must say good-by forever to the father she loved. It had been on Fairchild's tongue to send her some sort of message by the physician, some word that would show her he was thinking of her and hoping for her. But he had reconsidered. Among those in the house of death might be Maurice Rodaine, and Fairchild did not care again to be the cause of such a scene as had happened on the night of the Old Times dance.

Judge Richmond was dying. What would that mean? What effect would it have upon the engagement of Anita and the man Fairchild hoped that she detested? What--then he turned at the entrance of the interne with the batteries.

"If you 're going to be here all night," said the white-coated individual, "it 'll help me out a lot if you 'll use these batteries for me. Put them on at their full force and apply them to his cheeks, his hands, his wrists and the soles of his feet alternately. From the way he acts, there 's some sort of morphinic poisoning. We can't tell what it is--except that it acts like a narcotic. And about the only way we can pull him out is with these applications."

The interne turned over the batteries and went on about his work, while Fairchild, hoping within his heart that he had not placed an impediment in the way of Harry's recovery by not telling what he knew of Crazy Laura and her concoctions, began his task. Yet he was relieved by the knowledge that such information could aid but little. Nothing but a chemical analysis could show the contents of the strange brews which the insane woman made from her graveyard herbiage, and long before that could come, Harry might be dead. And so he pressed the batteries against the unconscious man's cheeks, holding them there tightly, that the full shock of the electricity might permeate the skin and arouse the sluggish blood once more to action. Then to the hands, the wrists, the feet and back again; it was the beginning of a routine that was to last for hours.

Midnight came and early morning. With dawn, the figure on the bed stirred slightly and groaned. Fairchild looked up, to see the doctor just entering.

"I think he 's regaining consciousness."

"Good." The physician brought forth his hypodermic. "That means a bit of rest for me. A little shot in the arm, and he ought to be out of danger in a few hours."

Fairchild watched him as he boiled the needle over the little gas jet at the head of the cot, then dissolved a white pellet preparatory to sending a resuscitory fluid into Harry's arm.

"You 've been to Judge Richmond's?" he asked at last.

"Yes." Then the doctor stepped close to the bed. "I 've just closed his eyes-- forever."

Ten minutes later, after another examination of Harry's pupils, he was gone, a weary, tired figure, stumbling home to his rest--rest that might be disturbed at any moment--the reward of the physician. As for Fairchild, he sat a long time in thought, striving to find some way to send consolation to the girl who was grieving now, struggling to figure a means of telling her that he cared, that he was sorry, and that his heart hurt too. But there was none.

Again a moan from the man on the bed, and at last a slight resistance to the sting of the batteries. An hour passed, two; gradually Harry came to himself, to stare about him in a wondering, vacant manner and then to fasten his eyes upon Fairchild. He seemed to be struggling for speech, for cooerdination of ideas. Finally, after many minutes--

"That's you, Boy?"

"Yes, Harry."

"But where are we?"

Fairchild laughed softly.

"We 're in a hospital, and you 're knocked out. Don't you know where you 've been?"

"I don't know anything, since I slid down the wall."

"Since you what?"

But Harry had lapsed back into semi-consciousness again, to lie for hours a mumbling, dazed thing, incapable of thought or action. And it was not until late in the night after the rescue, following a few hours of rest forced upon him by the interne, that Fairchild once more could converse with his stricken partner.

"It's something I 'll 'ave to show you to explain," said Harry. "I can't tell you about it. You know where that little fissure is in the 'anging wall, away back in the stope?"

"Yes."

"Well, that's it. That's where I got out."

"But what happened before that?"

"What didn't 'appen?" asked Harry, with a painful grin. "Everything in the world 'appened. I--but what did the assay show?"

Fairchild reached forth and laid a hand on the brawny one of his partner.

"We 're rich, Harry," he said, "richer than I ever dreamed we could be. The ore's as good as that of the Silver Queen!"

"The bloody 'ell it is!" Then Harry dropped back on his pillow for a long time and simply grinned at the ceiling. Somewhat anxious. Fairchild leaned forward, but his partner's eyes were open and smiling. "I 'm just letting it sink in!" he announced, and Fairchild was silent, saving his questions until "it" had sunk. Then:

"You were saying something about that fissure?"

"But there is other things first. After you went to the assayers, I fooled around there in the chamber, and I thought I 'd just take a flyer and blow up them 'oles that I 'd drilled in the 'anging wall at the same time that I shot the other. So I put in the powder and fuses, tamped 'em down and then I thinks thinks I, that there's somebody moving around in the drift. But I did n't pay any attention to it--you know. I was busy and all that, and you often 'ear noises that sound funny. So I set 'em off--that is, I lit the fuses and I started to run. Well, I 'ad n't any more 'n started when bloeyy-y-y-y, right in front of me, the whole world turned upside down, and I felt myself knocked back into the chamber. And there was them fuses. All of 'em burning. Well, I managed to pull out the one from the foot wall and stamp it out, but I didn't 'ave time to get at the others. And the only place where there was a chance for me was clear at the end of the chamber. Already I was bleeding like a stuck hog where a whole 'arf the mountain 'ad 'it me on the 'ead, and I did n't know much what I was doing. I just wanted to get be'ind something--that's all I could think of. So I shied for that fissure in the rocks and crawled back in there, trying to squeeze as far along as I could. And 'ere 's the funny part of it--I kept on going!"

"You what?"

"Kept on going. I 'd always thought it was just a place where the 'anging wall 'ad slipped, and that it stopped a few feet back. But it don't--it goes on. I crawled along it as fast as I could--I was about woozy, anyway--and by and by I 'eard the shots go off be'ind me. But there was n't any use in going back--the tunnel was caved in. So I kept on.

"I don't know 'ow long I went or where I went at. It was all dark--and I was about knocked out. After while, I ran into a stream of water that came out of the inside of the 'ill somewhere, and I took a drink. It gave me a bit of strength. And then I kept on some more--until all of a sudden, I slipped and fell, just when I was beginning to see dyelight. And that's all I know. 'Ow long 'ave I been gone?"

"Long enough to make me gray-headed," Fairchild answered with a little laugh. Then his brow furrowed. "You say you slipped and fell just as you were beginning to see daylight?"

"Yes. It looked like it was reflected from below, somewyes."

Fairchild nodded.

"Is n't there quite a spring right by Crazy Laura's house?"

"Yes; it keeps going all year; there 's a current and it don't freeze up. It comes out like it was a waterfall--and there 's a roaring noise be'ind it."

"Then that's the explanation. You followed the fissure until it joined the natural tunnel that the spring has made through the hills. And when you reached the waterfall--well, you fell with it."

"But 'ow did I get 'ere?"

Briefly Fairchild told him, while Harry pawed at his still magnificent mustache. Robert continued:

"But the time 's not ripe yet, Harry, to spring it. We 've got to find out more about Rodaine first and what other tricks he 's been up to. And we 've got to get other evidence than merely our own word. For instance, in this case, you can't remember anything. All the testimony I could give would be unsupported. They 'd run me out of town if I even tried to start any such accusation. But one thing 's certain: We 're on the open road at last, we know who we 're fighting and the weapons he fights with. And if we 're only given enough time, we 'll whip him. I 'm going home to bed now; I 've got to be up early in the morning and get hold of

Farrell. Your case comes up at court."

"And I 'm up in a 'ospital!"

Which fact the court the next morning recognized, on the testimony of the interne, the physician and the day nurses of the hospital, to the extent of a continuance until the January term in the trial of the case. A thing which the court further recognized was the substitution of five thousand dollars in cash for the deeds of the Blue Poppy mine as security for the bailee. And with this done, the deeds to his mine safe in his pocket, Fairchild went to the bank, placed the papers behind the great steel gates of the safety deposit vault, and then crossed the street to the telegraph office. A long message was the result, and a money order to Denver that ran beyond a hundred dollars. The instructions that went with it to the biggest florist in town were for the most elaborate floral design possible to be sent by express for Judge Richmond's funeral--minus a card denoting the sender. Following this, Fairchild returned to the hospital, only to find Mother Howard taking his place beside the bed of Harry. One more place called for his attention,--the mine.

The feverish work was over now. The day and night shifts no longer were needed until Harry and Fairchild could actively assume control of operations and themselves dig out the wealth to put in the improvements necessary to procure the compressed air and machine drills, and organize the working of the mine upon the scale which its value demanded. But there was one thing essential, and Fairchild procured it,--guards. Then he turned his attention to his giant partner.

Health returned slowly to the big Cornishman. The effects of nearly a week of slow poisoning left his system grudgingly; it would be a matter of weeks before he could be the genial, strong giant that he once had represented. And in those weeks Fairchild was constantly beside him.

Not that there were no other things which were represented in Robert's desires,--far from it. Stronger than ever was Anita Richmond in Fairchild's thoughts now, and it was with avidity that he learned every scrap of news regarding her, as brought to him by Mother Howard. Hungrily he listened for the details of how she had weathered the shock of her father's death; anxiously he inquired for her return in the days following the information--via Mother Howard--that she had gone on a short trip to Denver to look after matters pertaining to her father's estate. Dully he heard that she had come back, and that Maurice Rodaine had told friends that the passing of the Judge had caused only a slight postponement in their marital plans. And perhaps it was this which held Fairchild in check, which caused him to wonder at the vagaries of the girl--a girl who had thwarted the murderous plans of a future father-in-law--and to cause him to fight down a desire to see her, an attempt to talk to her and to learn directly from her lips her position toward him,--and toward the Rodaines.

Finally, back to his normal strength once more, Harry rose from the armchair by the window of the boarding house and turned to Fairchild.

"We 're going to work to-night," he announced calmly.

"When?" Fairchild did not believe he understood. Harry grinned. "To-night. I 've taken a notion. Rodaine 'll expect us to work in the daytime. We 'll fool 'im. We 'll leave the guards on in the daytime and work at night. And what's more, we 'll keep a guard on at the mouth of the shaft while we 're inside, not to let nobody down. See?"

Fairchild agreed. He knew Squint Rodaine was not through. And he knew also that the fight against the man with the blue-white scar had only begun. The cross-cut had brought wealth and the promise of riches to Fairchild and Harry for the rest of their lives. But it had not freed them from the danger of one man,--a man who was willing to kill, willing to maim, willing to do anything in the world, it seemed, to achieve his purpose. Harry's suggestion was a good one.

Together, when night came, they bundled their greatcoats about them and pulled their caps low over their ears. Winter had come in earnest, winter with a blizzard raging through the town on the breast of a fifty-mile gale. Out into it the two men went, to fight their way though the swirling, frigid fleece to Kentucky Gulch and upward. At last they passed the guard, huddled just within the tunnel, and clambered down the ladder which had been put in place by the sight-seers on the day of the strike. Then--

Well, then Harry ran, to do much as Fairchild had done, to chuckle and laugh and toss the heavy bits of ore about, to stare at them in the light of his carbide torch, and finally to hurry into the new stope which had been fashioned by the hired miners in Fairchild's employ and stare upward at the heavy vein of riches above him.

"Wouldn't it knock your eyes out?" he exclaimed, beaming. "That vein 's certainly five feet wide."

"And two hundred dollars to the ton," added Fairchild, laughing. "No wonder Rodaine wanted it."

"I 'll sye so!" exclaimed Harry, again to stand and stare, his mouth open, his mustache spraying about on his upper lip in more directions than ever. A long time of congratulatory celebration, then Harry led the way to the far end of the great cavern. "'Ere it is!" he announced, as he pointed to what had seemed to both of them never to be anything more than a fissure in the rocks. "It's the thing that saved my life."

Fairchild stared into the darkness of the hole in the earth, a narrow crack in the rocks barely large enough to allow a human form to squeeze within. He laughed.

"You must have made yourself pretty small, Harry."

"What? When I went through there? Sye, I could 'ave gone through the eye of a needle. There were six charges of dynamite just about to go off be'ind me!"

Again the men chuckled as they looked at the fissure, a natural, usual thing in a mine, and often leading, as this one did, by subterranean breaks and slips to the underground bed of some tumbling spring. Suddenly, however, Fairchild whirled with a thought.

"Harry! I wonder--couldn't it have been possible for my father to have escaped from this mine in the same way?"

"'E must 'ave."

"And that there might not have been any killing connected with Larsen at all? Why couldn't Larsen have been knocked out by a flying stone--just like you were? And why--?"

"'E might of, Boy." But Harry's voice was negative. "The only thing about it was the fact that your father 'ad a bullet 'ole in 'is 'ead." Harry leaned forward and pointed to his own scar. "It 'it right about 'ere, and glanced. It did n't 'urt 'im much, and I bandaged it and then covered it with 'is 'at, so nobody could see."

"But the gun? We did n't find any."

"'E 'ad it with 'im. It was Sissie Larsen's. No, Boy, there must 'ave been a fight--but don't think that I mean your father murdered anybody. If Sissie Larsen attacked 'im with a gun, then 'e 'ad a right to kill. But as I 've told you before--there would n't 'ave been a chance for 'im to prove 'is story with Squint working against 'im. And that's one reason why I did n't ask any questions. And neither did Mother

'Oward. We were willing to take your father's word that 'e 'ad n't done anything wrong--and we were willing to 'elp 'im to the limit."

"You did it, Harry."

"We tried to--" He ceased and perked his head toward the bottom of the shaft, listening intently. "Did n't you 'ear something?"

"I thought so. Like a woman's voice."

"Listen--there it is again!"

They were both silent, waiting for a repetition of the sound. Faintly it came, for the third time:

"Mr. Fairchild!"

They ran to the foot of the shaft, and Fairchild stared upward. But he could see no one. He cupped his hands and called:

"Who wants me?"

"It's me." The voice was plainer now--a voice that Fairchild recognized immediately.

"I 'm--I 'm under arrest or something up here," was added with a laugh. "The guard won't let me come down."

"Wait, and I 'll raise the bucket for you. All right, guard!" Then, blinking with surprise, he turned to the staring Harry. "It's Anita Richmond," he whispered. Harry pawed for his mustache.

"On a night like this? And what the bloody 'ell is she doing 'ere, any'ow?"

"Search me!" The bucket was at the top now.

A signal from above, and Fairchild lowered it, to extend a hand and to aid the girl to the ground, looking at her with wondering, eager eyes. In the light of the carbide torch, she was the same boyish appearing little person he had met on the Denver road, except that snow had taken the place of dust now upon the whipcord riding habit, and the brown hair which caressed the corners of her eyes was moist with the breath of the blizzard. Some way Fairchild found his voice, lost for a moment.

"Are--are you in trouble?"

"No." She smiled at him.

"But out on a night like this--in a blizzard. How did you get up here?"

She shrugged her shoulders.

"I walked. Oh," she added, with a smile, "it did n't hurt me any. The wind was pretty stiff--but then I 'm fairly strong. I rather enjoyed it."

"But what's happened--what's gone wrong? Can I help you with anything--or--"

Then it was that Harry, with a roll of his blue eyes and a funny waggle of his big shoulders, moved down the drift toward the stope, leaving them alone together. Anita Richmond watched after him with a smile, waiting until he was out of hearing distance. Then she turned seriously.

"Mother Howard told me where you were," came quietly. "It was the only chance I had to see you. I--I--maybe I was a little lonely or--or something. But, anyway, I wanted to see you and thank you and--"

"Thank me? For what?"

"For everything. For that day on the Denver road, and for the night after the Old Times dance when you came to help me. I--I have n't had an easy time. And I 've been in rather an unusual position. Most of the people I know are afraid and--some of them are n't to be trusted. I--I could n't go to them and confide in them. And--you--well, I knew the Rodaines were your enemies--and I 've rather liked you for it."

"Thank you. But--" and Fairchild's voice became a bit frigid--"I have n't been able to understand everything. You are engaged to Maurice Rodaine."

"I was, you mean."

"Then--"

"My engagement ended with my father's death," came slowly--and there was a catch in her voice. "He wanted it--it was the one thing that held the Rodaines off him. And he was dying slowly--it was all I could do to help him, and I promised. But--when he went--I felt that my--my duty was over. I don't consider myself bound to him any longer."

"You 've told Rodaine so?"

"Not yet. I--I think that maybe that was one reason I wanted to see some one whom I believed to be a friend. He 's coming after me at midnight. We 're to go away somewhere."

"Rodaine? Impossible!"

"They 've made all their plans. I--I wondered if you--if you 'd be somewhere around the house--if you 'd--"

"I 'll be there. I understand." Fairchild had reached out and touched her arm. "I--want to thank you for the opportunity. I--yes, I 'll be there," came with a short laugh. "And Harry too. There'll be no trouble--from the Rodaines!"

She came a little closer to him then and looked up at him with trustful eyes, all the brighter in the spluttering light of the carbide.

"Thank you--it seems that I 'm always thanking you. I was afraid--I did n't know where to go--to whom to turn. I thought of you. I knew you 'd help me--women can guess those things."

"Can they?" Fairchild asked it eagerly. "Then you 've guessed all along that--"

But she smiled and cut in.

"I want to thank you for those flowers. They were beautiful."

"You knew that too? I didn't send a card."

"They told me at the telegraph office that you had wired for them. They--meant a great deal to me."

"It meant more to me to be able to send them." Then Fairchild stared with a sudden idea. "Maurice 's coming for you at midnight. Why is it necessary that you be there?"

"Why--" the idea had struck her too--"it is n't. I--I just had n't thought of it. I was too badly scared, I guess. Everything 's been happening so swiftly since--since you made the strike up here."

"With them?"

"Yes, they 've been simply crazy about something. You got my note?"

"Yes."

"That was the beginning. The minute Squint Rodaine heard of the strike, I thought he would go out of his head. I was in the office--I 'm vice-president of the firm, you know," she added with a sarcastic laugh. "They had to do something to make up for the fact that every cent of father's money was in it."

"How much?" Fairchild asked the question with no thought of being rude--and she answered in the same vein.

"A quarter of a million. They 'd been getting their hands on it more and more ever since father became ill. But they could n't entirely get it into their own power until the Silver Queen strike--and then they persuaded him to sign it all over in my name into the company. That's why I 'm vice-president."

"And is that why you arranged things to buy this mine?" Fairchild knew the answer before it was given.

"I? I arrange--I never thought of such a thing."

"I felt that from the beginning. An effort was made through a lawyer in Denver who hinted you were behind it. Some way, I felt differently. I refused. But you said they were going away?"

"Yes. They 've been holding conferences--father and son--one after another. I 've had more peace since the strike here than at any time in months. They 're both excited about something. Last night Maurice came to me and told me that it was necessary for them all to go to Chicago where the head offices would be established, and that I must go with him. I did n't have the strength to fight him then--there was n't anybody near by who could help me. So I--I told him I 'd go. Then I lay awake all night, trying to think out a plan--and I thought of you."

"I 'm glad." Fairchild touched her small gloved hand then, and she did not draw it away. His fingers moved slowly under hers. There was no resistance. At last his hand closed with a tender pressure,--only to release her again. For there had come a laugh--shy, embarrassed, almost fearful--and the plea:

"Can we go back where Harry is? Can I see the strike again?"

Obediently Fairchild led the way, beyond the big cavern, through the cross-cut and into the new stope, where Harry was picking about with a gad, striving to find a soft spot in which to sink a drill. He looked over his shoulder as they entered and grinned broadly.

"Oh," he exclaimed, "a new miner!"

"I wish I were," she answered. "I wish I could help you."

"You 've done that, all right, all right." Harry waved his gad. "'E told me--about the note!"

"Did it do any good?" she asked the question eagerly. Harry chuckled.

"I 'd 'ave been a dead mackerel if it 'ad n't," came his hearty explanation. "Where you going at all dressed up like that?"

"I 'm supposed," she answered with a smile toward Fairchild, "to go to Center City at midnight. Squint Rodaine 's there and Maurice and I are supposed to join him. But--but Mr. Fairchild 's promised that you and he will arrange it otherwise."

"Center City? What's Squint doing there?"

"He does n't want to take the train from Ohadi for some reason. We 're all going East and--"

But Harry had turned and was staring upward, apparently oblivious of their presence. His eyes had become wide, his head had shot forward, his whole being had become one of strained attention. Once he cocked his head, then, with a sudden exclamation, he leaped backward.

"Look out!" he exclaimed. "'Urry, look out!"

"But what is it?"

"It's coming down! I 'eard it!" Excitedly he pointed above, toward the black vein of lead and silver. "'Urry for that 'ole in the wall--'urry, I tell you!" He ran past them toward the fissure, yelling at Fairchild. "Pick 'er up and come on! I tell you I 'eard the wall moving--it's coming down, and if it does, it 'll bust in the 'ole tunnel!"

CHAPTER XXIII

Hardly realizing what he was doing or why he was doing it, Fairchild seized Anita in his arms, and raising her to his breast as though she were a child, rushed out through the cross-cut and along the cavern to the fissure, there to find Harry awaiting them.

"Put 'er in first!" said the Cornishman anxiously. "The farther the safer. Did you 'ear anything more?"

Fairchild obeyed, shaking his head in a negative to Harry's question, then squeezed into the fissure, edging along beside Anita, while Harry followed.

"What is it?" she asked anxiously.

"Harry heard some sort of noise from above, as if the earth was crumbling. He 's afraid the whole mine 's going to cave in again."

"But if it does?"

"We can get out this way--somehow. This connects up with a spring-hole; it leads out by Crazy Laura's house."

"Ugh!" Anita shivered. "She gives me the creeps!"

"And every one else; what's doing, Harry?"

"Nothing. That's the funny part of it!"

The big Cornishman had crept to the edge of the fissure and had stared for a moment toward the cross-cut leading to the stope. "If it was coming, it ought to 'ave showed up by now. I 'm going back. You stay 'ere."

"But--"

"Stay 'ere, I said. And," he grinned in the darkness, "don't let 'im 'old your 'and, Miss Richmond."

"Oh, you go on!" But she laughed. And Harry laughed with her.

"I know 'im. 'E 's got a wye about 'im."

"That's what you said about Miss Richmond once!"

"Have you two been talking about me?"

"Often." Then there was silence--for Harry had left the fissure to go into the stope and make an investigation. A long moment and he was back, almost creeping, and whispering as he reached the end of the fissure.

"Come 'ere--both of you! Come 'ere!"

"What is it?"

"Sh-h-h-h-h-h. Don't talk too loud. We 've been blessed with luck already. Come 'ere."

He led the way, the man and woman following him. In the stope the Cornishman crawled carefully to the staging, and standing on tiptoes, pressed his ear against the vein above him. Then he withdrew and nodded sagely.

"That's what it is!" came his announcement at last. "You can 'ear it!"

"But what?"

"Get up there and lay your ear against that vein. See if you 'ear anything. And be quiet about it. I 'm scared to make a move, for fear somebody 'll 'ear me."

Fairchild obeyed. From far away, carried by the telegraphy of the earth--and there are few conductors that are better--was the steady pound, pound, pound of shock after shock as it traveled along the hanging wall. Now and then a rumble intervened, as of falling rock, and scrambling sounds, like a heavy wagon passing over a bridge.

Fairchild turned, wondering, then reached for Anita.

"You listen," he ordered, as he lifted her to where she could hear. "Do you get anything?"

The girl's eyes shone.

"I know what that is," she said quickly. "I 've heard that same sort of thing before--when you 're on another level and somebody 's working above. Is n't that it, Mr. Harkins?"

Harry nodded.

"That's it," came tersely. Then bending, he reached for a pick, and muffling the sound as best he could between his knees, knocked the head from the handle. Following this, he lifted the piece of hickory thoughtfully and turned to Fairchild. "Get yourself one," he ordered. "Miss Richmond, I guess you 'll 'ave to stay 'ere. I don't see 'ow we can do much else with you."

"But can't I go along--wherever you 're going?"

"There's going to be a fight," said Harry quietly. "And I 'm going to knock somebody's block off!"

"But--I 'd rather be there than here. I--I don't have to get in it. And--I 'd want to see how it comes out. Please--!" she turned to Fairchild--"won't you let me go?"

"If you 'll stay out of danger."

"It's less danger for me there than--than home. And I 'd be scared to death here. I wouldn't if I was along with you two, because I know--" and she said it with almost childish conviction--"that you can whip 'em."

Harry chuckled.

"Come along, then. I 've got a 'unch, and I can't sye it now. But it 'll come out in the wash. Come along."

He led the way out through the shaft and into the blizzard, giving the guard instructions to let no one pass in their absence. Then he suddenly kneeled.

"Up, Miss Richmond. Up on my back. I 'm 'efty--and we 've got snowdrifts to buck."

She laughed, looked at Fairchild as though for his consent, then crawled to the broad back of Harry, sitting on his shoulders like a child "playing horse."

They started up the mountain side, skirting the big gullies and edging about the highest drifts, taking advantage of the cover of the pines, and bending against the force of the blizzard, which seemed to threaten to blow them back, step for step. No one spoke; instinctively Fairchild and Anita had guessed Harry's conclusions. The nearest mine to the Blue Poppy was the Silver Queen, situated several hundred feet above it in altitude and less than a furlong away. And the metal of the Silver Queen and the Blue Poppy, now that the strike had been made, had assayed almost identically the same. It was easy to make conclusions.

They reached the mouth of the Silver Queen. Harry relieved Anita from her position on his shoulders, and then reconnoitered a moment before he gave the signal to proceed. Within the tunnel they went, to follow along its regular, rising course to the stope where, on that garish day when Taylor Bill and Blindeye Bozeman had led the enthusiastic parade through the streets, the vein had shown. It was dark there--no one was at work. Harry unhooked his carbide from his belt, lit it and looked around. The stope was deeper now than on the first day, but not enough to make up for the vast amount of ore which had been taken out of the mine in the meanwhile. On the floor were tons of the metal, ready for tramming. Harry looked at them, then at the stope again.

"It ain't coming from 'ere!" he announced. "It's--" then his voice dropped to a whisper--"what's that?"

Again a rumbling had come from the distance, as of an ore car traveling over the tram tracks. Harry extinguished his light, and drawing Anita and Fairchild far to the end of the stope, flattened them and himself on the ground. A long wait, while the rumbling came closer, still closer; then, in the distance, a light appeared, shining from a side of the tunnel. A clanging noise, followed by clattering sounds, as though of steel rails hitting against each other. Finally the tramming once more,--and the light approached.

Into view came an ore car, and behind it loomed the great form of Taylor Bill as he pushed it along. Straight to the pile of ore he came, unhooked the front of the tram, tripped it and piled the contents of the car on top of the dump which already rested there. With that, carbide pointing the way, he turned back, pushing the tram before him. Harry crept to his feet.

"We 've got to follow!" he whispered. "It's a blind entrance to the tunnel som'eres."

They rose and trailed the light along the tracks, flattening themselves against the timbers of the tunnel as the form of Taylor Bill, faintly outlined in the distance, turned from the regular track, opened a great door in the side of the tunnel, which, to all appearances, was nothing more than the ordinary heavy timbering of a weak spot in the rocks, pulled it far back, then swerved the tram within. Then, he stopped and raised a portable switch, throwing it into the opening. A second later the door closed behind him, and the sound of the tram began to fade in the distance. Harry went forward, creeping along the side of the tunnel, feeling his way, stopping to listen now and then for the sound of the fading ore car. Behind him were Fairchild and Anita, following the same procedure. And all three stopped at once.

The hollow sound was coming directly to them now. Harry once more brought out his carbide to light it for a moment and to examine the timbering.

"It's a good job!" he commented. "You could n't tell it five feet off!"

"They 've made a cross-cut!" This time it was Anita's voice, plainly angry in spite of its whispering tones. "No wonder they had such a wonderful strike," came scathingly. "That other stope down there--"

"Ain't nothing but a salted proposition," said Harry. "They 've cemented up the top of it with the real stuff and every once in a while they blow a lot of it out and cement it up again to make it look like that's the real vein."

"And they 're working our mine!" Red spots of anger were flashing before Fairchild's eyes.

"You 've said it! That's why they were so anxious to buy us out. And that's why they started this two-million-dollar stock proposition, when they found they could n't do it. They knew if we ever 'it that vein that it would n't be any time until they 'd be caught on the job. That's why they 're ready to pull out--with somebody else 's million. They 're getting at the end of their rope. Another thing; that explains them working at night."

Anita gritted her teeth.

"I see it now--I can get the reason. They 've been telephoning Denver and holding conferences and all that sort of thing. And they planned to leave these two men behind here to take all the blame."

"They'll get enough of it!" added Harry grimly. "They 're miners. They could see that they were making a straight cross-cut tunnel on to our vein. They ain't no children, Blindeye and Taylor Bill. And 'ere 's where they start getting their trouble."

He pulled at the door and it yielded grudgingly. The three slipped past, following along the line of the tram track in the darkness, Harry's pick handle swinging beside him as they sneaked along. Rods that seemed miles; at last lights appeared in the distance. Harry stopped to peer ahead. Then he tossed aside his weapon.

"There 's only two of 'em--Blindeye and Taylor Bill. I could whip 'em both myself but I 'll take the big 'un. You--" he turned to Fairchild--"you get Blindeye."

"I 'll get him."

Anita stopped and groped about for a stone.

"I 'll be ready with something in case of accident," came with determination. "I 've got a quarter of a million in this myself!"

They went on, fifty yards, a hundred. Creeping now, they already were within the zone of light, but before them the two men, double-jacking at a "swimmer", had their backs turned. Onward--until Harry and Fairchild were within ten feet of the "high-jackers", while Anita waited, stone in hand, in the background. Came a yell, high-pitched, fiendish, racking, as Harry leaped forward. And before the two "high-jackers" could concentrate enough to use their sledge and drill as weapons, they were whirled about, battered against the hanging wall, and swirling in a daze of blows which seemed to come from everywhere at once. Wildly Harry yelled as he shot blow after blow into the face of an ancient enemy. High went Fairchild's voice as he knocked Blindeye Bozeman staggering for the third time against the hanging wall, only to see him rise and to knock him down once more. And from the edge of the zone of light came a feminine voice, almost hysterical with the excitement of it all, the voice of a girl who, in her tensity, had dropped the piece of stone she had carried, to stand there, hands clenched, figure doubled forward, eyes blazing, and crying:

"Hit him again! Hit him again! Hit him again--for me!"

And Fairchild hit, with the force of a sledge hammer. Dizzily the sandy-haired man swung about in his tracks, sagged, then fell, unconscious. Fairchild leaped upon him, calling at the same time to the girl:

"Find me a rope! I 'll truss his hands while he 's knocked out!"

Anita leaped into action, to kneel at Fairchild's side a moment later with a hempen strand, as he tied the man's hands behind his back. There was no need to worry about Harry. The yells which were coming from farther along the stope, the crackling blows, all told that Harry was getting along exceedingly well. Glancing out of a corner of his eye, Fairchild saw now that the big Cornishman had Taylor Bill flat on his back and was putting on the finishing touches. And then suddenly the exultant yells changed to ones of command.

"Talk English! Talk English, you bloody blighter! 'Ear me, talk English!"

"What's he mean?" Anita bent close to Fairchild.

"I don't know--I don't think Taylor Bill can talk anything else. Put your finger on this knot while I tighten it. Thanks."

Again the command had come from farther on:

"Talk English! 'Ear me--I'll knock the bloody 'ell out of you if you don't. Talk English--like this: 'Throw up your 'ands!' 'Ear me?"

Anita swerved swiftly and went to her feet. Harry looked up at her wildly, his mustache bristling like the spines of a porcupine.

"Did you 'ear 'im sye it?" he asked. "No? Sye it again!"

"Throw up your 'ands!" came the answer of the beaten man on the ground. Anita ran forward.

"It's a good deal like it," she answered. "But the tone was higher."

"Raise your tone!" commanded Harry, while Fairchild, finishing his job of tying his defeated opponent, rose, staring in wonderment. Then the answer came:

"That's it--that's it. It sounded just like it!"

And Fairchild remembered too,--the English accent of the highwayman on the night of the Old Times Dance. Harry seemed to bounce on the prostrate form of his ancient enemy.

"Bill," he shouted, "I 've got you on your back. And I 've got a right to kill you. 'Onest I 'ave. And I 'll do it too--unless you start talking. I might as well kill you as not.--It's a penitentiary offense to 'it a man underground unless there 's a good reason. So I 'm ready to go the 'ole route. So tell it--tell it and be quick about it. Tell it--was n't you him?"

"Him--who?" the voice was weak, frightened.

"You know 'oo--the night of the Old Times dance! Didn't you pull that 'old-up?"

There was a long silence. Finally:

"Where's Rodaine?"

"In Center City." It was Anita who spoke. "He 's getting ready to run away and leave you two to stand the brunt of all this trouble."

Again a silence. And again Harry's voice:

"Tell it. Was n't you the man?"

Once more a long wait. Finally:

"What do I get out of it?"

Fairchild moved to the man's side.

"My promise and my partner's promise that if you tell the whole truth, we 'll do what we can to get you leniency. And you might as well do it; there 's little chance of you getting away otherwise. As soon as we can get to the sheriff's office, we 'll have Rodaine under arrest, anyway. And I don't think that he 's going to hurt himself to help you. So tell the truth; weren't you the man who held up the Old Times dance?"

Taylor Bill's breath traveled slowly past his bruised lips.

"Rodaine gave me a hundred dollars to pull it," came finally.

"And you stole the horse and everything--"

"And cached the stuff by the Blue Poppy, so 's I 'd get the blame?" Harry wiggled his mustache fiercely. "Tell it or I 'll pound your 'ead into a jelly!"

"That's about the size of it."

But Fairchild was fishing in his pockets for pencil and paper, finally to bring them forth.

"Not that we doubt your sincerity, Bill," he said sarcastically, "but I think things would be a bit easier if you'd just write it out. Let him up, Harry."

The big Cornishman obeyed grudgingly. But as he did so, he shook a fist at his bruised, battered enemy.

"It ain't against the law to 'it a man when 'e 's a criminal," came at last. The thing was weighing on Harry's mind. "I don't care anyway if it is--"

"Oh, there 's nothing to that," Anita cut in. "I know all about the law--father has explained it to me lots of times when there 've been cases before him. In a thing of this kind, you 've got a right to take any kind of steps necessary. Stop worrying about it."

"Well," and Harry stood watching a moment as Taylor Bill began the writing of his confession, "it's such a relief to get four charges off my mind, that I did n't want to worry about any more. Make hit fulsome, Bill--tell just 'ow you did it!"

And Taylor Bill, bloody, eyes black, lips bruised, obeyed. Fairchild took the bescrawled paper and wrote his name as a witness, then handed it to Harry and Anita for their signatures. At last, he placed it in his pocket and faced the dolorous high-jacker.

"What else do you know, Bill?"

"About what? Rodaine? Nothing---except that we were in cahoots on this cross-cut. There is n't any use denying it"--there had come to the surface the inherent honor that is in every metal miner, a stalwartness that may lie dormant, but that, sooner or later, must rise. There is something about taking wealth from the earth that is clean. There is something about it which seems honest in its very nature, something that builds big men in stature and in ruggedness, and it builds an honor which fights against any attempt to thwart it. Taylor Bill was finding that honor now. He seemed to straighten. His teeth bit at his swollen, bruised lips. He turned and faced the three persons before him.

"Take me down to the sheriff's office," he commanded. "I 'll tell everything. I don't know so awful much--because I ain't tried to learn anything more than I could help. But I 'll give up everything I 've got."

"And how about him?" Fairchild pointed to Blindeye, just regaining consciousness. Taylor Bill nodded.

"He 'll tell--he 'll have to."

They trussed the big miner then, and dragging Bozeman to his feet, started out of the cross-cut with them. Harry's carbide pointing the way through the blind door and into the main tunnel. Then they halted to bundle themselves tighter against the cold blast that was coming from without. On--to the mouth of the mine. Then they stopped--short.

A figure showed in the darkness, on horseback. An electric flashlight suddenly flared against the gleam of the carbide. An exclamation, an excited command to the horse, and the rider wheeled, rushing down the mountain side, urging his mount to dangerous leaps, sending him plunging through drifts where a misstep might mean death, fleeing for the main road again. Anita Richmond screamed:

"That's Maurice! I got a glimpse of his face! He 's gotten away--go after him somebody--go after him!"

But it was useless. The horseman had made the road and was speeding down it. Rushing ahead of the others, Fairchild gained a point of vantage where he could watch the fading black smudge of the horse and rider as it went on and on along the rocky road, finally to reach the main thoroughfare and turn swiftly. Then he went back to join the others.

"He 's taken the Center City road!" came his announcement. "Is there a turn-off on it anywhere?"

"No." Anita gave the answer. "It goes straight through--but he 'll have a hard time making it there in this blizzard. If we only had horses!"

"They would n't do us much good now! Climb on my back as you did on Harry's. You can handle these two men alone?" This to his partner. The Cornishman grunted.

"Yes. They won't start anything. Why?"

"I 'm going to take Miss Richmond and hurry ahead to the sheriff's office. He might not believe me. But he 'll take her word--and that 'll be sufficient until you get there with the prisoners. I 've got to persuade him to telephone to Center City and head off the Rodaines!"

CHAPTER XXIV

He stooped and Anita, laughing at her posture, clambered upon his back, her arms about his neck, arms which seemed to shut out the biting blast of the blizzard as he staggered through the high-piled snow and downward to the road. There he continued to carry her; Fairchild found himself wishing that he could carry her forever, and that the road to the sheriff's office were twenty miles away instead of two. But her voice cut in on his wishes.

"I can walk now."

"But the drifts--"

"We can get along so much faster!" came her plea. "I 'll hold on to you--and you can help me along."

Fairchild released her and she seized his arm. For a quarter of a mile they hurried along, skirting the places where the snow had collected in breast-high drifts, now and then being forced nearly down to the bank of the stream to avoid the mountainous piles of fleecy white. Once, as they floundered through a knee-high mass, Fairchild's arm went quickly about her waist and he lifted her against him as he literally carried her through. When they reached the other side, the arm still held its place,--and she did not resist. Fairchild wanted to whistle, or sing, or shout. But breath was too valuable--and besides, what little remained had momentarily been taken from him. A small hand had found his, where it encircled her. It had rested there, calm and warm and enthralling, and it told Fairchild more than all the words in the world could have told just then--that she realized that his arm was about her--and that she wanted it there. Some way, after that, the stretch of road faded swiftly. Almost before he realized it, they were at the outskirts of the city.

Grudgingly he gave up his hold upon her, as they hurried for the sidewalks and for the sheriff's office. There Fairchild did not attempt to talk--he left it all to

Anita, and Bardwell, the sheriff, listened. Taylor Bill had confessed to the robbery at the Old Times dance and to his attempt to so arrange the evidence that the blame would fall on Harry. Taylor Bill and Blindeye Bozeman had been caught at work in a cross-cut tunnel which led to the property of the Blue Poppy mine, and one of them, at least, had admitted that the sole output of the Silver Queen had come from this thieving encroachment. Then Anita completed the recital,--of the plans of the Rodaines to leave and of their departure for Center City. At last, Fairchild spoke, and he told the happenings which he had encountered in the ramshackle house occupied by Crazy Laura. It was sufficient. The sheriff reached for the telephone.

"No need for hurry," he announced. "Young Rodaine can't possibly make that trip in less than two hours. How long did it take you to come down here?"

"About an hour, I should judge."

"Then we 've got plenty of time--hello--Central? Long distance, please. What's that? Yeh--Long Distance. Want to put in a call for Center City." A long wait, while a metallic voice streamed over the wire into the sheriff's ear. He hung up the receiver. "Blocked," he said shortly. "The wire 's down. Three or four poles fell from the force of the storm. Can't get in there before morning."

"But there 's the telegraph!"

"It 'd take half an hour to get the operator out of bed--office is closed. Nope. We 'll take the short cut. And we 'll beat him there by a half-hour!"

Anita started.

"You mean the Argonaut tunnel?"

"Yes. Call up there and tell them to get a motor ready for us to shoot straight through. We can make it at thirty miles an hour, and the skip in the Reunion Mine will get us to the surface in five minutes. The tunnel ends sixteen hundred feet underground, about a thousand feet from Center City," he explained, as he noted Fairchild's wondering gaze. "You stay here. We 've got to wait for those prisoners--and lock 'em up. I 'll be getting my car warmed up to take us to the tunnel."

Anita already was at the 'phone, and Fairchild sank into a chair, watching her with luminous eyes. The world was becoming brighter; it might be night, with a blizzard blowing, to every one else,--but to Fairchild the sun was shining as it never had shone before. A thumping sound came from without. Harry entered with his two charges, followed shortly by Bardwell, the sheriff, while just beneath the office window a motor roared in the process of "warming up." The sheriff looked from one to the other of the two men.

"These people have made charges against you," he said shortly. "I want to know a little more about them before I go any farther. They say you 've been high-jacking."

Taylor Bill nodded in the affirmative.

"And that you robbed the Old Times dance and framed the evidence against this big Cornishman?"

Taylor Bill scraped a foot on the floor.

"It's true. Squint Rodaine wanted me to do it. He 'd been trying for thirty years to get that Blue Poppy mine. There was some kind of a mix-up away back there that I did n't know much about--fact is, I did n't know anything. The Silver Queen didn't amount to much and when demonetization set in, I quit--you 'll re-member, Sheriff--and went away. I 'd worked for Squint before, and when I came back a couple of years ago, I naturally went to him for a job again. Then he put this proposition up to me at ten dollars a day and ten per cent. It looked too good to be turned down."

"How about you?" Bardwell faced Blindeye. The sandy lashes blinked and the weak eyes turned toward the floor.

"I--was in on it."

That was enough. The sheriff reached for his keys. A moment more and a steel door clanged upon the two men while the officer led the way to his motor car. There he looked quizzically at Anita Richmond, piling without hesitation into the front seat.

"You going too?"

"I certainly am," and she covered her intensity with a laugh, "there are a num-ber of things that I want to say to Mr. Maurice Rodaine--and I have n't the patience to wait!"

Bardwell chuckled. The doors of the car slammed and the engine roared louder than ever. Soon they were churning along through the driving snow toward the great buildings of the Argonaut Tunnel Company, far at the other end of town. There men awaited them, and a tram motor, together with its operator,--happy in the expectation of a departure from the usual routine of hauling out the long strings of ore and refuse cars from the great tunnel which, driving straight through the mountains, had been built in the boom days to cut the workings of mine after mine, relieving the owners of those holdings of the necessity of taking their product by the slow method of burro packs to the railroads, and gaining for the company a freight business as enriching as a bonanza itself. The four pursuers took their places on the benches of the car behind the motor. The trolley was attached. A great door was opened, allowing the cold blast of the blizzard to whine within the tunnel. Then, clattering over the frogs, green lights flashing from the trolley wire, the speeding journey was begun.

It was all new to Fairchild, engrossing, exciting. Close above them were the ragged rocks of the tunnel roof, seeming to reach down as if to seize them as they roared and clattered beneath. Seepage dripped at intervals, flying into their faces like spray as they dashed through it. Side tracks appeared momentarily when they passed the opening of some mine where the ore cars stood in long lines, awaiting their turn to be filled. The air grew warmer. The minutes were passing, and they were nearing the center of the tunnel. Great gateways sped past them; the motor smashed over sidetracks and spurs and switches as they clattered by the various mine openings, the operator reaching above him to hold the trolley steady as they went under narrow, low places where the timbers had been placed, thick and heavy, to hold back the sagging earth above.

Three miles, four, five, while Anita Richmond held close to Fairchild as the speed became greater and the sparks from the wire above threw their green, vicious light over the yawning stretch before them. A last spurt, slightly down-grade, with the motor pushing the wheels at their greatest velocity; then the crackling of electricity suddenly ceased, the motor slowed in its progress, finally to stop. The driver pointed to the right.

"Over there, sheriff--about fifty feet; that's the Reunion opening."

"Thanks!" They ran across the spur tracks in the faint light of a dirty incandescent, gleaming from above. A greasy being faced them and Bardwell, the sheriff, shouted his mission.

"Got to catch some people that are making a get-away through Center City. Can you send us up in the skip?"

"Yes, two at a time."

"All right!" The sheriff turned to Harry. "You and I 'll go on the first trip and hurry for the Ohadi road. Fairchild and Miss Richmond will wait for the second and go to Sheriff Mason's office and tell him what's up. Meet us there," he said to Fairchild, as he went forward. Already the hoist was working; from far above came the grinding of wheels on rails as the skip was lowered. A wave of the hand, then Bardwell and Harry entered the big, steel receptacle. At the wall the greasy work-man pulled three times on the electric signal; a moment more and the skip with its two occupants had passed out of sight.

A long wait followed while Fairchild strove to talk of many things,--and failed in all of them. Things were happening too swiftly for them to be put into crisp sentences by a man whose thoughts were muddled by the fact that beside him waited a girl in a whipcord riding suit--the same girl who had leaped from an automobile on the Denver highway and--

It crystallized things for him momentarily.

"I 'm going to ask you something after a while--something that I 've wondered and wondered about. I know it was n't anything--but--"

She laughed up at him.

"It did look terrible, didn't it?"

"Well, it would n't have been so mysterious if you had n't hurried away so quick. And then--"

"You really did n't think I was the Smelter bandit, did you?" the laugh still was on her lips. Fairchild scratched his head.

"Darned if I know what I thought. And I don't know what I think yet."

"But you 've managed to live through it."

"Yes--but--"

She touched his arm and put on a scowl.

"It's very, very awful!" came in a low, mock-awed voice. "But--" then the laugh came again--"maybe if you 're good and--well, maybe I 'll tell you after a while."

"Honest?"

"Of course I 'm honest! Is n't that the skip?"

Fairchild walked to the shaft. But the skip was not in sight. A long ten minutes they waited, while the great steel carrier made the trip to the surface with Harry and Sheriff Bardwell, then came lumbering down again. Fairchild stepped in and lifted Anita to his side.

The journey was made in darkness,--darkness which Fairchild longed to turn to his advantage, darkness which seemed to call to him to throw his arms about the girl at his side, to crush her to him, to seek out with an instinct that needed no guiding light the laughing, pretty lips which had caused him many a day of happiness, many a day of worried wonderment. He strove to talk away the desire--but the grinding of the wheels in the narrow shaft denied that. His fingers twitched, his arms trembled as he sought to hold back the muscles, then, yielding to the impulse, he started--

"Da-a-a-g-gone it!"

"What's the matter?"

"Nothing."

But Fairchild was n't telling the truth. They had reached the light just at the wrong, wrong moment. Out of the skip he lifted her, then inquired the way to the sheriff's office of this, a new county. The direction was given, and they went there. They told their story. The big-shouldered, heavily mustached man at the desk grinned cheerily.

"That there's the best news I 've heard in forty moons," he announced. "I always did hate that fellow. You say Bardwell and your partner went out on the Ohadi road to head the young 'un off?"

"Yes. They had about a fifteen-minute start on us. Do you think--?"

"We 'll wait here. They 're hefty and strong. They can handle him alone."

But an hour passed without word from the two Searchers. Two more went by. The sheriff rose from his chair, stamped about the room, and looked out at the night, a driving, aimless thing in the clutch of a blizzard.

"Hope they ain't lost," came at last.

"Had n't we better--?"

But a noise from without cut off the conversation. Stamping feet sounded on the steps, the knob turned, and Sheriff Bardwell, snow-white, entered, shaking himself like a great dog, as he sought to rid himself of the effects of the blizzard.

"Hello, Mason," came curtly.

"Hello, Bardwell, what 'd you find?"

The sheriff of Clear Creek county glanced toward Anita Richmond and was silent. The girl leaped to her feet.

"Don't be afraid to talk on my account," she begged. "Where's Harry? Is he all right? Did he come back with you?"

"Yes--he's back."

"And you found Maurice?"

Bardwell was silent again, biting at the end of his mustache. Then he squared himself.

"No matter how much a person dislikes another one--it's, it's--always a shock," came at last. Anita came closer.

"You mean that he 's dead?"

The sheriff nodded, and Fairchild came suddenly to his feet. Anita's face had grown suddenly old,--the oldness that precedes the youth of great relief.

"I 'm sorry--for any one who must die," came finally. "But perhaps--perhaps it was better. Where was he?"

"About a mile out. He must have rushed his horse too hard. The sweat was frozen all over it--nobody can push a beast like that through these drifts and keep it alive."

"He did n't know much about riding."

"I should say not. Did n't know much of anything when we got to him. He was just about gone--tried to stagger to his feet when we came up, but could n't make it. Kind of acted like he 'd lost his senses through fear or exposure or something. Asked me who I was, and I said Bardwell. Seemed to be tickled to hear my name--but he called it Barnham. Then he got up on his hands and knees and clutched at me and asked me if I 'd drawn out all the money and had it safe. Just to humor him, I said I had. He tried to say something after that, but it was n't much use. The first thing we knew he 'd passed out. That's where Harry is now--took him over to the mortuary. There isn't anybody named Barnham, is there?"

"Barnham?" The name had awakened recollections for Fairchild; "why he's the fellow that--"

But Anita cut in.

"He 's a lawyer in Denver. They 've been sending all the income from stock sales to him for deposit. If Maurice asked if he 'd gotten the money out, it must mean that they meant to run with all the proceeds. We 'll have to telephone Denver."

"Providing the line's working." Bardwell stared at the other sheriff. "Is it?"

"Yes--to Denver."

"Then let's get headquarters in a hurry. You know Captain Lee, don't you? You do the talking. Tell him to get hold of this fellow Barnham and pinch him, and then send him up to Ohadi in care of Pete Carr or some other good officer. We 've got a lot of things to say to him."

The message went through. Then the two sheriffs rose and looked at their revolvers.

"Now for the tough one." Bardwell made the remark, and Mason smiled grimly. Fairchild rose and went to them.

"May I go along?"

"Yes, but not the girl. Not this time."

Anita did not demur. She moved to the big rocker beside the old base burner and curled up in it. Fairchild walked to her side.

"You won't run away," he begged.

"I? Why?"

"Oh--I don't know. It--it just seems too good to be true!"

She laughed and pulled her cap from her head, allowing her wavy, brown hair to fall about her shoulders, and over her face. Through it she smiled up at him, and there was something in that smile which made Fairchild's heart beat faster than ever.

"I 'll be right here," she answered, and with that assurance, he followed the other two men out into the night.

Far down the street, where the rather bleak outlines of the hotel showed bleaker than ever in the frigid night, a light was gleaming in a second-story window. Mason turned to his fellow sheriff.

"He usually stays there. That must be him--waiting for the kid."

"Then we 'd better hurry--before somebody springs the news."

The three entered, to pass the drowsy night clerk, examine the register and to find that their conjecture had been correct. Tiptoeing, they went to the door and knocked. A high-pitched voice came from within.

"That you, Maurice?"

Fairchild answered in the best imitation he could give.

"Yes. I 've got Anita with me."

Steps, then the door opened. For just a second, Squint Rodaine stared at them in ghastly, sickly fashion. Then he moved back into the room, still facing them.

"What's the idea of this?" came his forced query. Fairchild stepped forward.

"Simply to tell you that everything 's blown up as far as you 're concerned, Mr. Rodaine."

"You needn't be so dramatic about it. You act like I 'd committed a murder! What 've I done that you should--?"

"Just a minute. I would n't try to act innocent. For one thing, I happened to be in the same house with you one night when you showed Crazy Laura, your wife, how to make people immortal. And we 'll probably learn a few more things about your character when we 've gotten back there and interviewed--"

He stopped his accusations to leap forward, clutching wildly. But in vain. With a lunge, Squint Rodaine had turned, then, springing high from the floor, had seemed to double in the air as he crashed through the big pane of the window and out to the twenty-foot plunge which awaited him.

Blocked by the form of Fairchild, the two sheriffs sought in vain to use the guns which they had drawn from their holsters. Hurriedly they gained the window, but already the form of Rodaine had unrolled itself from the snow bank into which it had fallen, dived beneath the protection of the low coping which ran above the first-floor windows of the hotel, skirted the building in safety and whirled into the alley that lay beyond. Squint Rodaine was gone. Frantically, Fairchild turned for the door, but a big hand stopped him.

"Let him go--let him think he 's gotten away," said grizzled Sheriff Mason. "He ain't got a chance. There 's snow everywhere--and we can trail him like a hound dawg trailing a rabbit. And I think I know where he 's bound for. Whatever that was you said about Crazy Laura hit awful close to home. It ain't going to be hard to find that rattler!"

CHAPTER XXV

Fairchild felt the logic of the remark and ceased his worriment. Quietly, as though nothing had happened, the three men went down the stairs, passed the sleeping night clerk and headed back to the sheriff's office, where waited Anita and Harry, who had completed his last duties in regard to the chalky-faced Maurice Rodaine. The telephone jangled. It was Denver. Mason talked a moment over the wire, then turned to his fellow officer.

"They 've got Barnham. He was in his office, evidently waiting for a call from here. What's more, he had close to a million dollars in currency strapped around him. Pete Carr 's bringing him and the boodle up to Ohadi on the morning train. Guess we 'd better stir up some horses now and chase along, had n't we?"

"Yes, and get a gentle one for me," cautioned Harry. "It's been eight years since I 've sit on the 'urricane deck of a 'orse!"

"That goes for me too," laughed Fairchild.

"And me--I like automobiles better," Anita was twisting her long hair into a braid, to be once more shoved under her cap. Fairchild looked at her with a new sense of proprietorship.

"You 're not going to be warm enough!"

"Oh, yes, I will."

"But--"

"I'll end the argument," boomed old Sheriff Mason, dragging a heavy fur coat from a closet. "If she gets cold in this--I 'm crazy."

There was little chance. In fact, the only difficulty was to find the girl herself, once she and the great coat were on the back of a saddle horse. The start was made. Slowly the five figures circled the hotel and into the alley, to follow the tracks in the snow to a barn far at the edge of town. They looked within. A horse and saddle were missing, and the tracks in the snow pointed the way they had gone. There was nothing necessary but to follow.

A detour, then the tracks led the way to the Ohadi road, and behind them came the pursuers, heads down against the wind, horses snorting and coughing as they forced their way through the big drifts, each following one another for the protection it afforded. A long, silent, cold-gripped two hours,--then finally the lights of Ohadi.

But even then the trail was not difficult. The little town was asleep; hardly a track showed in the streets beyond the hoofprints of a horse leading up the principal thoroughfare and on out to the Georgeville road. Onward, until before them was the bleak, rat-ridden old roadhouse which formed Laura's home, and a light was gleaming within.

Silently the pursuers dismounted and started forward, only to stop short. A scream had come to them, faint in the bluster of the storm, the racking scream of a woman in a tempest of anger. Suddenly the light seemed to bob about in the old house; it showed first at one window--then another--as though some one were running from room to room. Once two gaunt shadows stood forth--of a crouching man and a woman, one hand extended in the air, as she whirled the lamp before her for an instant and brought herself between its rays and those who watched.

Again the chase and then the scream, louder than ever, accompanied by streaking red flame which spread across the top floor like wind-blown spray. Shadows weaved before the windows, while the flames seemed to reach out and enwrap every portion of the upper floor. The staggering figure of a man with the blaze all about him was visible; then a woman who rushed past him. Groping as though blinded, the burning form of the man weaved a moment before a window, clawing in a futile attempt to open it, the flames, which seemed to leap from every portion of his body, enwrapping him. Slowly, a torch-like, stricken thing, he sank out of sight, and as the pursuers outside rushed forward, the figure of a woman appeared on the old veranda, half naked, shrieking, carrying something tightly locked in her arms, and plunged down the steps into the snow.

Fairchild, circling far to one side, caught her, and with all his strength resisted her squirming efforts until Harry and Bardwell had come to his assistance. It was Crazy Laura, the contents of her arms now showing in the light of the flames as they licked every window of the upper portion of the house,--five heavy, sheepskin-bound books of the ledger type, wrapped tight in a grasp that not even Harry could loosen.

"Don't take them from me!" the insane woman screamed. "He tried it, didn't he? And where 's he now--up there burning! He hit me--and I threw the lamp at him! He wanted my books--he wanted to take them away from me--but I would n't let him. And you can't have them--hear me--let go of my arm--let go!"

She bit at them. She twisted and butted them with her gray head. She screamed and squirmed,--at last to weaken. Slowly Harry forced her arms aside and took from them the precious contents,--whatever they might be. Grimly old Sheriff Mason wrapped her in his coat and led her to a horse, there to force her to mount and ride with him into town. The house--with Squint Rodaine--was gone. Already the flame was breaking through the roof in a dozen places. It would be ashes before the antiquated fire department of the little town of Ohadi could reach there.

Back in the office of Sheriff Bardwell the books--were opened, and Fairchild uttered an exclamation.

"Harry! Did n't she talk about her books at the Coroner's inquest?"

"Yeh. That's them. Them 's her dairy."

"Diary," Anita corrected. "Everybody knows about that--she writes everything down in there. And the funny part about it, they say, is that when she's writing, her mind is straight and she knows what she's done and tells about it. They 've tried her out."

Fairchild was leaning forward.

"See if there 's any entry along early in July--about the time of the inquest."

Bardwell turned the closely written pages, with their items set forth with a slight margin and a double line dividing them from the events tabulated above. At last he stopped.

"Testified to-day at the inquest," he read. "I lied. Roady made me do it. I never saw anybody quarreling. Besides, I did it myself."

"What's she mean--did it herself?" the sheriff looked up. "Guess we 'll have to go 'way back for that."

"First let's see how accurate the thing is," Fairchild interrupted. "See if there 's an item under November 9 of this year."

The sheriff searched, then read:

"I dug a grave to-night. It was not filled. The immortal thing left me. I knew it would. Roady had come and told me to dig a grave and put it in there. I did. We filled it with quicklime. Then we went upstairs and it was gone. I do not understand it. If Roady wanted me to kill him, why did n't he say so. I will kill if Roady will be good to me. I 've killed before for him."

"Still referring to somebody she 's killed," cut in Anita. "I wonder if it could be possible--"

"I 've just thought of the date!" Harry broke in excitedly. "It was along about June 7, 1892. I 'm sure it was around there."

The old books were mulled over, one after the other. At last Bardwell leaned forward and pointed to a certain page.

"Here's an item under May 28. It says: 'Roady has been at me again! He wants me to fix things so that the three men in the Blue Poppy mine will get caught in there by a cave-in.'" The sheriff looked up. "This seems to read a little better than the other stuff. It's not so jagged. Don't guess she was as much off her nut then as she is now. Let's see. Where 's the place? Oh, yes: 'If I 'll help him, I can have half, and we 'll live together again, and he 'll be good to me and I can have the boy. I know what it's all about. He wants to get the mine without Sissie Larsen having anything to do with it. Sissie has cemented up the hole he drilled into the pay ore and has n't told Fairchild about it, because he thinks Roady will go partnerships with him and help him buy in. But Roady won't do it. He wants that extra money for me. He told me so. Roady is good to me sometimes. He kisses me and makes over me just like he did the night our boy was born. But that's when he wants me to do something. If he 'll keep his promise I 'll fix the mine so they won't get out. Then we can buy it at public sale or from the heirs; and Roady and I will live together again.'"

"The poor old soul," there was aching sympathy in Anita Richmond's voice. "I--I can't help it if she was willing to kill people. The poor old thing was crazy."

"Yes, and she 's 'ad us bloody near crazy too. Maybe there 's another entry."

"I 'm coming to it. It's along in June. The date 's blurred. Listen: 'I did what Roady wanted me to. I sneaked into the mine and planted dynamite in the timbers. I wanted to wait until the third man was there, but I could n't. Fairchild and

Larsen were fussing. Fairchild had learned about the hole and wanted to know what Larsen had found. Finally Larsen pulled a gun and shot Fairchild. He fell, and I knew he was dead. Then Larsen bent over him, and when he did I hit him--on the head with a single-jack hammer. Then I set off the charge. Nobody ever will know how it happened unless they find the bullet or the gun. I don't care if they do. Roady wanted me to do it.'"

Fairchild started to speak, but the sheriff stopped him.

"Wait, here 's another item:

"'I failed. I did n't kill either of them. They got out someway and drove out of town to-night. Roady is mad at me. He won't come near me. And I 'm so lonesome for him!'"

"The explanation!" Fairchild almost shouted it as he seized the book and read it again. "Sheriff, I 've got to make a confession. My father always thought that he had killed a man. Not that he told me--but I could guess it easily enough, from other things that happened. When he came to, he found a single-jack hammer lying beside him, and Larsen's body across him. Could n't he naturally believe that he had killed him while in a daze? He was afraid of Rodaine--that Rodaine would get up a lynching party and string him up. Harry here and Mrs. Howard helped him out of town. And this is the explanation!"

Bardwell smiled quizzically.

"It looks like there 's going to be a lot of explanations. What time was it when you were trapped in that mine, Harkins?"

"Along about the first of November."

The sheriff turned to the page. It was there,--the story of Crazy Laura and her descent into the Blue Poppy mine, and again the charge of dynamite which wrecked the tunnel. With a little sigh, Bardwell closed the book and looked out at the dawn, forcing its way through the blinding snow.

"Yes, I guess we 'll find a lot of things in this old book," came at last. "But I think right now that the best thing any of us can find is a little sleep."

Rest,--rest for five wearied persons, but the rest of contentment and peace. And late in the afternoon, three of them were gathered in the old-fashioned parlor of Mother Howard's boarding house, waiting for the return of that dignitary from a sudden mission upon which Anita Richmond had sent her, involving a trip to the old Richmond mansion. Harry turned away from his place at the window.

"The district attorney 'ad a long talk with Barnham," he announced, "and 'e 's figured out a wye for all the stock'olders in the Silver Queen to get what's coming to them. As it is, they's about a 'unnerd thousand short some'eres."

Fairchild looked up.

"What's the scheme?"

"To call a meeting of the stock'olders and transfer all that money over to a special fund to buy Blue Poppy stock. We 'll 'ave to raise money anyway to work the mine like we ought to. And it 'd cost something. You always 'ave to underwrite that sort of thing. I sort of like it, even if we 'd 'ave to sell stock a little below par. It 'd keep Ohadi from getting a bad name and all that."

"I think so too." Anita Richmond laughed, "It suits me fine."

Fairchild looked down at her and smiled.

"I guess that's the answer," he said. "Of course that does n't include the Rodaine stock. In other words, we give a lot of disappointed stockholders par value for about ninety cents on the dollar. But Farrell can look after all that. He 's got to have something to keep him busy as attorney for the company."

A step on the veranda, and Mother Howard entered, a package under her arm, which she placed in Anita's lap. The girl looked up at the man who stood beside her.

"I promised," she said, "that I 'd tell you about the Denver road."

He leaned close.

"That is n't all you promised--just before I left you this morning," came his whispered voice, and Harry, at the window, doubled in laughter.

"Why did n't you speak it all out?" he gurgled. "I 'eard every word."

Anita's eyes snapped.

"Well, I don't guess that's any worse than me standing behind the folding doors listening to you and Mother Howard gushing like a couple of sick doves!"

"That 'olds me," announced Harry. "That 'olds me. I ain't got a word to sye!"

Anita laughed.

"Persons who live in glass houses, you know. But about this explanation. I 'm going to ask a hypothetical question. Suppose you and your family were in the clutches of persons who were always trying to get you into a position where you 'd be more at their mercy. And suppose an old friend of the family wanted to make the family a present and called up from Denver for you to come on down and get it--not for yourself, but just to have around in case of need. Then suppose you went to Denver, got the valuable present and then, just when you were getting up speed to make the first grade on Lookout, you heard a shot behind you and looked around to see the sheriff coming. And if he caught you, it 'd mean a lot of worry and the worst kind of gossip, and maybe you 'd have to go to jail for breaking laws and everything like that? In a case of that kind, what'd you do?"

"Run to beat bloody 'ell!" blurted out Harry.

"And that's just what she did," added Fairchild. "I know because I saw her."

Anita was unwrapping the package.

"And seeing that I did run," she added with a laugh, "and got away with it, who would like to share in what remains of one beautiful bottle of Manhattan cocktails?"

There was not one dissenting voice!

The Codes Of Hammurabi And Moses
W. W. Davies

QTY

The discovery of the Hammurabi Code is one of the greatest achievements of archaeology, and is of paramount interest, not only to the student of the Bible, but also to all those interested in ancient history...

Religion   **ISBN:** *1-59462-338-4*   **Pages:132**
MSRP $12.95

The Theory of Moral Sentiments
Adam Smith

QTY

This work from 1749. contains original theories of conscience amd moral judgment and it is the foundation for systemof morals.

Philosophy **ISBN:** *1-59462-777-0*   **Pages:536**
MSRP $19.95

Jessica's First Prayer
Hesba Stretton

QTY

In a screened and secluded corner of one of the many railway-bridges which span the streets of London there could be seen a few years ago, from five o'clock every morning until half past eight, a tidily set-out coffee-stall, consisting of a trestle and board, upon which stood two large tin cans, with a small fire of charcoal burning under each so as to keep the coffee boiling during the early hours of the morning when the work-people were thronging into the city on their way to their daily toil...

Pages:84

Childrens **ISBN:** *1-59462-373-2*   *MSRP $9.95*

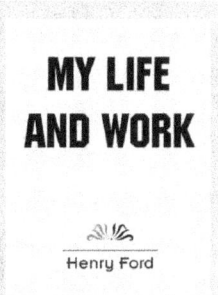

My Life and Work
Henry Ford

QTY

Henry Ford revolutionized the world with his implementation of mass production for the Model T automobile. Gain valuable business insight into his life and work with his own auto-biography... "We have only started on our development of our country we have not as yet, with all our talk of wonderful progress, done more than scratch the surface. The progress has been wonderful enough but..."

Pages:300

Biographies/ **ISBN:** *1-59462-198-5*   *MSRP $21.95*

The Art of Cross-Examination
Francis Wellman

QTY

I presume it is the experience of every author, after his first book is published upon an important subject, to be almost overwhelmed with a wealth of ideas and illustrations which could readily have been included in his book, and which to his own mind, at least, seem to make a second edition inevitable. Such certainly was the case with me; and when the first edition had reached its sixth impression in five months, I rejoiced to learn that it seemed to my publishers that the book had met with a sufficiently favorable reception to justify a second and considerably enlarged edition. ..

Pages:412

Reference   ISBN: *1-59462-647-2*   *MSRP $19.95*

On the Duty of Civil Disobedience
Henry David Thoreau

QTY

Thoreau wrote his famous essay, On the Duty of Civil Disobedience, as a protest against an unjust but popular war and the immoral but popular institution of slave-owning. He did more than write—he declined to pay his taxes, and was hauled off to gaol in consequence. Who can say how much this refusal of his hastened the end of the war and of slavery ?

Law   ISBN: *1-59462-747-9*   **Pages:48**

MSRP $7.45

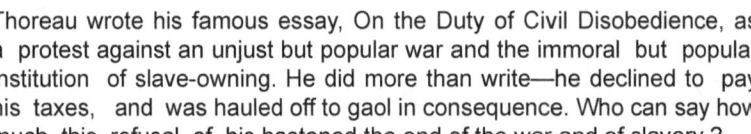

Dream Psychology Psychoanalysis for Beginners
Sigmund Freud

QTY

Sigmund Freud, born Sigismund Schlomo Freud (May 6, 1856 - September 23, 1939), was a Jewish-Austrian neurologist and psychiatrist who co-founded the psychoanalytic school of psychology. Freud is best known for his theories of the unconscious mind, especially involving the mechanism of repression; his redefinition of sexual desire as mobile and directed towards a wide variety of objects; and his therapeutic techniques, especially his understanding of transference in the therapeutic relationship and the presumed value of dreams as sources of insight into unconscious desires.

Pages:196

Psychology   ISBN: *1-59462-905-6*   *MSRP $15.45*

The Miracle of Right Thought
Orison Swett Marden

QTY

Believe with all of your heart that you will do what you were made to do. When the mind has once formed the habit of holding cheerful, happy, prosperous pictures, it will not be easy to form the opposite habit. It does not matter how improbable or how far away this realization may see, or how dark the prospects may be, if we visualize them as best we can, as vividly as possible, hold tenaciously to them and vigorously struggle to attain them, they will gradually become actualized, realized in the life. But a desire, a longing without endeavor, a yearning abandoned or held indifferently will vanish without realization.

Pages:360

Self Help   ISBN: *1-59462-644-8*   *MSRP $25.45*

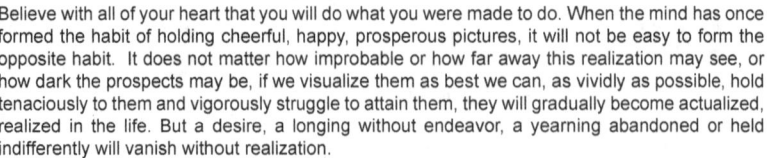
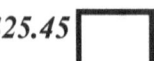

QTY

The Rosicrucian Cosmo-Conception Mystic Christianity by *Max Heindel*   ISBN: *1-59462-188-8* **$38.95**
The Rosicrucian Cosmo-conception is not dogmatic, neither does it appeal to any other authority than the reason of the student. It is: not controversial, but is: sent forth in the, hope that it may help to clear...   New Age/Religion Pages 646

Abandonment To Divine Providence by *Jean-Pierre de Caussade*   ISBN: *1-59462-228-0* **$25.95**
"The Rev. Jean Pierre de Caussade was one of the most remarkable spiritual writers of the Society of Jesus in France in the 18th Century. His death took place at Toulouse in 1751. His works have gone through many editions and have been republished...   Inspirational/Religion Pages 400

Mental Chemistry by *Charles Haanel*   ISBN: *1-59462-192-6* **$23.95**
Mental Chemistry allows the change of material conditions by combining and appropriately utilizing the power of the mind. Much like applied chemistry creates something new and unique out of careful combinations of chemicals the mastery of mental chemistry...   New Age Pages 354

The Letters of Robert Browning and Elizabeth Barret Barrett 1845-1846 vol II   ISBN: *1-59462-193-4* **$35.95**
by *Robert Browning* and *Elizabeth Barrett*   Biographies Pages 596

Gleanings In Genesis (volume I) by *Arthur W. Pink*   ISBN: *1-59462-130-6* **$27.45**
Appropriately has Genesis been termed "the seed plot of the Bible" for in it we have, in germ form, almost all of the great doctrines which are afterwards fully developed in the books of Scripture which follow...   Religion/Inspirational Pages 420

The Master Key by *L. W. de Laurence*   ISBN: *1-59462-001-6* **$30.95**
In no branch of human knowledge has there been a more lively increase of the spirit of research during the past few years than in the study of Psychology, Concentration and Mental Discipline. The requests for authentic lessons in Thought Control, Mental Discipline and...   New Age/Business Pages 422

The Lesser Key Of Solomon Goetia by *L. W. de Laurence*   ISBN: *1-59462-092-X* **$9.95**
This translation of the first book of the "Lernegton" which is now for the first time made accessible to students of Talismanic Magic was done, after careful collation and edition, from numerous Ancient Manuscripts in Hebrew, Latin, and French...   New Age/Occult Pages 92

Rubaiyat Of Omar Khayyam by *Edward Fitzgerald*   ISBN:*1-59462-332-5* **$13.95**
Edward Fitzgerald, whom the world has already learned, in spite of his own efforts to remain within the shadow of anonymity, to look upon as one of the rarest poets of the century, was born at Bredfield, in Suffolk, on the 31st of March, 1809. He was the third son of John Purcell...   Music Pages 172

Ancient Law by *Henry Maine*   ISBN: *1-59462-128-4* **$29.95**
The chief object of the following pages is to indicate some of the earliest ideas of mankind, as they are reflected in Ancient Law, and to point out the relation of those ideas to modern thought.   Religion/History Pages 452

Far-Away Stories by *William J. Locke*   ISBN: *1-59462-129-2* **$19.95**
"Good wine needs no bush," but a collection of mixed vintages does. And this book is just such a collection. Some of the stories I do not want to remain buried for ever in the museum files of dead magazine-numbers an author's not unpardonable vanity..."   Fiction Pages 272

Life of David Crockett by *David Crockett*   ISBN: *1-59462-250-7* **$27.45**
"Colonel David Crockett was one of the most remarkable men of the times in which he lived. Born in humble life, but gifted with a strong will, an indomitable courage, and unremitting perseverance...   Biographies/New Age Pages 424

Lip-Reading by *Edward Nitchie*   ISBN: *1-59462-206-X* **$25.95**
Edward B. Nitchie, founder of the New York School for the Hard of Hearing, now the Nitchie School of Lip-Reading, Inc, wrote "LIP-READING Principles and Practice". The development and perfecting of this meritorious work on lip-reading was an undertaking...   How-to Pages 400

A Handbook of Suggestive Therapeutics, Applied Hypnotism, Psychic Science   ISBN: *1-59462-214-0* **$24.95**
by *Henry Munro*   Health/New Age/Health/Self-help Pages 376

A Doll's House: and Two Other Plays by *Henrik Ibsen*   ISBN: *1-59462-112-8* **$19.95**
Henrik Ibsen created this classic when in revolutionary 1848 Rome. Introducing some striking concepts in playwriting for the realist genre, this play has been studied the world over.   Fiction/Classics/Plays 308

The Light of Asia by *sir Edwin Arnold*   ISBN: *1-59462-204-3* **$13.95**
In this poetic masterpiece, Edwin Arnold describes the life and teachings of Buddha. The man who was to become known as Buddha to the world was born as Prince Gautama of India but he rejected the worldly riches and abandoned the reigns of power when...   Religion/History/Biographies Pages 170

The Complete Works of Guy de Maupassant by *Guy de Maupassant*   ISBN: *1-59462-157-8* **$16.95**
"For days and days, nights and nights, I had dreamed of that first kiss which was to consecrate our engagement, and I knew not on what spot I should put my lips..."   Fiction/Classics Pages 240

The Art of Cross-Examination by *Francis L. Wellman*   ISBN: *1-59462-309-0* **$26.95**
Written by a renowned trial lawyer, Wellman imparts his experience and uses case studies to explain how to use psychology to extract desired information through questioning.   How-to/Science/Reference Pages 408

Answered or Unanswered? by *Louisa Vaughan*   ISBN: *1-59462-248-5* **$10.95**
Miracles of Faith in China   Religion Pages 112

The Edinburgh Lectures on Mental Science (1909) by *Thomas*   ISBN: *1-59462-008-3* **$11.95**
This book contains the substance of a course of lectures recently given by the writer in the Queen Street Hail, Edinburgh. Its purpose is to indicate the Natural Principles governing the relation between Mental Action and Material Conditions...   New Age/Psychology Pages 148

Ayesha by *H. Rider Haggard*   ISBN: *1-59462-301-5* **$24.95**
Verily and indeed it is the unexpected that happens! Probably if there was one person upon the earth from whom the Editor of this, and of a certain previous history, did not expect to hear again...   Classics Pages 380

Ayala's Angel by *Anthony Trollope*   ISBN: *1-59462-352-X* **$29.95**
The two girls were both pretty, but Lucy who was twenty-one who supposed to be simple and comparatively unattractive, whereas Ayala was credited, as her Bombwhat romantic name might show, with poetic charm and a taste for romance. Ayala when her father died was nineteen...   Fiction Pages 484

The American Commonwealth by *James Bryce*   ISBN: *1-59462-286-8* **$34.45**
An interpretation of American democratic political theory. It examines political mechanics and society from the perspective of Scotsman James Bryce   Politics Pages 572

Stories of the Pilgrims by *Margaret P. Pumphrey*   ISBN: *1-59462-116-0* **$17.95**
This book explores pilgrims religious oppression in England as well as their escape to Holland and eventual crossing to America on the Mayflower, and their early days in New England...   History Pages 268

QTY

The Fasting Cure *by Sinclair Upton*　　　　　　　　　　　　ISBN: *1-59462-222-1*　**$13.95**
In the Cosmopolitan Magazine for May, 1910, and in the Contemporary Review (London) for April, 1910, I published an article dealing with my experiences in fasting. I have written a great many magazine articles, but never one which attracted so much attention... New Age/Self Help/Health Pages 164

Hebrew Astrology *by Sepharial*　　　　　　　　　　　　ISBN: *1-59462-308-2*　**$13.45**
In these days of advanced thinking it is a matter of common observation that we have left many of the old landmarks behind and that we are now pressing forward to greater heights and to a wider horizon than that which represented the mind-content of our progenitors... Astrology Pages 144

Thought Vibration or The Law of Attraction in the Thought World　　ISBN: *1-59462-127-6*　**$12.95**
by William Walker Atkinson　　　　　　　　　　　　　　　　*Psychology/Religion Pages 144*

Optimism *by Helen Keller*　　　　　　　　　　　　ISBN: *1-59462-108-X*　**$15.95**
Helen Keller was blind, deaf, and mute since 19 months old, yet famously learned how to overcome these handicaps, communicate with the world, and spread her lectures promoting optimism. An inspiring read for everyone... Biographies/Inspirational Pages 84

Sara Crewe *by Frances Burnett*　　　　　　　　　　　　ISBN: *1-59462-360-0*　**$9.45**
In the first place, Miss Minchin lived in London. Her home was a large, dull, tall one, in a large, dull square, where all the houses were alike, and all the sparrows were alike, and where all the door-knockers made the same heavy sound... Childrens/Classic Pages 88

The Autobiography of Benjamin Franklin *by Benjamin Franklin*　　ISBN: *1-59462-135-7*　**$24.95**
The Autobiography of Benjamin Franklin has probably been more extensively read than any other American historical work, and no other book of its kind has had such ups and downs of fortune. Franklin lived for many years in England, where he was agent... Biographies/History Pages 332

Name	
Email	
Telephone	
Address	
City, State ZIP	

☐ **Credit Card**　　　　　☐ **Check / Money Order**

Credit Card Number	
Expiration Date	
Signature	

Please Mail to:　Book Jungle
　　　　　　　　　PO Box 2226
　　　　　　　　　Champaign, IL 61825
or Fax to:　　　630-214-0564

ORDERING INFORMATION

web: *www.bookjungle.com*
email: *sales@bookjungle.com*
fax: *630-214-0564*
mail: *Book Jungle PO Box 2226 Champaign, IL 61825*
or PayPal *to sales@bookjungle.com*

Please contact us for bulk discounts

DIRECT-ORDER TERMS

**20% Discount if You Order
Two or More Books**
Free Domestic Shipping!
Accepted: Master Card, Visa,
Discover, American Express

www.ingramcontent.com/pod-product-compliance
Lightning Source LLC
Chambersburg PA
CBHW080903020726
47502CB00008B/2332